THIS
WAS
NOT
THE
TRUTH

& Other Collected Stories

DREW GRIFFITHS

ISBN 978-1-54395-164-6 eBook 978-1-54395-165-3

For Rachel and her never ending spirit

&

Henry who never would settle for anything less

this was not the truth

Christopher/1997-1999

I waited.

I stood in the snow with only two shirts to keep me warm. Isaac had disappeared again. Our mother would be full of smiles for him. His face looked deep with long hours and cigarettes. I saw the car rumbling low from down the road. A rusted blue Olds still with real chrome. The car slowed, stopped, and he got out. I watched him circle around the hood. His slender fingers were tracing their way back toward me. He left the car running. In the lingering exhaust he found enough cover to get clean of it all and wrestle himself back into place and pretend he never left

"How's mom?"
"She misses you. I missed you."
"Are you sure?"
"I don't know."
I looked down.
I felt something rising up in my throat.
I was pulling at the insides of my pockets.
"I ask you for one thing."
"I am not a little boy anymore."
"Sometimes you act like it."
"I don't want to fight."
In my limp arms he could see it.
"Either do I."
"Why did you come back?"
I could not stop my mouth from asking.

"There is no other way."

"That's it?"

"That is it."

"Liar."

"Just let it be."

"Let's go home."

"Okay, let's go home."

I watched him walk back to the Olds. I climbed back into the truck. I knew that I had loved him. I watched him lead me back home. He drove with the window open slightly despite the cold. He was smoking again. The car moved smoothly for him. He took the long way home. He enjoyed another cigarette. There was only one light on in the house. Her bedroom was church to him. That was where he pleaded with her. That was where he begged her for forgiveness. That was where she gave him absolution. That is where no one could touch them. I understood he had nothing left. He jerked the car into park and did not wait for me. I watched him hustle up to the front door the keys jangling in his hand. She was waiting for him. He was so impatient, fumbling over the door lock. I took his bag out from the backseat of the car. He was already with her. I pushed my ear up against the door. I had heard it before. They talk in a way that I never understood. It sounded unconscious. I watched my breathing as they spoke, careful not to interrupt because I knew if I waited he would come to me tonight. I would hear him turn the knob slightly, and watch the light in the hall slip in through the space cutting right across my face. I waited and listened at her door.

"I missed you."

Her voice cracked against itself.

"I know."

"I was not happy you left again."

"I had to go."

"How could you."

"I can't right now."

"It doesn't matter, this is all that matters."

She was growing firmer in her tone.

I could hear them moving.

They stepped lightly like children around each other.

"I am sorry."

"It will be difficult."

"It will be."

"What about Christopher?"

"Don't, not right now."

"I understand."

"Are you ready?"

"I have nothing else."

"It is time then. Kneel."

"Everything smells so wonderful."

I pulled away from the door. It sounded as if they were crying. Our room was cold. I turned on the small lamp at the desk and there were shadows everywhere. I could see the outline of the Great Horn plastered to the ceiling above, calling me. It was everything I wanted.

When I woke up he was already gone. The house was full of the early summer sun and the smell of grease in a pan. I could hear men with garden tools. He was with her eating breakfast. I dressed quickly. His bed barely looked slept. I came down the stairs quickly. It was Sunday. I would have to wait. I stood in the doorway until they noticed me. They ate quietly with smiles and fast bites, toast, eggs, jelly, orange juice, and a coffee ring. They did not have time for anyone else. Sunday. He was naked to the waist she already had her Sunday dress on. I made my own breakfast and listened to the hiss of the iron as I ate my cereal. He stood over her in his only good shirt. I had never seen him wear it except on Sunday. Then he disappeared.

He took the keys from the counter. Isaac barely looked at me. He knew I could never say no when he was dressed like that. His shoes polished, pants freshly creased only ten minutes ago, even his skin looked freshly starched. I did not dare touch him that would have to wait. I watched from the hall as he backed the car carefully out of the driveway. There was a heavy cloud of exhaust that lingered after them. They would be gone for hours. The house felt so small without him. In the kitchen the dishes were still piled in the sink. I put the towel over my shoulder and turned on the faucet. The water ran hot almost immediately. I pulled my hands back quickly the dish broke against the side of the stainless steel sink. The cut was deep down the inside of my hand. A thick line like the great river and the blood ran quickly into the drain. I wrapped the towel around my hand. The blood was beautiful and heavy but I forced myself into the bathroom. I opened the medicine cabinet, hand lotion, aspirin, Band-Aids, Trojans, Gauze. I pulled the towel from my hand. The blood ran down the valley of my hand into the sink. The pain was a beautiful thing. I tried to turn on the faucet but before I turned the handle, all I could see was shining tips of the great valley.

I had not seen land for almost a week. We started at Pointe Noire in the Congo. It was hot even in the water as we helped push the boat to shore. The men at the shore had arms scarred by the sun and wrapped in muscle. I wiped my face with the rag in my pocket. My father was standing like a peacock his hat full with flamingo feathers bought in Ghana. The other men at the shore seemed to have the brightest smiles of all. I could not wait to see the valley. Father pulled some money from the pouch inside his shirt. It was barely dry enough to count. The men took the boat. He smiled. I handed my rope to a boy twice my height. At the shore I took my boots from around my neck and untied the laces. They smelled like ocean. Africa.

I woke up, towel stuck dry to my hand, as they tumbled through the front door. They were full of laughter and the incessant talk that comes with church. I would not be able to talk to Isaac until late. I knew he would want to be close to her. I could hear her start the talk of dinner and things about salad, fresh vegetables, chicken, hard boiled eggs, the cloth napkins, the good plates, the fine spices, preheating the oven, sautéing the greens, peeling the potatoes, homemade stuffing, communion, mary, jesus, pudding, whipped cream, fresh strawberries, the fine linen tablecloth, the upstairs candlesticks. He was a part of all these things. I turned my head back on the pillow and stared at the slender contours of the great horn. It was the most noble land mass I had ever seen, proud sure of its hip. A woman who has seen many children, a father with an eager lap to rest in. It was never desperate, simply waiting for us.

I stood at the top of the stairs. She was talking about how to baste the chicken. She was wearing her favorite apron, tied at the neck and the waist just above her hips. She still had on her dress. I was surprised to see her without shoes.

"Can I help?"

I did not dare cross the threshold.

"We have everything under control."

She did not turn, she refused to see me.

"I can set the table."
"Your brother will do it. He understands what I want."
I could smell the butter in the cast iron pan.

"Are you sure I can't do anything?"

I already knew the answer.

No. I waited. I wanted to smoke. I went to the hall closet and pulled at the pockets of his jacket in order to find his cigarettes. I knew he would have hid them from her. I took a desperate looking nail from the pack and slid it into the corner of my mouth. The pack of matches was nestled in the corner of the same pocket. I opened the front door quietly. I knew it didn't matter. I knew they couldn't hear me, not on Sunday. It was cool outside and the air smelled like our neighbors cut lawn. I folded over the match, one hand, and struck it with my thumb against the back of the pack. The initial inhale was full of sulfur and threatened a coughing spurt. I held the smoke deep and long and watched as the long stream pushed out past my lips. At the corner two boys were riding their bikes. I moved towards them turning over the matchbook in my hand and taking long drags every few steps. The boys had cards jammed in their spokes. Rat-ttt-rat-ttt-rat-ttt-rat-ttt. I listened to them ride in circles around their driveway. They looked like brothers, each with the other's smile. It was beautiful. They laughed and spun about on hard turns and half-done tricks. I stayed after the smoke was gone watching them ride as the sun set and bleached them out in a blanket of orange until all I had was shadows, long and sick like. I could still hear them laughing. Rat-ttt-rat-ttt-rat-ttt-rat-ttt-rat-ttt-rat-ttt. Rat-ttt-rat-ttt.

I sat next to him at dinner. Our chairs were close enough that our legs could touch. She was burning at the other side watching us. I spooned mashed potatoes on to my plate. The kitchen was hot from cooking all day. The perspiration was in a slight line on his upper lip. I was afraid to turn my head to look at him. I ate.

I ate as if I would never see food again. I shoveled greens, potatoes, chicken, gravy, and glasses of milk into my mouth. I dried my plate with hot biscuits and swallowed them almost whole but I could not look at him. I felt his leg pressing against mine but I did not turn my head. I could not give him away. When he adjusted his napkin, I felt his hand. I could not turn my head. She brought dessert without her eyes ever leaving the table and I ate because I thought I might never eat again. After she cleaned the table I watched him follow her upstairs. Neither of them had shoes on.

"Let me see you hand."

He came into the room with a cigarette. I offered him the bandage was still on my hand. He smelled the ends of my fingers.

"You smoked my cigarettes."
"I had to do something."
I pulled my hand back.
He made attempts for my wrist.
"What?"
"It's about the only thing we have left."
"Don't do that now."

Exhale. He stubbed the cigarette into the ashtray.
I watched his back as he leaned forward to open the nightstand drawer. He undressed to his briefs.
I pointed my hand towards the ceiling.
"This, this is Pointe Noire. This is where we start. Then to Kinshasa. Then we follow the river. It is a beast. Cuts through the heart of it all. We follow it all the way to the great valley."

Isaac looked back at me and I knew immediately it longer mattered.

She was smiling at the breakfast table. The pan was fresh with grease and fried eggs. The kitchen was full of light from the windows and he had a look that I had not seen in years. She poured orange juice into a tall glass and set it next to him. I opened the cabinet and removed a bowl. The cereal was stale as it came out of the box. There was no milk left in the refrigerator. I took a glass from the sink poured the orange juice and drank with my hips leaning against the counter. She was still wrapped in her bathrobe. I was wearing clothes from the floor. He had showered and shaved for the first time in two days. He looked just like our father. She forced her way through the kitchen for him. She brought him eggs, toast, juice, a cup of coffee, milk, and sugar. She smiled for him, and he made small motions with his hand while he ate. My father used to tell me that everything happens in the morning. Everything.

I watched him working in the yard that morning from my bedroom window. He had his head buried in a thick bush. Mary was sipping milk from a glass at the edge of the porch. My sister had just turned fifteen and the icing was melting off her cake onto a paper plate. It was not even noon yet. She watched our father work over the bushes. His bare chest was shiny with sweat and patched with dirt. He had on gloves and a thick handled pair of pruning shears were sagging in his pocket. The sun was filling up the yard from high overhead. I heard my mother humming old psalms in the kitchen. Isaac was sitting in the kitchen. I saw it all that morning. He looked so tired under that sun. He was tired and had given up. The pruning shears laying open in the grass she nearly cut her foot open. She held the glass for him, his mouth begging her. He had forgotten himself. She let the milk spill over the edges of his lips and roll down his chin and neck into the hair on his chest. She slid her slim hips over his body so quickly I almost pretended not to see it. If the muffins had been ready ten minutes earlier nothing would have happened. She would have not come out of the house to get him. She would have not seen them in the grass just past the hedge. My sister's blue bathing suit top spread out simply in the grass. She would have not screamed his name, Paul. I would have not broken the window and let it all coming crashing in.

"You will leave. You will pack and leave."

It was a voice I had never heard from our mother.

"I'm going with him."

She had a voice too young even for fifteen.

"I know you are."

"That is her decision."

He was drying his chest with a kitchen towel.

"Who are you to talk after what you have done to me."

"To you?"

"How could you?"

"I love her."

"Fuck you. You love her. Fuck you."

"I love him mother."

"He is your father Mary, your father you dumb cunt."

"I love him. That is more than you ever gave him. You are dried up."

"Cunt."

"You can never give him what I have. You destroyed all these boys."

"Mary you ruined me. You ruined this whole family."

When Mary left with him that night there was nothing. The house felt so small as I watched them. I thought Isaac would never let go of me. I was never so wrong. Everything happens in the morning.

After breakfast there was nothing to do. There was nothing to do except wait. In the sun on the porch I smoked a cigarette and waited. When Isaac came out of the house he had the keys in his hand. He looked at me, smoke left hanging, and said nothing. He did not dare open his mouth and tell me where he was going. He did not tell me what time he was coming home. He did not tell me that our mother was crying. He did not tell me anything. He knew everything and it was the only thing that he had left. I had to let him go. He always handled the car smoothly. I watched him turn the wheel flat flesh part of his palm on the wheel. He whipped it around and was past the corner before I exhaled. I wish I had taken another cigarette. It was not even noon yet and I was so tired. Tonight I would need Evelyn more than ever.

The people of Kinshasa were alive. They were full of energy and heart I had never felt before. Father was alive and laughing. I could not even belief it myself anymore. It was all amazing. The men moved about the tall unexpected buildings in business suits and smiles. The woman blushed modestly at our bare legs, and children followed us everywhere. Father had already booked our passage down the river to Kisangani. There was French everywhere. The men smiled and the women closed their eyes as we passed by. Father wiped his face with the cloth in his back pocket. The man at the boat office had eyes like the dead but it did not matter, the river was waiting for us.

My eyes snapped open. In the cooler nights, I stayed on the porch until the dark walked up the front lawn. I pulled myself up from the rattan bench. The air at night always smelled better. I looked in through the window. In the orange hallway light mother almost looked peaceful. She was just sitting there, absolutely still. I found it hard to believe she was even real. I was afraid of her now, caged like this. I walked into the front yard. The grass was gathering dew, in the last seconds of light it was hard to tell what was real anymore. I walked until to Evelyn's house. There was nothing to stop her anymore. She could have all of me. She could take everything.

"I can't come out with you."
"Why not?"
"You know why."
"I need you."
"Don't say that."
"Come down."
"I can't."
"Please."
"You have to be strong."
"I know."
"Is this what you want?"
"I need this."
"There is no end to this now."
"I know."
"It will be this way now."
"I need you."
"This will be it now."
"I know."
"It will be everything for us."
"I need you."
"I always loved you."
When she came out the front door her hair was still wet and her face was fresh from the shower. I felt her hand against me and convinced myself everything

would be good again. Her father's car smelled like tobacco. Her face looked very determined. The Cedar Pine's motel had only twelve rooms. I waited for Evelyn at the front entrance. In the window, I could see the desk clerk. He was wearing a red vest and looked tired. She smiled awkwardly as she approached the door. I knew she was worried but the routine was familiar enough. I smiled at the desk clerk and his face remembered me. There was a moment of indecision as he chose a key from the pegboard. Number 2, number 8, number 10, number 3. Always number 3. He handed me the key and I dug in my jeans for money. Evelyn was getting ice from the machine in a plastic bucket. I took the key and walked out to the room. The walkway buzzed with fluorescent lights and insects. We could hear two men in room number 9. I opened the door for #3, stepped into the dark musty room and undressed.

Evelyn was holding the ice bucket against her breasts. She was smiling. She placed the bucket down on the nightstand and moved across the room. The light in the bathroom was yellow and I turned away. When I turned back she was already undressed her skirt on the white tile floor. I could hear the shower running. She wanted to be ready. Her mouth was warm on the side of my neck. I closed my eyes again. Evelyn. I wanted to say her name. I wanted to scream out. Her hand was at the small of my back. The edges of her finger digging into my side, still tender from the last time. In her face she begged me not to let her. All that was left was for us to wait.

We had to wait for the boat in Kinshasa. It would be a day and a half if everything went right. The man at the boat office directed us to the Colonial Bungalows. The roof was a sheet of tin and the two rooms smelled like urine and cut grass. It was hot. The kitchen sink was full of black water. Father sat down carefully on the only chair. I watched him look at the room. His hand was broad and wide on his thigh. He pushed back his hat and wiped his brow. There was no reason to stay in the bungalows. Kinshasa was waiting for us. The sun hit my face like a match head as soon as we opened the door. There were beggars everywhere. My father pulled his billfold from his back pocket and slipped it against his thigh. Everyone was looking for the shade. There were soldiers leaning on their weapons by a fruit stand.

Evelyn was driving fast. I could not tell what she was thinking. I could not read her face anymore but I knew I could not go home yet. My clothes smelled like the motel. I wish I had another cigarette. There was nowhere to go. There was nothing I could do. Nothing I could do for her but give. Nothing I could do for any of them. Nothing I could for us. I could not look at her when I got out of the car. Her hands were still on the wheel. She would not move. Her eyes told me everything. I could not say no to something so beautiful. I would walk the rest of the way home taking my time around the quiet blocks, moving carefully not to disturb the fresh bandages. I knew Isaac would be home already. She would have had her fill of him already and be sleeping. The street before the house was wet from a summer shower. I liked the smell of it, after rain.

The front door was unlocked. I was surprised. The kitchen light was still on and there was the smell of smoke in the house. I was surprised. Isaac was sitting at the table. He was not wearing his shirt. I watched him from the hall, smoking, using a saucer as an ashtray. The smoke left his mouth slowly, elegantly. It was these things that made him dangerous. He could easily destroy what I had left.

Kinshasa smelled like garbage. The city was beautiful. The trees jutted out of the streets like ripe fruit in orange and blue. I could hear music vibrating down the crowded street. The rhythms were almost irresistible. I looked at father. He was sitting on the bed naked to the waist. He had been smiling since we reached shore at Point Noire. We had at least two days to wait for the boat. A soldier smiled as we passed by. He was resting against a cinder block building. His gun slack in the corner of his elbow. I was grateful that the sun was setting. The shadows were a great relief to everyone. I made sure to walk carefully. I watched father wipe his face again. The cloth stained and heavy with sweat. There was a bistro at the end of the block. There were four young girls outside. Their skin in the settling light looked like coffee with cream. Their perfume mixed with the dull smell of rotting garbage and fresh ash. Father took a feather from the tallest ones hair. He gave her an American dollar. When she smiled the white in her teeth was startling. She touched my cheek. I did not want to say anything. The dull ache of pain in my side was enough.

I took the cigarette from Isaac's hands. He lit the match and waited for the smell to dissipate. I inhaled heavily on the first drag. He did not look familiar anymore but it did not matter in the dark. The pain would only hurt in the morning. I followed him up the stairs to our room. He did not say anything and I knew it was all over for him.

In the morning, the sun would pull up over the tips of the peaks cresting like a wave in subtle hints of red, orange, lavender. We were only two days from the great horn.

Isaac/1996-1998

I had no time to wait.

Sunday morning pulled up over the edge of the windowsill. Christopher was still in his bed. His body looked small under the blankets. He did not like the mornings. I looked on the floor for my shorts. Mother was already dressed. There was breakfast on the table. Paul was watching television in the den. His plate was empty. I sat down and drank a large glass of orange juice. Mother slid two eggs onto my plate. The toast was already buttered. She always looked good on Sundays. I never liked wearing a suit. My eggs were runny. She always made them that way. Father always drove on Sundays. The window down slightly so he could smoke. Mother hated that. She always complained about the smell and the rattle in his chest. The church was just another place to him. It was everything for mother. She was everything for me. Sunday.

I watched her during the service. Her hands shook in her lap. The sweat beaded up on her. A row of tiny drops on her forehead, some just above her thin tight lips. He never moved. He never even seemed to breathe. Paul was too afraid to look at us. She could not have been more at peace. She told me that everything was written for us. She told me that soon she would need me more than ever, that all he wanted was an escape. The only thing he wanted was to take her family away from all the good she was doing. To destroy what she had made. Paul was nothing to me. She had shown me that.

The minister was a solid man. He had dark hair and a long face. When he spoke he gave long stares straight forward and his lips never trembled. I always listened to him. I never heard the words the way she could. Mother would smile at me during the service. She would turn her head just slightly so I could see. It felt wrong but I did not care. Father never looked at us. Africa. His books and maps were all he wanted. Africa. The minister always had dirt under his fingernails. The service ended. Mother was talking to him. She had her hands tied around themselves. When he talked he smiled in the way only a minister can smile. Father was sitting in the car with the rest of them telling stories of Flamingos and riverboats. I watched him from the edge of the church steps. He had a cigarette smoking between his fingers. It was always this way. In the car, on the way home, we never talked. Mother always focused on the passing cars.

She started dinner just before three. The turkey had been defrosting since last night. The organs were pre-packed in plastic. I was peeling potatoes over the garbage can. Christopher was standing in the doorway. She did not even know he was there. I said nothing. I peeled the potatoes. Father was in his study. We could smell the smoke. I could hear him unrolling his charts and maps. The sigh of well-worn paper. Christopher moved away from the door. I could hear them talking excitedly.

you see this. right here. this is where it will all begin. point noire. it opens right into the mouth of the congo river. it will be great. we will go when it is fall there just us. i like that. me too. this is the capital kinshasa we won't be there long. then we take the boat. right. it should take us a couple days. maybe a week. maybe more then kisangani. that is where the real trip starts. kisangani. we leave the river and move towards ethiopia. axum. maybe. the people of st. mary of zion say they have the ark of the covenant they say that it has been there for thousands of years brought back to the mother homeland by solomon's son. menelik. son of the queen of sheba.

Mary has eyes just like mother. She would be thirteen in almost two weeks. Father always said everything happens in the morning. Christopher left his plate in the sink. I watched him leave the kitchen. I had cigarettes in my jacket pocket. Mother wore yellow gloves to wash the dishes. I dried. Every time she handed me a dish she smiled. She was wearing her apron over her dress. Mary was staring at the television. When the dishes were finished mother would smile and go upstairs to change. Mary would wait long enough to hear her door close and then go to father. Confirmation. Christopher would take two cigarettes from my jacket and go outside. The kitchen was empty. The house was so full with stillness it felt small. She was waiting for me. The hallway felt cold. Mother had changed, brushed her hair straight and smooth to her shoulders. She was sitting at the edge of the bed. The leather book was clasped between her hands. She was almost trembling. I knelt down beside her. She took my head into her lap. Her stockings were soft on smooth thighs. She opened the book. I closed my eyes, she adjusted her hip. It was an effort not to cry. Mother. Rebekah. She began to read.

let him kiss me with kisses of his mouth. more delightful is your love than wine. your name spoken is a spreading perfume this is why mother loves you. draw me. i will follow you eagerly. bring me isaac to your chambers. with you i rejoice and exult i extol your love it is beyond wine how rightly i love you. on my bed at night i sought him whom my heart loves i sought him but did not find him you are beautiful my mother you are beautiful and there is no blemish in you you have ravished my heart my mother my bride you have ravished my heart with one glance of your eyes your lips drip honey let my son come to his garden and eat its fruits.

I was tired. It was always this way. Christopher would return home soon. I could hear father with Mary in his study. The usual sounds. She would leave frustrated and full of anticipation. I rolled up into my bed. The sheets smelled of detergent and cigarettes. There was a pack of Camels in the nightstand drawer. I closed my eyes to light the match. The smell of sulfur and cigarette smoke drifted from me. I lay on my side towards the window. The streetlights had a fantastic glow as the fog settled in. I slid my hand down my thigh. I could not believe what I could do. I did not want to wait any longer.

I sat up in bed and lit another cigarette. Christopher had that simple look on his face. He was thinking of Africa. The jungle, the river, the mountain pass, the ark of the covenant, Saint Mary of Zion, the son of Solomon. It was the only thing that kept him moving forward, that and Evelyn. I handed him the cigarette. When he inhaled he always kept his eyes closed. He smiled and handed the cigarette back to me. He had such fine hands. Long thin fingers and smooth palms. I know he had been with her, his shirt poorly concealing fresh bandages. There was no other place for him to go. No one else would listen to him. She must know everything. There was nothing to do but wait for the morning. Mary's birthday was coming. Confirmation. The sun was tipping over the edge of the window his shadow was everywhere.

It was the first morning that felt like summer. The sun rose quickly and the heat was already pressing into the house. Rebekah was already being stubborn fighting about the air conditioner. Paul loved the heat. The heavy presence of it. The smell of a slight sweat. The sound of ice in a glass. The ring left on a table. Mary's new blue bathing suit. Mother was finishing breakfast. Christopher never liked the mornings. I could see it in his face. He always looked afraid. I sat down at the table. She placed a plate next to the bowl of plain cereal. The pitcher of milk was wet. Her hands were red again. She had been praying for something. I ate slowly. She put strawberry jelly on two pieces of toast for me.

When father left for work Mary could not stop herself. No one wanted to look. The car struggled to start. There was too much anticipation. She ran from the house, her bare feet, to the car as he pulled out of the driveway. He stopped only for a minute. She was still dressed for bed. When she leaned into the window he placed his hand against the side of her face. I looked back to the kitchen. Christopher was alone at the table. Mother refused to turn around. Mary grabbed at his arm and kissed the rough palm of his hand. Her feet were bleeding slightly from the sharp stone driveway. He left her there for us. She would be thirteen in two days. No one would help her wash her feet. I stood over her as she sat on the porch step.

"You're bleeding."
"I know."
"It's a sin."
"I love him."
"You do not."
"You don't know what love is."
"You think we don't see things. You think she doesn't see things you think she doesn't know."
"I love him I love him."
"You are going to destroy us, you'll break her."
"Let her pray."
"You best be careful."
"Do you think I don't know about it? We all know even Paul knows."

"Don't."

"We see your face the way you look at her."

"Don't talk about what you don't understand."

"You're no prophet and I am not Mary. I never wanted to be."

"You don't understand what you are saying."

"She wanted that she ruined me. She can't love anything anyone."

"She loves me."

"She is killing you. She will kill you like she tried to kill me."

"What. You don't understand what you are saying.

"I understand his is the only way out."

I had to leave in order not to hit her. My hand was trembling. I could not find Rebekah. The kitchen was empty. The house seemed so small. I looked for Christopher. The study was empty. The maps were scattered over the table. A thick black line along the path. I could not find mother. She had left the book at the edge of the bed. I held it between my hands. The leather felt warm. It was soft and smelled of her. I started to cry & ran from that house. If it were not for Christopher I would have never stopped. We might have all been saved.

I found Christopher wandering in the street. He was smoking a cigarette. I did not look at him. I took the cigarette from his hand and inhaled heavily and slipped it back between his fingers. He was barely moving but I could hear him breathing. Inhale. Exhale. Smoke. The smell of tobacco came from him. So much had happened and it was still just the morning. He wanted to see Evelyn and I could not deny him. I went into the house to get the keys. Christopher stomped out his cigarette. The car was unlocked. I waited for him to settle before starting the engine. It was close enough to walk. I knew that. We both understood that much but this moment was all he had left to give me.

"It's all over isn't it Isaac?"

"I don't know."

"Why don't you want to come with us?"

"I can't leave her now. I can't do that."

"It was all planned. We have everything charted."

"It's not real."

"But I can see it so clearly."

"It's not the truth."

"It's all I have."

"You got to stop doing this. It's not going to end well."

"Please, just start the car."

Christopher walked to the front door. There was no doorbell. He knocked and waited. I wanted him to look back towards the car. It would have meant everything. I never saw his face after she opened the door. She smiled. Her hair was long and a muddy brown. She always looked thin no matter who she was with. Small breasts. Small hips. So well controlled. She had fine lips. He waited at the door for her while she went back into the house. He looked uncomfortable. He could not find his feet. He never went inside. When she came back she had a small sturdy black bag with her. She put her hand up against his side carefully inspecting the situation. Evelyn.

When he came back to the car he sat in the backseat with the small bag between them. Her eyes were dark in her face. She kept her smile subdued. She kept her face from me. I could not tell what she already knew. I looked at Christopher in the rear view mirror. He was watching the road flash by. There was an uneasy anticipation in the car. There was nothing left for me anymore.

I stopped the car at the corner. The motel vacancy light was a cheap red. They got out of the car quickly. In her hand she was holding the small bag tightly. I watched them walk. There was always a certain space between them. He opened the door to the motel office. The lights were just beginning to make a difference. I watched Christopher take the key. He handed it to her. The motel clerk barely looked at them. There was a small color television on the desk. They left the motel office. She handed him the bag. It looked even smaller swinging against his thigh. She unlocked the door for him. Room number three. I watched him wait. He stood there with her shadow. I watched him move to her. The door lingered open. I turned off the ignition. The car stumbled and then went quiet. I closed the car door softly. The grass was thick. Their room light was on. I waited at the door.

"Your brother?"

"It will be fine. There is nothing he can do anymore."

"Take off your clothes."

"I feel really cold."

"Does it still hurt?"

"No."

"Don't lie to me."

"I don't have much time, my father."

"I need you."

"Get on the bed."

"We will live in grass huts with the sun on our backs."

"You can't get to lost this time, make sure you stay with me before. . . "

"I know. Kiss me first."

"Please do it now."

"OK. Just let me get ready."

"That's it, I can see the river. I can see the whole fucking valley. Everything is so beautiful."

"Christ, look what you made me do. Christopher. Jesus. There is too much blood."

I ran from the door and started the car. The motel door opened. His face, his skin, it never looked so white. She was holding the bag, it was the only time I ever saw anything real on Evelyn's face. He walked around and opened the passenger door behind me. I looked at him through the mirror. His bottom lip was trembling. When she opened the door he did not move. I did not dare say anything. There was no life left in her. They kept the bag between them. When Evelyn got out of the car he did not move to the front seat. I waited only long enough for her to get clear of the car door. She took the bag with her. The car smelled like lilacs. I noticed it was beginning to rain. Christopher got out of the car quickly. I watched him stumble towards the house. The porch light was already on. I knew Rebekah was waiting there for me. I suddenly felt as if everything was so getting very small. Once inside the house I knew I was already buried.

The stairs were littered with shadows. I looked back as I helplessly climbed the stairs. Christopher was lost to me. He was holding his side. I could not see his hands in the dark. I wanted to cry. I swear there was blood on the carpet. I waited for a breath at the top of the stairs. He did not move. He only tilted his head towards the light in the study. He was already gone leaning up against the railing in the red morning light along the river in Kinshasa. He had told me the story so many times before. He was watching the men gather around the smoke stack. Black and long with a strong head. They played cards and tossed stories about Chantal, and Francine. There were six barges strapped to the sides of the

Colonel Ebaya. They were alive with people crawling and spooning. The slept on mats. They lived under tarpaulins. He was sitting in a chair at the edge of the deck. The sound was an uneven rush of disease and love. He had been on the river for five days already. He had buried all of us just outside Kinshasa. He was waiting for Kisangani. He was waiting for Axum. The light of the Zion. There was nothing to keep him anymore.

The light was on in Rebekah's room. I was ready to give up anything.

She was reading the leather book. Her legs were hanging from the edge of the bed. I watched her. I did not speak. I did not even chance to breathe more than a whisper. She did not look up once. Everything in that room seemed so much smaller. She just waited. I moved to the edge of the bed and knelt by her feet. They were clean, just washed, against my lips.

Evelyn/1998

I could not wait.

He was late. Already fifteen minutes. I could not wait any longer. Dad was doing a restless walk in the kitchen with a cup of warm coffee. I had not seen mother all day. He did not like Christopher. He said things. I could not wait any longer. He said things. I was wearing the dress that Christopher liked. The one that lay smooth against my breasts rested well between my thighs. I could not let him know. I could not wait. Dad was pouring another cup of coffee. I did not ask him where my mother was. It wasn't the first time. Six months ago she left in the middle of church. Dad didn't even turn to look. He didn't even watch her. She walked right down the middle of the pews her flats just barely making a sound. That was not the first time. I knew she would leave. The preacher was slipping into the psalms. The beauty of love. It made Christopher sick. It gave his mother everything she wanted. Dad poured a third cup of coffee.

I packed the bag slowly. Everything was ready for him. The bag was packed and waiting at the edge of my bed. I did not know when he was coming. His brother had driven the last two times. Christopher was still afraid to drive. His mother disapproved of me. I have seen her in church. The man who cleans the rectory has told me about her he tells me that she is not right. The man says people talk about her they say don't be fooled because she is always praying... Her husband is not like my father. He has a normal job. He smiles when he sees me. He is obsessed with maps and charts. Christopher says he is always looking for something. I have not seen my mother for almost three weeks. It was only July, the heat was unbearable and it was not even noon yet. I walked to the kitchen barefoot. The tile was cool against my skin. My father was looking into his cup of coffee. There was a pitcher of milk on the table. I turned the sink and let it run cold. We needed groceries. I knew that afterwards I was always hungry. I had packed the bag slowly. This thing it started like everything else.

I first saw him at the spring farmers market. Christopher was waiting for his brother. He had a small expression. I watched him from across the street while my mother was buying fruit. I don't know how long I watched him with his hands jammed into his pockets. Isaac was scolding Mary about something they both looked desperate about. It was the way Christopher was watching them that cut right through me. That look on his face was starving. Mary was younger. She was younger than both of them. She had a jeans and a blue bikini top on. Isaac was yelling suddenly. Christopher looked as if he would simply disappear at any minute. I should have known it would not be easy. I went to him, left my mother. When I touched his arm I felt blessed again. He turned to me his face full and desperate. I kissed him lightly on the sides of his face. I left my mother and went with him. Isaac stopped yelling long enough for Mary to slap him. Her hand small, fragile, but not without merit. I left my mother and went to him. This man could give me what I needed and nothing else could save me.

I filled a large clean glass with the ice and ran it under the sink. The water was cool. I was anxious. My father was drowning in another cup of coffee. I could not help him. I had packed the bag slowly. I drank the water slowly leaning against the kitchen sink and closed my eyes and could see him bleeding. I could not stop myself. I could only wait. I had packed the bag slowly.

Christopher was always talking about Africa. Pointe Noire, Kinshasa, Kisangani, The River, The Jungle, The Albert Nile, The Nangeya Mountains, Mount Pelekech, Lake Turkana, The Great Rift Valley, Nazret, Axum. Axum. St. Mary of Zion. The Ark. I could only do my best to hold on. Solomon. Menelik. Sheba. Menelik. Son of Sheba. Son of Solomon. He carried the light across the desert that could ruin us all.

His mother had become convinced and Isaac was full of spite. The past winter had been brutal for everyone. By the summer we were done spending our time dancing around each other. The first mark was on his face and it barely bled but afterwards Isaac would not look at him the same. I waited outside the motel.

The wind sounded like a round of applause. Christopher walked towards me begging for me to not hold back.

I packed the bag slowly. It was light. I put it down at the bottom of the stairs. I had not seen my mother in six weeks. My father left his coffee cup on the kitchen table, his cigarette still burning in the ashtray. The house felt like a weight. I could not sit. I could only wait. Everything I did was for my sister, for Teresa.

Isaac was impatient with one hand jammed in his pocket the other cupping his cigarette. He had a lean, feminine body. He was not at all like Christopher. His legs were to long for his torso and his neck raised his head at awkward angles. The sun was hot even for a summer morning. Christopher was sitting on the curb smoking a cigarette. There was a book open next to him. I was holding a glass of orange juice. The asphalt was warm against my bare feet. I could hear kids riding their bikes around the corner. I went to him. He held out his cigarette but did not look up. I took a long drag and he took the glass of orange juice from my hand. He waited for the cigarette and I took another drag. The curb was rough against the bare backs of my legs. I let him look at me. I wanted him to. Isaac saw everything. I put the cigarette between his lips. He inhaled and kissed me.

What are you reading?
A book about Africa.
What about Africa?
About Menelik.
Who?
Menelik.
Who is that?
He is the son of Solomon
Who is his mother?
The Queen of Sheba.
I don't believe you.
Most people don't.
Tell me more.
Why?
I want to know.
Why?
I want to know about you, about Africa.

Ok but not now, not here.

How can you be so still?

I'm waiting.

Waiting?

For Africa.

We sat on the curb and smoked two more cigarettes. The sun was getting hot. I wanted to see his maps. To see the slender form of the river. I wanted to hear about the Congo. I wanted to touch him. He was always afraid to touch me. He was afraid to hurt me. I left him on the curb. It was still morning. My father was screaming for the newspaper. I ran upstairs to Teresa's room and told her everything Christopher had promised me.

salvation. i need you to save me. the light you see must be beautiful. bring your hand to me. let me heal you. bleed for me. let me heal you. i will repent for you. i will be punished for you. let me take your pain. let me hold it inside me. i need your light. i need your salvation. the congo will be beautiful. the clouds are preaching a heavy rain across the mountains of nazret. in axum they will wait for us. st. mary of zion. show me the way. i will follow you. the winding river will be our lover. the great big ship with its hordes will be our children. the smokestack will breathe life for us. the sun will shine for us and the heart of the jungle will sing. it will all be for us.

The day was long and the noon sun seem to stretch forever. Ever since my mother returned I waited for dark. In the dark it was difficult to tell what was happening. I could barely see her in the dark, the television buzzing around her in the background. She was smoking. I wanted a cigarette. The bathroom light was casting into the hallway. I looked for my father. I heard him breathing. The sounds of his shallow gap lungs in the hallway. I barely recognized him lying there. Face turned away from the door. Back scattered with scars and welts. I moved to kneel at the edge of the bed. I tried to touch him. His hand. I tried to see him but he was gone, his shame crippling him. I packed Teresa a bag while he lay motionless in the other room. Underwear, a bra, her favorite blouse, a pair of socks, a skirt, jeans, a bottle of perfume and her toothbrush. I left it at the edge of her bed. I blame him for everything. My mother was watching the television her face proud, her hand wrapped in a towel with some ice. Teresa was trying to keep the gash in her face from opening again. He did not move when he spoke to me.

Is she gone?

She is watching TV.

Is she going to leave?

I don't know.

Did she say anything?

No.

Is Teresa

Did you try to stop her?

I couldn't.

Did you just sit there?

Stop it.

Did you just let her do it again?

Look at me what can I do.

Didn't you try to stop her?

I am too tired. I was too late.

You are always too tired, you are always too late.

Stop Evelyn. Please just help me up.

Why, why, why should I.

I am your father.

You are nothing, you are nothing but piss and shit and tears.

I am your father.

You are weak, you are nothing, nothing, you couldn't save me, and you couldn't save us.

I tried.

You had your chance, you had your chance with Teresa.

I had to choose, I couldn't take anymore.

So you just let her do it.

Look at my back, look at my face. I am dying.

Why didn't you take us away?

I did all I could for both of you.

You did nothing, all you had to do was take us away.

I did everything for you. You don't understand.

Teresa was just begging for you to save her.

I tried.

I am not waiting for you anymore. I will save us both.

I went to Christopher and he held me until I fell asleep. Sometime in the night, I felt his body leave me. I felt the empty warm space he left in the motel bed. The stillness that remained after him. I know he went to Isaac to try and save him. He could not see it was too late for his brother. I would make sure it was the last time. I needed him more than he understood. I slept in that bed for almost two days. I sweated into his sheets. I watched the sun slide up over the windowsill and slip back down beneath the horizon. I waited for him to come and touch me and then pretended I did not need him. I had to be strong. I watched him dress in the dark. His body a rickety shadow. I listened to his breath as he slept on top of the blankets. His shallow chest bare and fragile. I cupped his hand against my breasts. I let my heart pull his rhythm into mine. I could feel the blood between us. His hands so precious. All of that pain as he told me the story.

we wade down the river in a sickly boat. it is a nation alone. a class system, a infrastructure, a poverty stricken ghetto. i watch him sit over the edge. his feet swinging near the brown muck. it isn't even water. when it came rushing out of the tap in our room we laughed madly. i took his whole body next to mine. there was so much heat. give me your mouth. give me your skin. give me your hands, your feet, your back, your scars, your scabs, your blood. i will swallow it all. i will take everything from you. i will take it all. i will have it and laugh. you will show me the way down the river. your tender feet bathed in blood and the brown river. our lover. my savior.

In the summer I did not sleep. I waited for him. I waited for him to come to me. My father would kill himself. I had not seen my mother in three weeks. I packed the bag slowly. It was ready for him. I was up before the sun had a chance to breathe. I could hear my father sleeping. I went to watch him. His body lost in the empty space next to him. I took some money from his wallet and his cigarettes from the dresser. I slipped into the wooden bench on the porch. I inhaled sulfur and felt like gagging as I watched the match go out. I held the smoke as long as I could. I felt it build up inside me. I counted in my head. I waited as long as I could. I exhaled a sleepy stream of smoke. It was still just the morning. Teresa always loved the mornings.

I remembered in the first weeks of an especially cold winter I let Teresa sleep in the bed with me. She didn't care that she was too big for us both to be comfortable. She stood in her pajamas her feet wrapped in two pairs of our fathers socks. The pillows sighed heavy and quick. I felt her warm breath all over my face. It was a nice bed. She had an old stuffed elephant in her hands, the stuffing coming out of one arm. I looked at her face. She had the smile of early Sunday mornings. I watched her eyes slip close and her bit lips slide apart. She breathed like a bird. I waited until I felt her sleeping. I tried to leave the bed without an absence. I moved slowly letting the blankets fill up my space. I put an extra pillow where my body was. Teresa held her hands tightly to her chest. Nine years old. I closed the door to my room. The hinges had a slight creak. The nightlight was solemn at the end of the hall. They were sitting together in the kitchen. I slipped into a chair at the end of the table. They were holding cups of coffee close to their chests with both hands. I smiled at her still dangling shoes in the left hand. They were talking together about Teresa. They smiled as they looked at me. I watched my father slip his hand along the outside of my mother's fingers. They were talking together. The kitchen floor was cool against my bare feet.

The morning faded quickly with the heat. I shook off my daydream as I felt the sticky heat summer roll up the front porch. I could hear the rattle of the air conditioner. I finished the cigarette and buried the butt in the dirt of a potted plant. Father was already waiting for his coffee. He stood in front of the coffee pot. His hands lying scared at his sides. The slow drip, then the hot stream. He moved like this.

We met at the motel for the first time in a spring thaw. The ground was heavy and wet with early morning showers. There was a low fog riding on the street and I waited for him in the front office. He walked this time. The desk clerk was watching a small television. There was a newspaper open on the desk. This was the first time. The desk clerk looked away from the television. I had a small dark blue dress on. I went outside to wait for him. I had cigarettes in the bag. It took me two hours to pack the bag. I was careful. I knew what I wanted. I placed the bag on a small bench outside the motel office. The cigarettes were resting on top. I saw Christopher at the edge of the sidewalk just as it curved. He saw me but he did not change his pace. He did not run. I smoked and watched him. His long sharp angled body with his hands jammed into his pockets. When he got to me, close to me, he took the cigarette from my mouth. He inhaled quick and long. The desk clerk looked up from his television. Christopher put the cigarette out and went inside. I did not move. I closed my eyes. It will become the routine. Christopher smiled at the clerk. He made a simple motion towards me. He would shrug. He reaches into his pocket. Forty-Five dollars. The clerk would barely look away from his television. He would hand him a key for Room number 3. Christopher would take the key, his one hand still in his pocket. A smile and then he would leave. I could hear the clerk's television when the motel office door opened. He was holding the key in his left hand. I picked up the bag from the bench. It was lighter than I remembered. It got lighter every time. Room number 3.

The door stuck. Christopher would push against it with his body before it opened. He would eventually call it our chapel, our St. Mary of Zion. A simple room. A bed, a dresser, a bathroom, one chair. I would not need more. We needed barely. I put the bag down at the edge of the bed. The dresser. The ark. The cigarettes. I put them on the dresser. Christopher was waiting in the middle of the room. I move to him. I took his hand and slid it under my dress. I was willing to give up a little now. He did not even breathe. I undressed him and laid him on the bed. He waited patiently for me.

Are you cold?
No.
Do you need anything?
No.
You have to be strong.
I know.
For us.
I know.
For all of us.
I will.
This will save us, this will be everything.
I am ready.
Are you afraid?
Yes.
Do you trust me?

Yes.

Then tell me everything.

The motel clerk did not look up when Christopher placed the key back on the desk. His face was white and cool. It was easy that time. The first time. The blood barely there. We did it quickly without words or instruction. He bit his lip till it bled. I had to work to hold him down.

Teresa was drinking a milkshake cool and long. She had her hands wrapped tightly around the tall glass. I put my books down and walked up behind her. She smiled and looked back at me. I kissed her lightly on the cheek. She had a chocolate at the corners of her mouth. I smelled the grill in the backyard. Charcoal and lighter fluid in the house. I played with her hair for a minute. Her shampoo smelled like cherries. In the backyard father was wearing a green apron and standing over the grill. There were glasses of lemonade sweating on the picnic table. I sat down on the end of the bench. Mother had her hands full of potting soil and herbs. She was growing her garden already. Basil, oregano, parsley, thyme, carrots, peppers, wild flowers, and one squash plant. I smiled as she waved at me. My father was chattering with the coals. It was wonderful. We ate with mouths full of conversation. Father was working and mother was keeping herself busy with gardens, neighborhood social calls and books. Teresa always had her games. She played them constantly. She played them at the table, in the car, at her school desk, in her bed before sleep, on the floor in the living room. They changed like a puzzle. Animals and angels. Insects and marshmallows. Horses and flying saucers. Everything was hers and we gave it to her. She smiled and the room was full.

Isaac was desperate. I had been watching him all week when Christopher wasn't looking. His face was full of ticks and jumps. I did not seem him sleep once the week I stayed with Christopher. His body was full of convulsions at night. Twists and fits that made my skin stand up. He made noises I never heard. Deep and racked with hurt. Then he would go to Rebekah. He would go to her in the middle of the night. He would go to her with his face down. He had given up. Given in. I could hear him shuffle out of the room. Christopher was like stone next to me. His father was almost ready to leave. Mary was smiles and sidelong glances. She ran to him like a dear. Her feet bare and scarred from the gravel. His hands had broad strokes on her thighs. I remember them in the yard. Always too close to each other. Christopher told me in flat painless words about them. He said her top was lying in the grass. He said his mother would not cry. He told me what Mary said. I am leaving. I am leaving with him. We are leaving. We can't stay here. I love him. I love him. We're not like you. Not like any of you. I see you with that new girl. What has she done to you? Look at your hands. Father he needs me. I can escape. Look at your hands. Isaac is gone now. He is nothing now. Mother was so desperate that she ruined him.

I pulled the blanket aside. Christopher had his hand on my stomach. I looked at it. The marks were still raw. I moved out from under his hand. The space in the bed seemed so small. The light from Rebekah's room made an angry line in the hall. I moved towards it. I wanted to see them. I wanted to know everything. I crouched at the door. She was sitting up in bed, her bare feet flat on the rug. I watched Isaac move in the room. My legs were beginning to ache. He moved to her carefully. She did not move. There was a leather book in her lap. She did not look at him. She did not look at the book. Her face was still. Isaac knelt next to her. He was careful in his movements, slow, deliberate his eyes focused desperately on something past what this was. She began. It was soft, so soft and with a simple mindedness. He put his hands down on her lap at the edges of the book. She moved slightly making herself accustom to him. He was breathing like a small animal. I watched her breasts rise under the thin camisole. Her lips moved with a no emotion. She read from the leather book until he was crying his face buried in her thighs, Rebekah still and calm. She was all he had left. She was everything to him now. She read from the book until his devotion satisfied her and the prayers echoed with the ecstasy of Sunday sermons. She was with words I had never heard before. I admired her in the sketched bedroom light. In that light she had everything she ever wanted.

Christopher was still in bed. He had barely moved. The space I left in the bed was still there for me. He would not touch it. I moved to be next to him. His body was warmer than I expected. He sometimes can surprise me. I knew what I had seen would break him. It could never be the same anymore.

Where did you go?
To the bathroom.
I don't believe you, where did you go?
To smoke.

Kiss me.

No.

You didn't smoke.

No.

Where did you go?

No.

Tell me.

No.

I want to know.

No.

You went to see them?

No.

You had to know didn't you?

No.

You think I don't know?

No.

Tell me.

No.

You had to know.

No.

Now I have no secrets left.

I know.

Then tell me.

No.

She has ruined him, I tried to give him the river.

I felt him against me. He was full of heat and anger. It would be the only time like this. I had never felt him like that before. Full of so much blood. I could not stop myself. He was stronger than I thought. He was stronger than anyone knew.

Rebekah/1964-1998

I should have waited. I left the house early in the morning. Paul had just washed the Oldsmobile. The chrome shine was beautiful. I let him open the door for me and watched him walk around the back of the car. He traced his hand around the edge of the fender. He opened the door and nestled the bag of groceries on the floor behind his seat. I waited to hear the ignition. It sounded wonderful as it turned over, a low and subtle rumble. I could feel it in my feet. I crossed my legs once before he moved the car into drive. It was hard not to look at him. His face was slender. I put my hands in my lap and watched the house disappear quickly. The green shutters and the heavy picket fence were the last things to leave me. I was going with Paul to a town called Air. The Olds was rumbling low down the highway. I had never lived anywhere else except summer camp, nine years ago, when I was twelve. I placed Paul's hand on my stomach. He could feel Isaac kicking. I knew from the beginning it would have to be a boy. A girl would never feel this way. He smiled and drove with his arm resting out the open window. The drive was only two hours but that was far enough from everything. Paul promised to take care of me. We were married for two days. The Justice of the Peace had a pleasant comfortable smile when he read the vows. My mother did not cry. My father was happy to give me away. He held my arm with a strong march of a retired soldier. His metal was pinned just below the pocket on his only gray suit.

Jun/78

Dear Julie,

For the first time you are wrong. You were wrong. Paul says I listen too much to you. I don't know but it doesn't matter. This town we are in is beautiful. You should see the street. A row of houses that look like candy. Blue, white, yellow, lime, there is even a little pink house at the end of the row. There are kids riding their bikes in the street and the grass looks like a big green carpet. I know California is far from us but I would love you to visit, maybe when the baby is born. You should see it all. Paul is going to be a great father. I know that it will be a boy. Isaac. A good name for a boy. I know what you would say but it feels right. He's going to be a great man. I know it. A mother can feel it. He'll be everything I want. I will show him the book and Paul will show him how to play baseball. I want to have picnics in the backyard and plant a garden. Can you see it, carrots, peppers, maybe a watermelon, a row of corn if it will grow. We can have barbecues and talk to our neighbors. Paul says he is going to buy me a car once we get settled. A little one. Maybe one of those new Japanese ones. It will be great. I know it will.

Jul/79

Air is a simple town. A suburb of a suburb. A town with nothing to offer except quiet streets. He had already moved our things into the house. The sofa from my grandmother. A new dinette set as a wedding gift. Dishes, glasses, a washing machine, his tools. I liked the house. It had an empty look. A space for me and Isaac to grow. I can see where he will take his first steps. I can see where he will sit on the floor and watch television. Paul insisted on buying a new set. There are too many knobs. It has a wonderful glow. I guess it will be okay. I don't want Isaac in front of that thing too much. He is going to read the book. I know he will love going to church. Father wants him to be a soldier. All medals and yes sir no sir. I don't know. I don't think I like that. I don't want him to end up like James. There is no war. We can be real family. We will stay together.

April/76

It's 2am. I can just barely see the clock. I can hear the hands waiting, eager to turn. She has been taking about leaving again. Disappearing. That's what people call it. Mother had an episode. All those questions again. What did you have for breakfast. Did you eat a banana today. Did you eat lunch. Who did you eat with. What are they doing. Where did you go. What were their names. How do you know them. Why are you doing tonight. Where are you going. Who are you going with. When are you coming. When are you leaving. Who will drive. Are you taking the bus. Do you have enough money. What are you wearing. Why don't you talk to me. Why do you lie to me. Why don't you go watch television with your father. Why don't you like television. Why are you never home. Where do you always go. What's that in your pocket. I should have gone with my sister to California. Anything not be like her.

May/81

Dear Julie,

We finally have flowers in the garden. I tilled the ground myself by hand. Isaac held the packet of seeds. He is almost three. His little hands were so eager to grow. Paul has been working double shifts now at the auto plant. Isaac helps me make his lunch in the mornings. He is amazing. I wish you could see him. He looks so much like our brother before James was lost. California seems so far away from here. I tell him about you. I tell him about your letters. I tell him how you are making something amazing out of your life. He talks about you like you are right around him. He says your name all the time now. He wants you to write him letters.

Sept/73

Daddy looks dead. When he falls asleep in front of the television I hear him talking. He says things I never thought a man should say. I wish Julie was here to talk to at night.

Sept/78

Paul told me he could not get away from the plant. He told me that the line would shut down without him. He told me that he did it for us. He said all of this while he was holding Isaac... Three hours old. The neighbors had to drive me to the hospital. I don't even know their last names. They are in the waiting room. They have big smiles and flowers. The husband is smoking something cheap. Paul had grease on his hands still. I took Isaac from him. I did not want him to see his father like that. I didn't mind the labor. The pain was to remind you that life is not just something between your legs. Paul didn't even bring me anything. The husband gave him a cheap smoke. The wife was full with congratulations. She was already too old. I could see it in her face while they drove. Her smile was turned knotted angry at the edges. She could not stop looking at the husband. A longing full of resent. It was probably not his fault. She is probably a desert.

Oct/79

The house is full of noises. I hear them all the time. They live in corners, in closets, behind the walls in the pantry. Paul tells me I am just crazy because of the baby. The baby. He is always telling me the baby is making me crazy. The baby has me crazy. The baby. Isaac is all I have. Paul says he is not right. Paul says babies are suppose to cry at night. Paul says that we should take him somewhere. I know he is good. I know that his doesn't need to cry. I hear noises in the house. I called a man to come look at the house. To look at the pipes. To look in the walls while Paul was at work. The man could not look at me straight. His eyes were always moving away.

Jun/80

Julie

Paul has been painting the house on the weekends. He starts at 8am on Saturday. Every Saturday for two weeks. I asked him if we could go somewhere. He says the house needs to be painted. I said the house is new. He says the other houses look better. Our house needs to look better. I know he still loves me. Sometimes I just need to get out of this town. The woman next door has no children. She is older than me. She says that her and her husband don't want children. What kind of people don't want children. The husband goes to work every morning to an office where he doesn't need a tie. I wish Paul had a job like that. He says it is not honest work. Honest work. When are you coming to see the baby. I have your picture in Isaac's room. I want him to know you. I don't care what Paul says.

Oct/73

Daddy walks around the house with all that weight on his face. They should have never let James go. Today he looked like a ghost. His clothes look empty when he is in the them. I hear him at night. In his bedroom. He screams into his pillow. He screams until he gives in. He screams Dolce. They should have never let him come home.

Aug/70

I hate the summer. The heat makes things happen. Mother and father are desperate. I watch them from the kitchen. The walk in circles around things. They walk in circles around the couch. They sit. Then they walk in circles around the chair. Then they sit. Then they walk in circles around the coffee table. They walk, they say nothing. It is all waiting. Sometimes if the heat breaks we have a good day. In the car with the windows down towards a park. Sometimes we go nowhere and that is just as good. Mother says it is too hot to cook. We eat cold chicken and wet lettuce with ranch dressing. Sometimes French. Once James swallowed a small bone. He started screaming. He said it was going to choke him. He said he was afraid to die. I thought he was going crazy. Two weeks ago, Sunday, the church fans were broken. Everyone was wilting over, rumpled sleeves, and dresses folding into woman's thighs. I watched the preacher exhaust himself. It was fantastic. James had already left. A month had gone by without him. Julie was in California for more than a year. I had letters. At least a dozen from Julie. Three from James. My brother writes like a dying poet. Every word seems to hurt him, to just barely make it on the page.

Sept/80

Julie
The house is full of noises.

Nov/97

Paul is desperate now. He wants her. I see it. I see it. He thinks I don't see it. I see it. I see it. I see the way he looks at her. I see the things he buys her. He thinks I won't notice. New underwear in the laundry. Perfume on her clothes.

Mar/82

All Paul talks about is fucking. He only wants to fuck me. He only wants my pussy. He only wants my tits. His dick runs around like a jackhammer. He looks at me while I cook dinner. Cunt. He looks at me while I shower. Cunt. He looks at me while I sleep. Cunt. Pussy. Pussy. That is everything. Isaac won't stop crying.

Nov/79

Julie
I took Isaac to church today. It was the first time. Paul stayed home to watch football on the television. I wouldn't tell him but I was glad. I didn't want him between us. Sundays will be our day. Our day to be alone. I had not been to church since the pregnancy. The church in Air is white. It is a large white church. It looks just like the churches I see in movies. Clean and tall at the crest of a

hill. There is a subtle path that leads up to two large oak doors. Elm trees are everywhere. Orange, red, in the fall like the lord was calling to us. I carried Isaac in my arms. I wanted to cry he looked so beautiful.

April/81

Paul is talking about Africa again. He has his maps all over the floor, the table, the desk. There are thousands of colors across the floor. He holds Christopher in his arms and says those words. Zaire. Ghana. Ethiopia. Morocco. Angola. Burundi. Rwanda. I watch him. He takes his hand and traces across rivers, through mountain ranges, over plains and deserts. He sits and talks to him, holding him. Isaac is crying for me.

July/79

Rebekah

Things in California are sunshine. The weather here is great. Everything is great. I am working overtime now trying to make things happen. I will try to come and visit soon. I can't wait to see Isaac. He must be wonderful. You must be wonderful right now. I am sorry for such a short letter. Things here are crazy. You know how it is. Always have something to do. Always have somewhere to go. That's how this business works. Anyway, I will write soon.

Julie

Apr/74

I listened to him all night. He was dying. I tried to pray for him.

Mar/80

I did it for you. I did it for you. I didn't want him. I didn't need another. I have Isaac. Isaac is everything to me. I know you don't love him. I know you watch us at night. His body sleeping next to mine. I can hear the ice in your drink as you walk in the hallway. He is beautiful. I won't end up like them. I can't. So I did it for you. I did it for you. He will be yours. He will be yours. He will be my sacrifice. He will be my cross. He will be my burden. He will be Christopher.

Jun/81

I made muffins today. Isaac sat at the table, with a glass of lemonade, drawing in his book. Blueberry. It was our favorite. The kitchen smelled wonderful. Paul was working weekends now at the plant. He had been promoted. He says it is a very important job. He says the plant can't run without him. On Sundays he doesn't come to church with us. He stays at home. He watches television and mows the lawn. I will not let him get to Isaac. Isaac is already reading the book. Just a few words but it is enough. I read to him every night. He sits in bed with his head in my lap. His favorite is our psalms.

Apr/96

Julie

My daughter is a whore. Today I caught her with a boy. She is only thirteen. Thirteen and she let him take her clothes off. She was lying there naked with him on top of her. He didn't even bother to take his shirt off. He was nothing. She never comes to church. I slapped her. I slapped her face until it turned red. She did not cry. She would never cry. She is nothing inside. She was just lying there and laughing. Naked. She never once tried to cover herself. My daughter is a whore. All I have now is Isaac.

Jul/78

Today we had a barbecue. Paul and I outside at our little wooden picnic table. Paul had worked on the yard all week. My flowers are in bloom. Air is wonderful. It is wonderful here. Paul is happy. I am happy. I can't believe it. We talked about Isaac today, Paul kept touching my stomach all afternoon. We talked about buying a new car. Japanese maybe. He insists on buying American. He says that it is the right thing to do. He says we need to support our country. He says my father would want us to buy American. He says what would James think. He would have been twenty eight this summer.

May/81

I know it's a boy. It has to be but not like Isaac. He will be Paul's. He will try to make Paul happy. At night when we have nothing to talk about he stares at the television. I read Isaac our psalm. Paul drinks. It is not a problem. It is just something new for him. He loves to look at the bottles. They are lined up. They have a precise order. There are certain glasses. I want him to be settled. We have air conditioning now.

Julie

Christopher is sleeping. He is such a burden. He is always needing something. He is nothing like Isaac was. Isaac only needed me. Christopher needs all the time. Paul is working constantly now. He only cares about work and his maps. He sits with Christopher in that room. Maps everywhere. There are books with pictures of naked breasts. I told him I do not want Isaac to see that. Things like that are not right. Isaac only needs me. This house seems so small now. I want to come and see you. I want to see the sun in California. It must be wonderful. Everything here is so small. All the people you see. Everything must be wonderful for you. Paul is building a deck. It has replaced the bottles. I have nothing except Isaac. Paul has his job, his maps, his books. Christopher. He can have the body. It is my sacrifice.

Mar/98

Paul is lost. I lost him to her. Mary has something I could never give him. I won't blame him, I won't admit I was wrong. It's her, she did it to hurt me. She knew it was the only thing left she could get from me.

Sept/72

I am scared for him. I watch him moving around the house like he is unsure if he is real. Dad always slaps him on the shoulder. How ya doin son. Good to have you back James. Mom makes him eggs. You hungry wants some eggs. Are you tired you want some eggs. I can't talk to him anymore. He is always turning that word over in his mouth. Dolce. Dolce. Dolce. He knows too much now. I know he can tell. I know he sees it. I have to get out of here.

Sep/97

I see them together. I see the way they move. I still have Isaac.

Aug/72

He had a car. That was all that mattered to me. It was nothing great an old Plymouth with a dozen nicks and dents scattered down the side. It was a car. I didn't care about anything else. I put my tongue in his mouth after only ten minutes. He didn't even say a word. He shifted the car into drive and took a wide turn onto the street.

Nov/98

This is it. This is it. This is all of it. I know it is like this now. I know everything now. I know about him, and Isaac. I know about everything. This is it. This is the end of it. I've lost it all. I can't live without him. I don't care about anything else. Everything here seems so small. We didn't need anyone else. We didn't need anyone. He was mine, I was his. It was beautiful. It was pure. It was the right way. Now it is nothing. Nothing. I am nothing. My body is nothing. My mind is lost to me. My body is nothing. I am ugly now. My pussy is a curse. I will change everything. I will do it for Isaac.

Nov/70

Paul was the only one who would look at me. He didn't know anything about me. When I told him he said he didn't care. He had an Oldsmobile and a place to go.

Sept/68

James left today. In the middle of the morning with nothing but a small bag and his boots tied together over one shoulder. He had a look on his face that I had never seen. Father was talking low and close to him. Mother was turning a cup of coffee around in her hands. He looked so thin that morning. The sun cut past his body and barely left a shadow. Father was trying his best not to smile. I could almost see it at the corners of his mouth. I had talked to him about it. I had told him I would miss him. I told him I didn't want him to leave. He was everything to me. He did not want to go. He said it was the best for him. He said it would help him. He would get rid of the junk. It would turn his mind the right way. I tried not to cry in front of him. He took his hand and pressed it against my check. Don't forget about me. I can't. You will. I won't. You will grow up and forget. I promised him I would never forget.

May/70

Mother looked beautiful this morning. Her hair was wrapped up around her head like a movie star. She had on a slender sundress and stockings that I had never seen before. They were not from the local pharmacy. She was wearing lipstick. I did not kiss her goodbye. I did not want to change anything about her.

Aug/98

I can't believe that she came from me. That cunt. That cunt. She came from me. I ripped her out of my pussy. I ripped her out of me and this is what she does. She is a cunt just like her mother. She is just like her mother. Weak. All she has is between her legs. She doesn't know anything else. I haven't shown her anything else. I haven't given her anything else. That is all I have to offer. All I had left for Paul, all I can do for Isaac. She is a bitch. I can smell her pussy on his hands. Paul still comes to me and tries to get between my thighs. I know he is fucking her. He has fucked her already. Mary is fifteen. She begged him for it. I watched her. When he comes home from work. The way he holds her. The way she hides her hand between them. Cunt. I am a cunt. She is a cunt. We are something thicker than blood.

May/95

Christopher is sixteen now. He has rejected me. Paul has won him over with his charts and maps but it won't last. I can see everything about Paul now. The way he looks at Mary and waits. That is all he has. I will keep Isaac safe.

Aug/98

Mary watches everything. She watches and dreams of escape. She waits for the day that Paul will take her from me. From us. I know I cannot stop it. I know it will come and I have failed her, I have given her nothing else to wait for. I can ruin it all.

Mar/90

Dear Julie
When are you coming to visit. When will I ever see you again. I know things are very busy for you now. I know that being your type of woman takes a lot of work. Isaac no longer reads your letters to me. He keeps them to himself now. He loves them. He loves everything about you. He keeps telling me that one day he will leave here for California.

Aug/94

Christopher. He is fifteen. Almost a man. Never quite a boy. He doesn't know what to do with himself. I watch him walking around the house. Everything seems so small. He is not at all like his brother. His body is all angles. James was made of angles. Paul has something new now. In the hallway by the bathroom he holds his towel in his arms waiting just to hear the water to turn off. He has only mumbles and news about the weather. Only strangers talk about the weather. I always see him alone. I picked him up outside the school and he was waiting alone. Christopher just waits. He says hello. He says hello with such finality I am afraid to say anything else to him. He knows how I cursed him, cast him aside. He felt it when he was still inside me. I know he felt it when I screamed his name. This is why he hates me. This is why he will do anything to hurt me. He is not strong enough to hit me. He will wait. He is so good at waiting. That is why he is always at Isaac, begging him to follow those ridiculous maps. I see them together on the porch, their lips barely move sharing whispers about the long dark river. When Isaac is with me it is not like before. He does not have the same ease in the dark. There is a reluctance in his hands. Isaac is threatening me with California. Julie. Julie. Why did you have to be so glamorous. You can't have him either. My own sister.

Dec/80

I like to think that he still loves me. He tells me he is trying to get better, to fix things, but even my cunt won't work for him anymore.

May/80

Julie

Paul built a bench. It is made of teak. It is wonderful. We sit at nights when it is not too cool. In the summer we will use it more. It smells wonderful. He bought himself tools. He loves his tools. This is the thing for him now. Tools. He has dozens hung precisely in the garage. Tools. I don't understand. He is happy. That is good enough. I know that things now are hard with Isaac. Paul says there is more money coming soon. The plant wants him to be something. He says they have plans for him. I am satisfied with that. He loves his tools. He loves working in the yard. The deck. The bench. He always has projects. He has a book series. It tells him how to build things. He is obsessed with them. Every night I see him reading in his underwear and t-shirt. He looks handsome sitting with that single light on. It is nice in our home now. Not so much talk of Africa.

Sept/72

That backseat of his old Plymouth felt like a cheap motel. The leather smelled like cigarettes and beer. I rode those bench seats until our bodies were too slippery to keep together. I did not love him. I did not even want him. I just needed something. I would do anything not to end up like her. I let him stay inside me long afterwards. He said it made him feel safe. I would do anything not to go home.

Mar/71

It was the first year without a party. It was the first year without any friends. There was no cake. There were no cards. There were no hats. My mother said it was better this way. Birthday parties are for little girls. You are too old. My father bought me a watch from the drugstore. He said it was to help me be responsible. My mother gave me a pamphlet. She said I need to be prepared. She showed me pictures of things I had to buy. She gave me twenty dollars. I never had twenty dollars. She said the woman at the drugstore could help me. She said it was natural. She said to never talk about it. I was afraid to ask her anything. My father sat in the other room watching televised sports. I had already been to the drugstore three months ago. That is where I met him. The first time. He drove me home in his Plymouth. Julie told me to be careful. She told me everything in her letter. She told me what to buy. She sent me money. She did not send me a pamphlet. She sent me condoms. She told me how much it would hurt. She told me never to tell mother.

Aug/68

The church was bursting with noise. All the people singing. All the people so alive. I did not care. I did not care what they thought. I looked down to my parents as I stood up. The people all around me clapping. They just sat there staring at the floor. I opened my mouth and let Him in. I let Him in for the first time. I knew that he had blessed me. I sang. I felt all of my body moving. I felt the blood. I felt the body. I felt everything that was around me. I felt a part of everything that was Him. I looked at them just staring at the floor. I heard my heels clicking against the hardwood floor. The woman next to me was sweating. She was more alive than anyone I had ever seen. Her eyes were closed but she knew about everything around her. She knew the walls. She knew the floor. She knew how many steps to the alter. She knew all the men and women in the choir. She knew all the boys with angel faces. She knew all the girls with sweat in their Sunday hair. I wanted to be her. I wanted to have a part of her. I got as close to her as I could. I put my body right next to hers. I felt heat. I felt something stronger my legs barely able to stand. She knew I was there. She reached out her thick arms and pulled me to her. In her heart I heard the blood. I found everything I was hoping for. I felt my mother pulling at my dress. She was wrenching on my arm. She would never know what it was like. When I left her breast and stumbled into my mother I have never felt so cold. I never could be like her. Afterwards in the car they said nothing. I looked out the window. People were all lined up outside the big oak doors, talking, shaking hands, embracing. I knew He was staring right at them. He was looking down at them. He was full of such joy. I gave everything up to him.

Dec/73

Julie

I should have listened to you. I should have been careful. I should have listened. Why do you have to be in California. James is nothing anymore. Dolce. Dolce. Dolce. I hear him crying. I tried to tell him. I know he knows everything. I couldn't even see him anymore. He is not ours anymore. James. I tried to tell him but he was nothing. He is nothing. I do not know what to do. I can't tell them. I am sorry. Please do not deny me. I am sorry for everything. I am sorry for what I did. I am sorry for what I have to do. Please forgive me.

Dec/81

I have given up everything except Isaac. I have given Paul a boy of his own but he is already chasing me around with his hard on and I am scared.

Jun/98

It happened today. I know it is not the first time but today I saw them. She was undressed. Her blue bikini top laying in the lawn. I was holding a tray of muffins. She was on top of him. Her back was shiny and wet. I did not know what else to do. I watched them pack their bags. Her clothes still looked so small. He took everything he could in one bag. His head was always at the ground, his eyes always searching. He knew what he had done. They took the truck. I don't blame him. I should have never let him inside me.

Jan/83

I sat naked in the chair in our bedroom. My body was still wet from the shower. He did not even wash his hands. I am a cunt. We did it standing up in the bathroom. Afterwards he urinated in front of me. Nothing good can come from this.

May/80

I read to Isaac. It was the words that made him smile. The psalms.

Apr/75

The building was white. The cab driver asked sheepishly if he needed to wait.

Sept/72

Paul loves that car. I see him at the end of the block his head in the engine. His face smeared with grease and sweat. He looks nice without his shirt. The hair on his head is so blonde. I watch him with his tools. Each one is clean. He has a place for each one. He has a rag for the oil. He has a rag for the transmission. He has a pan for the oil. He has a pan for the transmission. There is no grease in his parents' driveway. He has a rag to polish. He has a rag in his pocket for his face. His hands are well used. I have never seen his mother.

Mar/71

I never told them anything. I bought a magazine with pictures of naked woman in it. I kept it between the mattress and the box spring. I pushed it all the way to the middle. The woman in the pictures had amazing skin. Her breasts did not hang. Her legs did not shake. Nothing on her moved. She was perfectly still in every motion. She was in control of her body. She was in control of her life. Men wanted her. Women wanted to be her. Everyone wanted to be with her. There was an expensive car in the picture. On one page she was with naked with two soldiers. She had something everyone wanted. My father found me looking at the magazine. He took it from me. He looked at the pages. He looked at me. I never saw him look so frightened of himself. He said she was a cunt. He told me she was just a piece. He told me decent women don't shave between their legs. When he told my mother she made me see a psychologist. He asked me embarrassing questions and then sent me home with a pamphlet and a note. Dear Rebekah's Mother your daughter is normal. My parents folded the letter and placed it in a kitchen drawer full of rubber bands and coupons.

Mar/97

Isaac is getting restless. He is always moving around the house. The house seems so small now. My sons spend hours whispering to each other. Paul is just furniture now. If it was not for Mary he might be dead. They are waiting. Everything is a piece of glass. The light distorts their faces. I must save Isaac.

Apr/75

I drew in a breath that felt like it would burn me. Then it was over. It was done. I tried to find my legs to get off the table. The building was white. The doctor's face was desperately reassuring. Everything was steel and modern. He took it from me, it was too easy. The cab driver helped me to the car. He closed my door. When the car started it was the most comforting sound I could have heard but I knew a daughter would have ruined us.

Oct/73

James. I watched him put that spike into his vein. Every day. When he came home I asked him with my face full of tears. What did you do. What was it like. Did they scream. What does it feel like. He told me everything. When father asked him he only said it was war. War. When I asked him he said it was shit. Everything was shit. His friends dying was shit. The Vietcong was shit. The USO was shit. The napalm was shit. The only thing that kept him alive was the junk. The junk made the jungle paradise. The junk made the bullets move slow. The junk made the sunsets last as long as possible. The junk kept his body alive. The junk killed his soul. The junk made him forget Dolce and the institution. In a place where there is no God there is the junk.

Aug/98

I saw them. They might have known it. I don't think they cared. I don't even know her name but she has taken Christopher like a vampire. He is living on pain and fever dreams. I won't let them get to Isaac.

Oct/88

Rebekah

California is so amazing and everything here are going well. I wish you could visit with Isaac and the family but I am just so busy these days between the set and promo reels I am not sure when would be a good time. Sorry for such a short letter but I have to dash.

Julie

Oct/73

Paul proposed. It was romantic enough. He did get on one knee. He said it was the right thing to do. He had been following me for months. Taking me to lunch, taking me to dinner, to the movies, the store. Anywhere. He would have driven me to California if I was not afraid to ask. He would do anything for me. Wash my clothes. Take out the garbage. Polish my shoes. Lick my pussy. He said it was because he was in love with me. Anything is better than staying here. There is nothing to stay for without James. Julie says we can come to California. She is too busy for us. I do not want to ruin her dreams. He says we are moving to a town called Air. It will be nice enough.

Feb/73

James. I failed you. I should have never left you there alone.

Jan/72

The choir was alive. They floated above the preacher cradled in his arms. He held them all as their voices streamed out and into the pews. Then He entered me with honest devotion. I opened myself up to him. I let the hymns run through my body. I felt their voices in my fingers. I felt their voices behind my eyelids. I felt him in my stomach. I let him penetrate me and then rush out my mouth in praise. I danced with him.

Jan/99

The house seems so small. Christopher is dead. They are gone now. I am here with Isaac. With so much blood. There is nothing now but blood. This is my only burden. I cannot cry for him. I cannot pray for him.

Apr/75

I will do anything for forgiveness.

Paul 1998

I refused to wait anymore, the secrets in this house are crushing me. I spoke to Christopher last night, he is lost to me, that girl now owns him.

We can leave together. All three of us
That's not how it works
Why not
It is not that easy I love Mary.
Don't tell me that.
My son My daughter it will be beautiful
I won't do that I will not be part of that perversion
Look at all this blood My son
Axum

Mary has fantastic eyes and when I watch her all I can see is the deep brown of the Congo in her eyes. There is nothing else but Africa in her eyes.

I don't blame them, I don't blame anyone. It is not their fault, things happen. People are like machines in that way. They break when they get tired. They break for no reason, the fan belt snaps in your car, a screw falls out of your chair a light bulb goes out. Smoke comes out of the television. It is like this, it is the way it goes. You can't blame them, they did their best, they are just broken. They sit there in their chairs, they bought them at the furniture store outside of town. Ten years ago maybe, I remember the trip. All talking in the car about what kind of chairs they could afford. Dad had just gotten a big bonus from the office. They hadn't bought anything in five years. They didn't know what things cost. They knew about eggs, milk, bread, groceries, gasoline, new tires, sparkplugs, vacuum bags, laundry detergent, t-shirts, socks, aspirin, insulin, underwear, nails, hammers, screws, a snow-shovel for the winter bought last during the hottest month of summer. They didn't know about a car, a television, a radio, a sofa, a vacuum a washer or dryer. At the store he held the money tightly in his hand inside his pocket. It was the largest thing he had ever carried in one hand. He looked like a rabbit in the headlights. I had twenty dollars folded in my wallet. I had been saving for my trip. The only thing I had bought was my book and my map. That is all I wanted. They wanted leather. They could not afford two leather chairs. They had to settle for a floral pattern and a plain looking colonial pattern. Dark blue and off white, they were awful next to each other. My parents bought them. He refused to have them delivered. It was ridiculous to have them on the roof of the station wagon. Two ugly chairs flying down the highway at no faster than forty-five mph. People passed us flashing their lights. They looked awful next to each other. I think when I was seven I cornered a squirrel in the corner of the yard between the metal shed and the fence. I stared at it. It was just a rodent. I didn't want to hurt it, it was shaking. Maybe five minutes. No more than ten. Then it just stopped, it just stopped shaking and fell over. I picked it up. It was stiff. When I brought it inside she started screaming. That high pitched shrill only a forty-year-old mother has. Over and over. I just held it out to her and she hit me in the face with a dishtowel. I think I wanted to cry but nothing happened. I just stood there until my arms got tired and then put the squirrel on the table. We stood there staring at it. When he came home he looked at both of us and then at the table. He went to the closet, shoebox, shovel. It was all over in five minutes. He was an efficient caregiver. After that they started doing strange things around me. I always wished I had a sister. That would have been nice. A brother would have been difficult. A sister would want nothing I have. I could talk to her, ask her about things. I could talk to her about them. She could show me what to do.

There is a place in Ethiopia. It is small and hidden. Hidden enough that they are left alone. The ark of the covenant is there. It is a small temple. Mt. Saint Mary of Zion. There is only one man at the temple who has seen it. He is an elder priest, his vow is to protect the ark. No one else has seen it. There are others there, they help take care of him bring him food. When he gets old, too old he will train someone new. No one tries to enter the temple. No one outside of the single priest has seen the ark. There are many Ethiopians who worship this way. There is a festival every year. I read that the Ark has emerged once in the last hundred years during the festival. Follow the Congo River all the way into the interior of Africa and then go overland into Ethiopia. I just put a down payment on a house. It is not too far from the town they live in now. Air. A town called Air. I tell people that. It is a nice house. Front yard. Back yard. I will build a picnic table and a deck. There is a new plant opening in the town. I can work there. I will start on the floor working with the machines and men with dirty under their nails. I don't mind work. I rebuilt the engine in the Olds. I will move to management eventually. Stay late. Work hard. Buy nice things. A little Japanese car for Rebekah. She will like that.

I hated living in that house with those damn chairs. They were like tombs. They waited there. They were always waiting for something. They would sit and stare at the television or just the mantle. They were always looking for something. One day mother told me she always wanted something else. I asked her if she loved me. She did not answer me. I pulled at her arm until there were tears in her eyes.

Isaac is not a normal boy. He does not do things. He sits watching her like she has wings. He will not talk to me, he will not do anything with me. He is only five but he should want to play things that boys play. He wants to listen to the psalms. He should to things boys do with their fathers.

We moved into the house and she seemed so happy. The neighbors brought us things, cake, pie, tools, some milk, it was a holiday. I never had a holiday before. Rebekah laid contact paper down in all the cabinets and drawers. The bathroom, kitchen, the laundry room, the bedrooms. The cabinets in the garage. The wallpaper was new. The house still smelled slightly of paint I was glad.

I put my maps in the spare room. I would hang the important ones. The others they would be for discussion. Rebekah is happy. The baby's things are in the room next to ours. The crib and toys, things baby's need. I like watching her. She is beautiful. Her legs are lean and dark. The color has come back to her skin. After her visit to the doctor she looked ill for a full two weeks. She says she will cherish this time forever. She would do anything for him. I will get tools and build a deck. A play-set. Things that husbands do. The plant is expanding and my boss says I can move up to management now. They still sit every night in their chairs.

They have not tried to visit. I don't talk to them. There was a girl across the street. Before Rebekah. She had a dad with long hair. I stayed at her house twice. I told them that I was with someone from school. The dad with the long hair was always relaxed. That is what he called it. I never saw her mother. I don't think he had a job. She worked at a dress shop after school. She said she liked it there. The people were nice. We would talk. It was simple enough.

Girl: How was your day?

Me: Good I guess.

Girl: You guess.

Me: I guess.

Girl: You want to come over after I finish work?

Me: I guess.

Girl: Yes or no?

Me: Yes.

Girl: Good.

She was nice. She had a tattoo of a bird on the inside of her thigh. She showed me a lot of things. Once we were lying naked in her bed. The sheet was on the floor. It was hot and I could smell her all around me. Girl: You want to do something new?

Me: I guess.

Girl: Yes or no.

Me: Yes.

Girl: Wait here.

She left the bed and I watched her for a minute. I thought about Africa while she was gone. When she came back she had a smooth small bag with her small dangling in between her legs as she walked back to the bed. She pushed my mouth together with her hands. I stuck out my tongue. She put it on my tongue and I held it inside my mouth. She took two. We waited ten minutes. She lit candles. It was hot. She turned on music. It was hot. Then she climbed on top of me.

Girl: Go slow. Slow. Slower. Slow.

Me: Okay.

Girl: I love you.

Me: Okay.

We did it like this for twenty minutes.

Girl: Can you see that?

Me: What?

Girl: It is beautiful.

Me: What?

Girl: Close your eyes.

Me: Okay.

Girl: Are you going to cum?

Me: Soon.

Girl: Wait for me.

Me: Okay.

Girl: You feel good inside me.

Me: Okay.

We did it like this for ten more minutes.

Girl: Are you ready?

Me: Yes.

Girl: Cum with me.

Me: Okay.

Girl: Oh god it's beautiful.

Me: . . .

She lay down next to me afterwards. I never felt more uncomfortable. The dad with the long hair was making coffee in the morning. He smiled at me. I smiled back and left holding my shoes in my hand. He didn't say anything that a dad with short hair would say. I bought a new map at the bookstore. It was two towns away. I had to drive twenty-five miles. The bookstore in town only had magazines.

The National Geographic is good. They are helpful. I need more. Nazret. It is not an easy place to find. It is not on all the maps. There are almanacs. Encyclopedias. They are out of date. Too general. It is hard to find out anything real about the place. I have a new book on the ark. It is hard to find the truth. They sound real. King Solomon and the Queen of Sheba. Menelik the son. He brought the ark back. Sheba. They said that Menelik brought it back to Ethiopia during his reign. The shotel is the priest's only weapon. No one has ever tried to get inside. If it's true, if it's only true. We will start at the entrance to the river. Kinshasa. The trip can take up to 35 days. The boat is just a barge really strapped against other barges. It is a small floating city. There are grills and barrels everywhere for cooking. This one family is twelve in all. The air in the cabins is unbreathable. Most sleep out on the deck despite the mosquitoes and the flies. We can use the foam rubber mattresses. Mary has fantastic eyes. When I watch her all I can see is the deep brown of the Congo in her eyes. There is nothing else but Africa in her eyes. She was wearing a flowered dress today. Light, cream with crushed red flowers. It is the only thing her mother gave her since she turned thirteen.

I met Rebekah at school. We went to the same school. Once we talked about how children have to do everything they can to not grow up and be their parents. She went to the church on Sundays. She told me her brother was sent away. Her sister was helping to make movies in California. Talking about them was like strangers talking about the weather. There is a house at the end of the block with almost no front lawn. There is a family of five living there. Two boys. One girl. Every Saturday they sit on the front porch hanging there feet into the bushes. They are always talking. They smile at each other. The parents, a dad with short hair and a mom with a modern look always seem happy. They have the smallest house but don't seem to care. I like that. The girl is always running from the boys. They play music.

The girl with the dad who had long hair loved music. She always had music. That seemed important. I had a picture of girl in my locker. I found her in a magazine. She was wearing half a bathing suit. It was pretty. I don't know why I kept it. It didn't seem important. It only seemed like the right thing to do. I met Rebekah's father in a hardware store. It was a place men went. I was buying nails. He spoke to me like he had known me.

Him: How's that Olds treating you?

Me: Okay I guess.

Him: Nothing like American.

Me: I guess.

Him: My daughter says you are in the metal shop.

Me: Yes.

Him: There's a job at my plant I can get you.

Me: Okay.

Him: You never know one day you could be management.

Me: Okay.

Him: Great, I'll get the paperwork going.

He was buying wires and a wrench.

Me: Okay.

Him: I'll tell Rebekah you'll call.

I paid for the nails. The hardware store man was smiling. I watched her playing with Isaac. They had the same look. They are the same. He is everything to her. I watch them and I am not there. I am never there. I work. I told her that I would build a deck outside, something for Isaac to play on. I bought tools and filled the garage with them. All the husbands in Air have tools in their garage. All the wives wear white aprons and take walks with their children. Rebekah does not go on walks. She keeps Isaac to herself. He doesn't play with other children. He only is with her. She reads to him.

More delightful is your love than wine
With you I rejoice and exult I extol your love
On my bed at night I sought him whom my heart loves
Let my son come to his garden and eat its fruits
Your very figure is like a palm tree

Nothing I do can help him. I bought enough tools to fill the garage. We have two cars now. The Olds and a new ford truck. It is a good truck. It fits in nicely. The plant is already expanding. She got another letter today from Julie in California. It is all dreams. Movie sets, rented cars with drivers, the makeup chair and catered lunches. She reads them to Isaac. Hollywood. I asked her to stop but she reads them while I am at the plant. Church on Sunday while I am still sleeping. These are the things she does to me. It seems so unnatural. I started smoking today.

When I watch Mary all I can see is the deep brown of the Congo in her eyes. The movements of the river when she moves. She was wearing a flowered dress today. Light, cream with crushed red flowers. It is the only thing her mother gave her since she turned thirteen. In the summer the sweat gathers just the small of her back.

The Olds rumbles low down the road. Real chrome. Leather seats. I picked her up around the corner from the school. Christopher is falling in love with Africa. He has plastered a map to his ceiling. We only talk about Africa. The Congo and the ark. We will start at Point Noire. The river will be excruciating. The trip overland might break us. He never complains. His eyes are full of hope and light. He is jealous of Isaac. I see him watching the two of them. She is ruining him. She is turning Christopher into her pain. Rebekah thinks I do not see these things. She thinks I am stupid. They think I am stupid. I see what she does with Isaac. The psalms. That is no excuse. I can hear boys riding their bikes. Circling around each other just down the street. Playing cards in the spokes. I didn't think they did that anymore. It is such a peaceful sound.

He bought the Olds for me from a man he used to know. It was three hundred and fifteen dollars. It barely ran. I worked hard on making it a car. I wanted to drive to school. I wanted to take the girl who had the father with long hair. I rebuilt the engine out of parts from the scrap yard. Rebekah first saw me working in the driveway with grease on my hands. I think she liked that. A man who did real work. Her father worked at the old plant. He wore a tie. He did not work with his hands. He worked with a typewriter and forms. Her mother was furniture in that house if she was there at all.
Rebekah: Are you listening to me.
Me: Yes.
Rebekah: Are you?
Me: Yes.
Rebekah: I don't want to end up like her. In the house all day. No one to love me. I don't want children that hate me.
Me: Okay.
Rebekah: Are you listening to me.
Me: Yes.
Rebekah: Of course.

I never owned a television until I was too old to care. When I was little other kids had television. I listened to my mother read Johnny Tremain, Anna Karenina, The Old Man and the Sea. Sixteen years old. I liked the sound of the plant. I liked the rhythm of it. The hiss of the lever. The hard push of the metal. It was assembly. Hsss. Clink. Hsss. Clink. The boat made sounds like that. The captain always swearing as he steered that beast down the Congo. Noises coming from every space. Spitting out between the metal sheets that held her together. From the cans that cooked dinner. From the old and heartbroken engine. Without the sounds we would have to listen to the crying. Without the crying all you could hear is the jungle. On Fridays Rebekah did not eat meat. We could never go to dinner on Fridays. There was a drive-in movie theater in Air. On the Waterfront is a great movie. Marlon Brando.

I bought a bag of marijuana from a boy in the high school bathroom. I gave it to the girl whose dad had long hair. She smiled and took me into her bedroom. That seem to be the way things worked. They sat in their damn chairs all night. They did not go upstairs. They did not eat dinner. They did not even have a glass of water. They sat there staring at each other. He had his shirt off. She left her shoes on all night. I know it was me. They know it was me. They refused to say anything. They refused to talk to me. That was when everything came together. Those damn chairs. They couldn't even afford leather. One afternoon the school had called. I was sitting at the kitchen table. Lemonade and Ritz crackers. She hung up the phone crying. Then he came home.

Him: What's wrong.

Her: There was a problem at school.

Him: What now?

Her: There was some sort of a fight.

Him: So what?

Her: Some boys were making fun of him.

Him: Boys will be boys.

Her: Paul wouldn't . . .

Him: Just say it already for christsake.

Her: Paul wouldn't fight.

Him: Figures.

Her: He just stood there he . . .

Him: He what.

Her: They beat him until . . .

Him: Until what for chirstsake!

Here: He shit himself.

He took off his shirt and handed it to her. He could never understand anything. I know all he was thinking about was that he wanted leather. They had no idea. I drove the Olds to Air. I want to see the house. The neighborhood was nice. There were families. There were kids playing in the yard. The grass was green and thick. Flowers along the front walks. Rebekah could have a garden. Flowers in the front. Herbs and vegetables in the back. I met Anna. She was sitting on the front steps of the school. The Olds was running loudly but she still came up to the window.

Me: You need a ride?
Anna: Okay.
Me: Where are you going?
Anna: Anywhere.
Me: Let's go.
The clutch was burning out. I pushed the car into drive. Anna had long hair. She was wearing blue jeans and a plain blouse. She was crazy. We drove for almost five hours to nowhere. I pulled over into a parking lot and we fell asleep in the front seat. I woke up and Anna was wearing just her underwear leaning up against the side of my car.
Anna: Tell me Paul who are you going to be?
Me: I don't know.
Anna: Take off your clothes with me.
I undressed and piled my clothes on the car hood.
Me: This is kind of weird.
Anna: Now you can't hide from me Paul.
Me: Shit. Sorry. I . . .
Anna: Paul I have seen an erection before.
Me: I wasn't trying to . . .
Anna: Is that what you want from me.
Me: I don't know.
Anna: Is that what you want from this, because sexy is easy.
Me: I want to go to Africa, to Axum.
Anna: I don't think the bus goes there.
Me: Anna I think there is something wrong with me.
Anna: You look beautiful to me.
I started the car. There was a heavy fog lying waist high in the parking lot. The next week I took Anna to the bus station one town over from Air. The bus rattled away. She only had one bag. I watched her settle into her seat. They were plastic and red.

Today Christopher started plotting the route. He has a compass, rulers, guides, tools, he has a book on cartography. He is being very careful. When I watch him I am a amazed. He wants more books. I took him to the town library. There is no real knowledge in Air. It is in the deepest part of the Congo we might lose ourselves. It is important to keep going. It is important to come out on the other side shining with the sun full on your face. The jungle, to the plains, to the mountains, and into the cradle of Axum were Mount St. Mary of Zion will breathe life into our very skin.

I pulled on the edge of my paper. Test scores.
Counselor: I believe your test scores do not reflect your abilities.
Me: I guess.
Counselor: You know you can do better.
Me: I guess.
Counselor: These are the things that keep boys like you out of college.
Me: . . .
Counselor: You should pay more attention to your studies.
Me: . . .
Counselor: These things are important.
Me: I guess.
Counselor: You do want to go to college.
Me: . . .

The girl whose dad had long hair did not smell like the other girls at school. I kissed her in the girl's bathroom on the second floor. I bought her flowers and gave them to her, I drove her around in the Olds. I was nice to her friends. These are things that people do when they want something. She was waiting for me after work. I drove her to the next town. She took her clothes off in the woods behind the public park. Her breasts were small with large nipples. She looked healthy. Her skin was a deep chestnut color. I made love to her twice. The first time with a condom. The second time I was thinking about Axum. She smiled brilliantly in the hard orange setting sun. In Sunday school they told us about the ten commandments. I asked questions. This is why they stopped going to church. You are not allowed to ask too many questions. Rebekah wears white to church. Her parents don't wake up on Sundays. Not since James. They do not know what happens to her there. They could never understand. There is no way to get closer to someone than to sit in his favorite chair.

Christopher will be a great son. He will grow up to love me. He will understand me, I will be a successful father this time. I will work no matter how long. I will make money for our trip. Every week I will save money for us. Rebekah can have Isaac. I watch them together. He can't even see without her. Christopher will be strong.

Mary is laying in the sun, face down on a towel in the yard. Her top is undone. Last night she came to me while I was working on the Olds. Half-dressed and crying about how her brothers hated her. She felt sick and I told her about Anna. I told her about Axum.

When Rebekah brought Christopher home I had already laid the valley in his crib. He would grow up beneath the mountains and stars of Nazret. The crib was made of sandalwood. I had bought it the day Rebekah told me. She was crying. They once told me that nothing comes from hoping. I taught Christopher everything I knew. I showed him the maps. I read him the books. I told him stories I had learned. He bought more maps. He studied cartography. He made his own maps. He studied the river. I followed him from the dirt in Kinshasa up the river. He kept the mosquitoes away from our bed at night. The river is a snake, black and without conscience. It can ruin a man. In the sheets of the bed Rebekah leaves all she needs to say to me. She only wants Isaac. I am still a father. He is still my son. I know this much was true. These wall spill secrets at night. She reads to him from the book

Let him kiss me with kisses of his mouth
Your name spoken is a spreading perfume this is why mother loves you
You are beautiful my mother you are beautiful
Your eyes are doves behind that veil your hair
Your lips are scarlet your breasts are twin lilies
Your very figure is like a palm tree
I eat your honey

There is a new family down the street. I have noticed them moving in. They have nice things. Sofa. Chairs. Dining table. Beds. Linens. Everything looks nice. They have two cars, a nice ford truck and a new foreign sports car. They have two girls. One looks close to Christopher age, maybe a little older. The other is young. A small girl. They are both beautiful. Everything they have looks beautiful. I told

Rebekah about them. She did not care, she was with Isaac. I brought Christopher up to the window. We watched the movers, the father helping with boxes and lamps. The mother with her beautiful girls safe and settled in the front yard. Christopher was old enough to understand. All of the books, maps, charts, stories, pictures, ideas, mysteries. He understood all of it. He loved me. We spent hours with Africa while Rebekah and Isaac made bread in the kitchen. Africa in the study, the map now above his bed. The chorus plotted in thick blue lines snaked along with the Congo and then passed traveled with well-worn fingers through the mountains and to Nazret. Axum. A brilliant star waiting for us. Africa was his life. Then things change. Everything changes.

In the dark Mary told me everything about Evelyn and Christopher.

Isaac is getting restless. He can drive now. He is getting very restless. He still clings to her, he cannot let her go. At night he is still her little boy. He still will not talk to me. His mother has convinced him of this. They still have Sunday but everything is not quite the same. He is restless, looking for something. I know he must hate himself. The thing that he has done. The stars are dim and full of struggle tonight. I watch them. There is no flicker, just a yearning. Ready to explode burn out and make their claim on time. They have traveled endlessly in order to burn out. I see men on the side of the road. Gas stations, convenience stores, phone booths. They look desperate. I don't want to look desperate. I swear everything in this house seems to be getting smaller. There is no room to breathe anymore. Even the kitchen table seems smaller. There are too many secrets now. There is so much noise. I can hear them talking through the walls. Secrets, smiles, and a long glance. Isaac is writing letters to Julie still. There seems to be something missing in her. I have doubts but I am always listening. This whole house is getting smaller. It cannot contain this anymore. This is the truth. Evelyn is around more often. Christopher has left me with no choice, he has given up everything. She does not know what she has done. I hear them beneath the great map.

The sun on the temple St. Mary.
Now you can show me.
You don't understand.
Then teach me, show me the dark heart, give me its salvation.
Oh god, oh god, oh god.

There is so much blood.
That is how I know.

Julie 1999

Rebekah,

The cigarettes are killing me. I should have never started but it is better than the rest of the shit that is floating around this town. My name in lights. That is what I always wanted. Never thought it would be next to the words, nude, girls, and go-go. It has been a while since I hit the runway. That is how it was when I got here. That is the truth. Well not the whole truth. There is a lot more to say about that. I guess it was about James really. I just couldn't be in the house with what was going on. I know you had an idea. You were young. He did everything he could to hide it from you. I guess we all did. I didn't want to be a part of that anymore. That is why they sent him away that goddamn treatment and then the war, the army that was such bullshit. How could that have helped him. It was just more of everything he didn't need. My little faggot. That was Dad's favorite nickname for him. We never told you. Everyone thought it was better that way. Send him to the war that will straighten him out. He was already using by then. The army that just made it easier. Shooting up between his toes. I watched him once in the bathroom. I was only, you were only ten maybe. I thought I was going to vomit. He never cared about me the way he cared about you. That is not the real reason for any of this. I am sure it is all part of it but what did it, what made him crazy was Dolce. Dolce. He was beautiful. The two of them in all that shit. He loved him. Then he went to hell. They all went to hell. They found each other fast. Boys like James always find each other fast. The others I don't think they cared. Everyone was so fucking scared then. Mom, Dad, Me and you there in the middle of that storm. I know what they did to you. The psychiatrists, the shit they put on you. You were too young to be scared. So I started writing these letters. My Hollywood career, bright lights, screen tests, producers, scripts, it was all shit. I had to give you something. It felt good. When you wrote back. Those letters seemed so happy. You were proud of me. I guess after a while it was selfish. It made me feel good to make up this life for myself. I kept it going. How could I tell you the truth. There are some things that we should never say. I use to tell James that. I took my clothes off for money. I did other things for money. That was a long time ago. Now I am happy. I don't know anything about movies except what the kid at the video store tells me. I don't have a house in Malibu and a beautiful downtown apartment. I never married a producer. I never even dated an intern. They don't want strippers or girls from a town called Air. I knew that when I left. You knew it when you married Paul. We all have to find a way out. That is what all of us want. So I lashed my boat to a dream. I am happy now. I have a husband. We got married in Reno. I live in a nice house just north of Sacramento. I am getting rid of my Hollywood post office box. I know this is not the way to tell you the truth. Isaac has been sending me letters since he was ten. I don't know if you know this. He tells me things. You are my sister. This thing you are doing it isn't you. It's wrong. Isaac is desperate to escape, make sure you let him go. This is my last letter. I cannot be a part of this shit our family is always in. You broke those boys. You gave birth to them and then you have resented it ever since. I don't know what happen to you. I don't know where everything went so very wrong.

Aug/99

Aunt Julie

Evelyn is going to bleed him. Christopher. My brother. I love him now. His hands, his side, he is always bleeding. This is what she does to him. I have seen them. At the motel. Always in the same room. He begs her. She has a black bag. A small black bag. She is never without the bag when they are together. He makes no sounds. He makes no movements. She has him now.

Jun/99

Dearest Isaac,

I know you are hurt. I know you are confused. You must leave that house. Everything there is wrong. Leave. Leave. Don't look back. Don't go back. I am trying to send money. I cannot afford much. I hope it arrives in time. My money is tied up in different projects right now. That is the way Hollywood works. Take it and buy a bus ticket. A train get a cab to anywhere but there. I love you.

Nov/99

Dearest Isaac,

Don't let her ruin you. I know she is your mother. She is my sister. You cannot let her touch you. You cannot let her do anything to you that you don't want. Nothing. It is hard for me to read the things that you write. I believe you. I never doubt you. You have never lied to me. Isaac do what you can for now. I will try to help. I don't know what to do. Maybe I can send money. Don't let her touch you anymore.

Jun/99

Aunt Julie

I have never fucked your sister. This is the truth. None of that was true.

Nov/99

Julie

This is the truth. I have nothing left. Paul is gone. He has taken Mary. I am alone. That is the truth. I never meant to hurt Isaac. I gave him everything. I gave up everything for him. He was the most beautiful thing I ever had. I loved Isaac. I gave myself to him. I offered him everything. I opened my body to him to eat from. I gave him my blood. He took everything from me. This is the truth. I placed his head against in the inside of my thigh. I showed him what I had given up for him. He had chosen to give it back to me. Christopher is dead. I watched him grow. I fed him. Changed him. I never touched him. He was my burden. I gave him to Paul and Paul let that girl Evelyn ruin him. He could not save him. Christopher came home his face like ash. Then he was gone. This is true.

Dec/99

Rebekah

This is my last letter. Please do not write to me anymore.

Sep/99

Aunt Julie

Your sister is nothing but lies. Everything she has told you is a lie. Everything. I am leaving soon. I need your help.

Julie

Paul has done it. I know it has been obvious. I don't know why I denied it. I made him leave. He took that cunt with him. The two of them in the Olds. She wasn't even wearing any shoes. Cunt. She is nothing more than the space between my thighs.

Rebekah

Sister. You are dead inside. Something has removed your womb and now you are nothing but a shell. They were your children.

Aunt Julie

This was the truth.

Christopher betrayed me. He never loved me He showed me Africa and the glory of the mountains of Nazret and then took it from us for her. Everything was beautiful in that place. She has turned him. Bandages. Blood. He gave up everything to escape this.

Rebekah is all I have now. I know I can never leave her. Your family, this blood has ruined me. The house seems so small now. There are voices everywhere. Rebekah. She waits in the light. I can never leave her. I know this is the truth.

let him kiss me with kisses of his mouth. more delightful is your love than wine i sought him but did not find him i will rise and go about the city in the street and crossings i will see him but i did not find him. let my son come to his garden and eat its fruits. i heard my lover knocking. isaac isaac isaac your very figure is like a palm tree.

This was the truth. This was what we were waiting for.

Melody

Leslie's left hand was throbbing. The car had just appeared before her, the man and his dog sitting contently in the passenger seat. The car she had struck was an Oldsmobile, tan, with tan interior, and a brown stripe down the side. She grabbed her throbbing hand with the other and put her knuckle in her mouth. It felt good.

The police kept asking her where the other car's driver was. Why the car was no longer running. What the car was doing in the middle of the street.

"Was it parked?" The officer's badge had dull shine.

"No."

"No, then where is the driver?"

"There was a man. A man and a dog."

"There is no one in that car, Miss."

"I saw them, they were just there."

"What's your name, Miss?"

"Leslie, Leslie Dulin."

"Miss Dulin, have you been drinking?"

"No, Sir."

"Then please tell me how this car got here, where its driver is, and how this whole thing happened. Or am I supposed to believe it just came up out of thin air?"

"Yes."

The officer shifted his hat and sighed into the silence.

The alarm clock woke Leslie out of a heavy sleep. Her eyes were tired, and she felt something in her throat. She could not tell how long she had been choking. She grabbed her head and tried to scream. Her voice was chirped with the bird in her throat. It was small and fit easily in the palm of her hand. The wings and body were still underdeveloped, and it shivered from the cold. She punched her hand into the pillow on her bed and built a nest of her blanket. The chick looked content.

She brushed her teeth for ten minutes to get the taste out of her mouth. Her mother had folded her clothes neatly and left them beside her bed in the laundry basket. She had lost ten pounds in the last month, and her jeans rested lazy on her hips. She did not mind the added feeling of sex it brought her.

"I made breakfast for us." Her mother was laying two white plates on the table.

"Thanks." Leslie looked at herself in the plate and scratched at her eyelid.

"Stop that, you'll get an infection." She scooped eggs onto the plate from a large blue pan.

"Why Ma'am, you shouldn't have." Leslie's voice was high with a bad southern drawl.

"What did you say?"

"Nothing."

"Don't be fresh with me, girl. What did you say?"

"Nothing."

"I don't like your tone today."

"What tone?"

"Don't be playing fool with me." Her mother's old traditions were spilling out with into her accent.

"What?" Leslie was staring into her plate at the beautiful sad face. Her long blonde hair strung into several long braids. Her eyes were familiar to Leslie.

"What is with you girl? I swear dismorning I heard you singing and now you look like you about to cry." Her mother sat at the table and rubbed her fork with her napkin. Leslie pulled back on the surprise of her tears.

"You know I don't sing." She picked up her fork.

"Well I heard someone chirping away up there, an old song from, well from before your time. I don't even know where you could heard it, but I'd recognize it anywhere." She stabbed a large chunk of scramble eggs.

"I wasn't singing."

"Eat up, or you'll be late for school."

Leslie heard the bus before it was at her block. The engine was old and rattled loudly. It felt good to be outside. She wrapped her hands around her elbows and waited at the end of her driveway for the bus. There were other kids standing along the street, all waiting. She saw him walking his dog. It was the fourth day in a row. This time he walked directly past her and maybe smiled. The bus smelled like the summer, and the vinyl seats were already warm and stuck to the backs of her arms. She closed her eyes and leaned against the back of the seat clutching herself. *Stop, stop singing.*

The servants had been running with buckets all day. It was raining harder than it had been all season, and it was only July. Martha, perhaps the oldest, was sitting in the porch rocker stripping ears of corn for dinner. Her hands looked marvelously young to Lilly.

"Hello, Miss Lilly." She tossed the husk of corn into a large white bucket.

"Hello, Martha." Lilly pulled at the front of her dress.

"We'll burn the husks later in the fire. Makes a wonderful smell. Your father enjoys it." She took the cleaned ear of corn and dropped into a large cast iron pot of water and salt. Lilly moved forward on the porch and felt the mist of the rain blowing into her face. She ran her tongue over her narrow lips and smiled at the dirty flavor.

"You going to see Mr. James tonight, Miss Lilly?" She could hear the corn slide into the pot. Lilly leaned against the peeling white post. She pulled on the front of her dress again.

"I don't know. This rain. Men don't like the rain."

"Don't be ridiculous, Miss Lilly. No little bit of rain will keep a man from a peach like you." Martha's lips curled back in a little cackle. A rhythmic sound like cracking eggshells. Lilly only purred a little.

"Oh, Martha, you talk too loose sometimes."

"I don't mean no offense, Miss Lilly." Martha put her eyes on back on the corn.

"Don't apologize Martha. You know I'm just fooling with you." Lilly pulled on the front of her dress again.

"What's wrong Miss Lilly?" Martha slipped the last ear of corn into the pot, and Lilly listened to the slow thud it made against the bottom of the pot.

"Nothing, Martha. Nothing at all. Did you put something under my mirror Martha?" Lilly felt something creeping up inside her.

"You know I did, Miss Lilly, and you better stop pulling on your dress before you just come right out of it." Martha wrapped her two marvelous hands around the edge of the pot and lifted it to her breast. She rested the heavy iron against her stomach and disappeared around the corner of the porch.

"Martha, how come you always can see inside?"

Martha was in the kitchen smiling.

Lilly heard the barn door metal locks clanging against themselves as the wind picked up the bottom of her dress. She moved to the end of the porch running her hand against the slick railing. Her father had painted the spindles two days ago on her nineteenth birthday.

Lilly slipped once in the wet grass, feeling the water against her breasts brought goose bumps down through her hips. She gathered herself and enjoyed the rain on her back as she lay in the grass. The barn door was left open since her father brought the two oldest cows to the slaughterhouse. Lilly put the bolt back in the door lock and ran back to the house slip sliding through the wet savanna.

"Miss Lilly, look at you." Martha was hovering over the stove as Lilly through herself into the kitchen with a shudder. "What were you doing out in the rain?"

"The barn door was left open." Lilly sighed heavily and enjoyed the smell of spice that filled her nose.

"Why didn't you ask Wilson or Larry?" She watched Martha motion over the pot. Her thin arm circling around with the steam in odd circles and smiles. Her left hand fondling with the crooked cross that hung about her neck. Lilly always thought it looked like it was melting.

"I don't need a boy to close the barn door. Besides I like the rain." Lilly rung her hair into the sink.

"Apparently you do." Martha squeezed her hand around the wooden relic that hung around her neck. Lilly felt it sharply in her chest at first before the dull resonance began to fill her belly. Martha grabbed Lilly by the wrist and turned her hand up. The blood was dark and smooth like milk. "You done and gone cut yourself, Miss Lilly." Martha brought the hand to her face. Lilly could not remember the blood in the grass. Martha took her apron and patted the inside of Lilly's hand. The blood was drying quickly against the coarse cloth. Lilly looked into her hand at the crooked shape that had been formed. The cut ran perpendicular to the smooth line that crossed her hand. The top of the fresh line curled back and pulled the top town melting into the middle of her hand. Lilly felt the ache in her stomach stronger now and she began to bleed. Martha held her hand tight in her own.

"Oh, god, oh god, Martha stop." Lilly yanked her hand away from Martha's young wrist.

"Miss Lilly I didn't mean no cause." Lilly pulled further away and pressed her hand into her aching belly. "Don't be foolish girl, let it come through. Take them in Miss Lilly, don't be afraid." Lilly felt the blood run down her thigh.

"Martha you got to stop before Daddy finds out."

"Child, no man can understand."

Lilly used the back stairs to reach her room with Martha's help. Martha's youngest was watching the pots. Lilly's room was remarkably cold and steam came out of the buckets that had been gathering warm rain. The ache in Lilly's belly was quiet now. She looked out herself in the mirror. Her eyes seemed larger and full of wild color. Her breasts were swollen and sticky under the wet dress. Martha had left a new dress on the back of the large rocking chair. Lilly peeled the dress from her back, and the air of the room swept over her tightening her skin.

Her body had become slim in the last week, and the curves of her mother were coming through the soft flesh of her thighs and hips. She perched her hands at her sides like the ladies at the market and stepped back from the mirror. She smiled enjoying the way her sex had become full and her waist narrow. She pulled out a pair of old dungarees from her childhood and slid them on. They swung low below her waist, and she smiled as her patch peeked past the waistline.

"Miss Lilly, supper is ready." She heard Martha's voice from the bottom of the stairwell. Lilly undressed quickly and rolled the jeans away. She pulled a new slip from the armoire and fell into it. The silk felt fabulous. She crawled into the dress that Martha had set aside and stormed down the stairs clumping her heavy tread heels on the bare wood.

"Sorry." Lilly dropped into her chair heaving.

"You know I don't like when you're late to the table, Lilly."

"Sorry, Daddy. I had to change."

"Why?"

"I had to close the barn door. I didn't want the chicks to catch cold."

"You know that is why I have all these boys around. I don't pay them for nothing." Her father slipped the fork past his mustache. His voice was full.

"Yes, Daddy." She unfolded her napkin and slipped it onto her lap. Martha was still bringing dishes to the table while her father had started devouring the potatoes. The largest plate, the harvest plate, was piled with steaming corn.

"Will there be anything else, Sir?" She stood quiet in the doorway.

"No, Martha thank you. You can go." Lilly felt her disappear. Her brothers ate like dogs, hanging their mouths close to the plates, arms like windmill blades. Her mother ate like her ancestors, slow and paced with a smile between bites. The brothers left the table immediately, shuffling to the kitchen for seconds and stories with Wilson and Larry. Lilly watched her father bury his face into an ear of corn. Her mother stared empty into her glass.

"The rain was just gruesome today, dear." Her mother pressed her napkin to the corner of her mouth. She had begun wearing lipstick when the sickness took her north for the first time. The doctors said it would improve her self-confidence. Henry thought it made her ugly. It had been difficult at first, but she began to enjoy the feeling it gave her. New men looked, even smiled.

"Yes, yes mother." Lilly watched the juice from the roast congeal in her plate.

"Today at the Montgomery's house their little boy did the most ghastly thing. He came running in covered in mud and swinging some dead rodent in his hand." Her mother began to shake her head.

"Lillian, boys will be boys. They been killing things since before we can understand." Her father swallowed a large biscuit.

"It doesn't mean they should throw it around like a raggedy doll, Henry." She sipped slowly from the sweating glass of water.

"Yes, Lillian, of course not." Henry swallowed a mix of potatoes and meat before belching quietly under his moustache.

Wilson was holding it. His hand gripping the leather strap. His ancestors finally spilling off his back like water. The leather sweated shiny, and Wilson had not smiled so proudly since the day that everything was declared different. The horse snorted heavy and in the fresh morning the animal's breath looked thicker than normal. Wilson only struck the whip lightly against the horse's rump charging the beast onward in a short trot. The distance from the barn to the fields was almost two miles, but Wilson always enjoyed the early morning ride.

The sun was breaking slow over the edge of the horizon. The orange cast creaking slowly over the thick fields, and breezy wheat that shifted to meet the glow. The Dupree's plantation had not grown cotton since 1863, something that seemed so much less important to Wilson now. Brownie, the horse, was an old Clydesdale that came from a northern man along with his coffin. Wilson kicked his boots into the huge sides of the horse, like the hull of a boat. The animal let go a snort of steam and pushed up over the hill. The Dupree fields rose like shining gold salvation in the mornings. The sun had reached the round hub of the hill and sent its light rolling down the green wet meadow until it crashed and tumbled into the field and furrowed through ruts and troughs until streaming out the other end.

To Wilson there was nothing more beautiful than the Dupree field in the early morning. The heavy wet lit wheat dripping shine until it was burned away, and the day's work smiled at Wilson and old Brownie. Wilson took the dirt path around the field to the stock shed. It was the first day that sun had shown on the fields in almost a week and the path was slow, and there she was.

Wilson found the Dupree's in Alabama while they were moving their family towards a second plantation that the first Henry Dupree had purchased before the war. A wheat plantation. Jason Dupree, Henry's brother, was the first to tell Henry that wheat will never grow in Alabama, and that is why it had come so cheap. Henry, first a businessman, second a husband, and lastly a father, could not ignore the price.

The family had broken down across from the courthouse where Wilson was examining his ancestry cracked and scarred across the back of a wooden post. The Dupree's convoy of farm trucks and one brilliant Cadillac had come to a grinding halt with the lead truck driven by the largest brother. He emerged from the steaming vehicle, his mouth full of cuss as he removed his hat to wipe his forehead. At once all four doors of the Cadillac swung open and a sweeping white storm swirled from the back passenger side. She had her hair pulled up underneath a large wide brimmed white hat with a silver silk ribbon knotted around her neck. Wilson felt the sun on his neck for the first time and used his hand to blanket his eyes.

"Excuse me?" The man with the steaming truck motioned towards Wilson. Wilson turned his head dropping his hand to his side. He felt his fingers clenching. It had been a hundred years since the Dupree's had grown cotton, and hundred and fifty since Digbee Dupree had owned a slave. Wilson stood still clinging to the post. He shifted his eyes. There were wisps of hair darted around her eyes like baby's breath.

"Excuse me, Sir?" He moved forward and replaced his hat. "I'm Digbee Dupree the III, I was wondering if you could help us?" Wilson looked at him as his hand found a pocket. The man was huge and emerging from his shirt with thick skin and a ruff of chest hair that ran up his neck. "You see the truck been steaming for a while and its just plain quit now. You know where we can get some water?" He ran his hand along his face pulling at the weak beard that was coming in.

"Can you take both of us?" Wilson felt the post leave him.

"What?"

"I can't go without her."

"Sir, are you all right?"

Her face broke hard against the edge of the shadow that the hat was bringing.

"Digbee, did you find some water?" Henry tried to shake the heat from his coat.

"I don't know, Father."

"You don't know?"

"Well I asked this man here, but I think he might not be quite right." Digbee pushed back the brim of his hat.

"Not right?"

Wilson had removed his shirt and moved to the rear of the courthouse. The pump had been in use since before Lee, and now that Mr. King was marching through the South, there were more thirsty men than ever. When Wilson returned, he had his shirt half-full of water and half full of sweat. He raced to the truck holding the wet bundle like a bag of scorpions. The radiator hissed and spit steam until Wilson rammed the soaking shirt into the open cap. The Dupree's watched him with odd sustain.

They picked up Martha only a mile from the courthouse, and they both rode in the rear of the second son's, Daniel's, truck. There was no talk of wages, but Wilson knew that these large, silent, white people no longer understood the post. They never did, and Martha whistled an old singsong melody through her teeth.

He could see only the hat when he closed his eyes, the silver silk ribbon strangely detached from her neck dancing with two small frayed ends of blonde. Wilson tried not to see her, to push the emotion out from his mind where it didn't belong. Control, control.

"You better not have eyes for that pretty white girl." Martha put her hand on Wilson's bare shoulder. The heat was tremendous.

"Martha don't be foolish."

"Foolish? What you think I love for a hundred years and ain't seen all lies that can be seen through?" Martha laughed her cackle. Her smile showing small wrinkles around her eyes.

"Don't worry about me Martha. You ain't my mama."

"I know baby, I know."

The Dupree plantation house was a large two-story mess that sprawled across half dozen acres like a wild flower. With white columns and thick green shutters, it was ominously friendly. The trucks pulled up in front of the large wraparound porch, and the motors hummed till they went quiet. The house sighed, and Martha called for Sarah.

The Dupree's new home had been built before the great nation's war. The Dupree's family had purchased the home as a second residence for family and a small supplemental income when times grew rougher during the brief period of reconstruction. There was never much suffering in their lineage. Henry emerged from the huge Cadillac like a weary beast carrying his hulking frame uncomfortably. The two boys leaped from their truck to their father's side excited for instructions. With a few languid arm movements, the boys began removing suitcases from the Cadillac's trunk.

Wilson crawled out of the back of the truck half-naked, his skin shiny with sweat and pride. He reached out for Martha, but she had already made her way towards the Cadillac. Wilson drove one truck towards the fields. The two brothers followed him in the other. Wilson watched Lilly Dupree, her feet barely moved the dust while she walked up the path towards the house. The silver silk had come untied and tickled her neck. There was hair in her eyes. Wilson spent a minute with one slouching stocking before speeding off down the narrow road.

Martha worked the house with Mrs. Dupree removing beautiful china and stemware from preciously wrapped boxes. The tissue was more expensive than anything she had ever worn except at the wedding.

"Now Martha, it is Martha right?" Her voice was like cracked glass.

"Yes, Ma'am, Martha."

"Right, well Martha, look this is where the glasses go, and here this space will be for the china understand." She placed one of each item in its prearranged place.

"Now be careful. This china has been in the Dupree family since that catastrophe at the island." She smiled rather formally. "It's probably older than you."

"I doubt that, Ma'am."

Wilson had kept his mouth closed when the Dupree brothers told him earlier that the Dupree plantation in Alabama grew wheat. The truck rumbled loud over the narrow path, and Wilson knew he would break his back fixing the road and still need help. It came up on him like fresh morning, and he almost drove the truck into the gully that ran alongside the road. The wheat was more than waist height and flowed like the tide until it blended into the horizon. The Dupree brothers ran their truck alongside of Wilson and smiled as they studied their field.

> *Wheat in Alabama. Martha it must be here.*
> *Child don't be so easy. One miracle don't make a saint.*
> *You better call Sarah.*
> *I be doing everything in good time.*
> *I'll need Larry to fix this road.*
> *Don't be worryin' about that now boy. Just help those boys with their wheat.*
> *It's amazin' woman. Amazin'. It must be here.*

Wilson heard the Dupree brothers rip a long strip of rubber as they sped off towards the tool shed. The doors had practically rusted off the hinge but the wood, the wood remained.

"Well I'll be damned. Digbee, this poor bastard ain't got one inch a rot in her." Daniel slapped the side of the shed with the flat of his hand, and a roost of barn owls screeched their way from the rafters.

"Let's get started." Daniel was holding a shiny red toolbox that looked fresh from a hardware store. He smiled and handed Wilson a claw hammer. "You think you can get those rusty hinges off without wreckin' that wood?"

"Yes, Sir." Wilson shuffled quickly towards the barn.

"Daniel, name's Daniel, and this is Digbee. We call my father Sir."

Leslie had been late for history at least a dozen times within the month and her teachers were growing impatient. There would be another letter sent home this week, and her mother would not understand.

"So the car just came out of nowhere?" William ran a slender hand through her loose blonde hair.

"Yeah, I mean I know it sounds stupid, but just like all of a sudden there was an Oldsmobile in front of me." She was looking out across the field.

"No, no, it's cool I understand I see things sometimes." He smiled plainly and slid a pack of Camels from his shirt pocket.

"Can I have one of those?"

"You smoke?"

"Maybe." Leslie took the filtered cigarette from the pack and stuck it between her lips. William struck a match in the cup of his hand for her, and she inhaled deeply. The smoke was a welcome relief.

"You never told me you smoked."

Leslie inhaled deeply again and watched the smoke lift out over the summer heat. William readjusted himself, looked at Leslie, and slouched back against the fence. His head had been throbbing since last week. His mother told him it was because he was not sleeping well, always talking about the island, the fire, and the serpent. He only knew about his nightmares. William closed his eyes and placed his hand against his lips.

"So, when did you start smoking?"

"William," Leslie turned to him and wrapped her arm around his waist. Her lips were warm from sitting in the heat, and William felt the sweat from her upper lip.

I love you.
I know.
Can you hear the voices?
Yes baby. Yes.

Leslie stood up and turned her skirt back around. She was smoking another cigarette, and her throat was beginning to hurt. William was still lying naked in the grass.

"You're beautiful." Leslie smiled and slid her hand close on his thigh. "I'm going back to class now."

"Why?" William whined slightly not wanting to move from his serenity. His swelled at her attention.

"I am already in trouble enough." She smiled and entertained the idea for a minute before standing back up. "Come see me tonight." William blinked. She was gone. It felt nice to be naked in the grass, and William stretched his tired limbs. The sun had risen directly above him, and now the heat was making his whole body sweat. He smiled and drew thick on his cigarette again. He left some of himself in the field and got dressed. William had been done with school for almost a month now attending classes on an irregular basis using the school as a social hall. He was tolerated by most of the staff because of the incident, and because of this, he respected their obligation.

He walked his bike home, enjoying the unusual cool breeze that had moved in while they were making love. William's mother was still at work when he propped the bike up against the aluminum siding. She would not be home for another three or four hours. The Dandelion Diner was only five blocks from the small stray house that William lived in. His mother, Lydia, worked the midday shift because hungry lunch rush customers tipped well if she smiled and wore her uniform a little too small.

Prior to the incident, William used to ride his bike to the Diner after school and eat tuna sandwiches with the local customers. Some of them smiled awkwardly when he stopped in for money or a coke. William was an exceptional student even after the incident. He was in love with literature and jazz. He played the trumpet, like his father, and even acted in several school plays all before the visions started again. His mother said they were simply nightmares. William, like his father, knew better.

The house smelled like stale Pine-Sol and cigarettes. There was a pack of Parliaments resting on the coffee table along with a letter from the school.

Dear Mrs. Lourds,

As I am sure you are aware of due to our prior communications, your son William Jr. has not been in regular attendance at school. We have overlooked the severity of his absences in the past due to the incident, but his new string of absences is inexcusable. I know that under the current circumstances involving the incident, we have overlooked this attendance problem as long as William performed well on his tests and assignment. I am sorry to say that after recent conversations with William's teachers, he has been failing to complete these tasks as well. I am now forced to expel William from Westminster High School and Choir College. My deepest condolences and regrets. William is a wonderful mind and deserves more than the past incidents have left him.

Jim Reed,
Principal

William put the letter in the ashtray and felt comfort as it burned.

William Sr. had finished seminary early and before anyone expected. The projects had been tough but were always a constant reminder of God. William felt proud in his suit. The heat was oppressive in New York City but hardly mattered anymore. It was William Jr's birthday and his own anniversary. He had been married to Lydia for five years tomorrow and was enjoying the relief of minor success. He had bought her a new diamond for her engagement ring, something he promised himself years before. Lydia was sitting in the dark living room with the thick shade pulled tight. Preacher Boy was nestled closely, his lips at her breast. The fan made an irresistible ticking sound, and he began to hum a singsong melody.

William's feet pronounced his arrival with a rhythm at the front door. He removed his hat and rubbed his forehead with the back of his arm. He hung his hat on the rack aside the door.

"Lydia . . ." There was urgency in his voice. William felt his feet begin to go, and his body pulled hard to the left. He grabbed the coat hanger, and his hand gripped tight on the post. Lydia pushed Preacher Boy aside and ran to her husband.

"Are you all right?" She leaned forward towards him, her breasts heavy and loose against her blouse.

"I, I was just then he. . . it must be the heat." William pulled himself upright his hand still holding the wooden post.

"Was it another vision?" Lydia pulled him forward with her eyes.

"I told you, they're not visions, just some dream. Damn it woman, close your shirt." William could not let go of the post.

"You used to like it when I wore it loose."

"What's Preacher Boy gonna think?"

"I hate when you call him that." She pulled on the collar of her shirt.

"Let me see that tit." He reached forward with his free hand.

"William."

"Let me see it."

"He's in the other room." She pulled harder against the collar of her shirt.

"Damn it, let me see your breast, Lydia." William grabbed at her shirt and pulled it open tearing one of the seams. Lydia's nipple was swollen and full.

"Goddamn it baby, you did it again."

"I couldn't help it."

"You couldn't help it?"

"He was shivering in fits, William." Lydia pulled back her shirt from William and began to move down the hall.

"Where are you going?"

"I don't want to have this here." She disappeared behind the bedroom doorway. William's hand could not leave the pole, and his head was still reeling from the sight of his father bleeding.

"Preacher Boy, I need you."

Wilson stopped to eat in a small restaurant outside of Princeton, New Jersey. The trees had grown thick with autumn leaves exploding with colors that Wilson had never seen.

The restaurant was almost empty except for one small white boy in the back booth. Wilson waved, and the boy was gone. The menu was coated in plastic, and Wilson was amazed at his choices. He earned money on his journey from Carolina pulling odd jobs for anyone who would let him. It was mostly desperate blacks and opportunistic whites who in a time of economic difficulty saw past black or white if the end result was green. Wilson ordered a tuna fish sandwich, a glass of milk, and a bowl of tomato soup. The waitress was a young girl with a sharp smile and thin slit eyes. She brought Wilson his food and left him to eat quietly. Wilson swallowed the slender sandwich in several bites and moved to the thick red soup. He slurped happily as the chef watched him eat with a mixed look of appreciation and apprehension. It was only 1952.

When Wilson first arrived on the island with the others, he was relieved to feel the chains leave his neck only to have them fasten his ankles. They had been stolen from the center of the jungle by a Belgian expedition who sold them to British entrepreneurs. They took turns him, Sarah, Larry, and especially Martha keeping the small seed alive in a palmful of dirt. Each shared their small ration of water to feed it and fertilized the dirt with their own excrement. The boat was two weeks of complete darkness. They would survive as long as it could grow. They had planted it just outside the workhouse when they arrived on the island keeping it close to the wall, so it would not become trampled. It grew, and they breathed easier.

"Have you told Sarah yet?" Wilson was filthy with dirt from the day's work.

"In due time, child. We need to be sure." Martha was stripping peapods on the front porch of the Dupree plantation.

"Since when you never not been sure, Martha."

"Oh child, don't be fresh, you know these things take time." Martha pressed a fresh pea against her tongue.

"That is the problem, you are always wasting time, just like in the village."

"You don't know nothing, child, about the village."

"Stop telling stories woman."

"You just keep your eyes from that pretty little girl."

"You just keep your nose out of my business." William slapped his hand against his thigh and light cloud of dust rose up from the back porch. He left Martha with her peas and danced around the corner of the porch. She had just been in from the yard, and the hem of her dress was stained with dandelion ends. Wilson removed his hat and wiped his forehead with the back of his sleeve.

"Miss Lilly."

"Wilson."

"Yes, Miss Lilly?"

"Oh, nothing, Wilson. You just look so sorry standing there like that."

"Just tired, Miss Lilly. Just tired."

"How's the road coming?"

"It'd be easier with a little help."

"That is a matter you will have to take up with my father."

"Oh, it's no problem Miss Lilly. Just me talking, that's all." Wilson slipped his hat back on and pushed it up away from his eyes.

"The yard looks nice this evening." She pushed some hair away from her face. "I like it when the sun's low and there are shadows everywhere."

"Shadows are special people, Miss Lilly."

"Oh Wilson, you and Martha always talking those stories of yours." Lilly propped herself against the white railing.

"Not stories, Miss Lilly. What Martha says, these things are true. People just don't pay attention. Always in a rush and too busy with working. There are things all around us that people just don't see." Wilson moved forward on the porch feeling the boards and his legs weak. Lilly turned her head towards him. Her hair had come unraveled with the pressing night and flushed out her face. Wilson felt himself stir and held to himself.

"Like Voices?" Her own was unsure.

"You hear the Voices, Miss Lilly?" Wilson thought of running.

"No, no, I just heard Martha talking about crazy things." She grabbed Wilson's arm. He tried to ignore it.

"Is it a bad thing, Miss Lilly?" Wilson felt a sudden shiver, and Lilly slid her hand against his flat chest.

When she arrived in the jungle for the first time, she was full of flash and smiles, big and bright for everyone. It was her eyes that were only for Wilson. She walked out of the jungle at sunset when the glow that surrounded her was barely becoming visible. Martha knew what she was right away. The others had a sense of it. They were not completely without influence. Wilson was in love. Her eyes pulled on him, and his feet could barely meet the ground when she placed her slim white hand against the flat of his chest resting so comfortably against his heart. She would keep him warm until the sisters came and took their child. It would not be the first sacrifice she made in his name.

Wilson gathered soft leaves to make the bed larger and smiled when she showed him how to make love for the first time. When the child would be born it would be divine, it would be more than a beautiful baby. When it would die in the arms of a stranger in the sweat of a jungle path, it would not matter. All that they had to do was wait for the return of her Grace.

Lilly was gone like smoke. Wilson felt a heavy sigh in him and watched the rest of the sun disappear behind the hills of the Dupree plantation. *Wheat in Alabama, Larry ain't never gonna believe this.* Wilson used the back entrance and played downcast eyes at Martha as she labored over the stove. The Dupree's had added servants' quarters in the 20's mainly to hide their bootleg liquor during prohibition. Wilson had discovered a large bottle of whiskey hidden in a fake hollow of his closet. The rooms were sizable enough, more than he had ever seen on the island.

There was a cast iron tub in the bathroom located at the back of the hall. The whiskey felt rough in his throat as he sipped sitting naked in the just warm tub. The road was under his nails. Wilson used a soft piece of soap that Miss Lilly had given him. He was happy to have her scent with him. *That girl is gonna be the end of all of us.* Wilson laughed, his mouth full of white teeth and liquor. He dressed in lazy summer clothes that hung loose from his waist and shoulders. Martha had placed dinner on the small wooden butcher-block table in the kitchen quarters.

Wilson felt the rim of the plate warm against his hand. The food was a wash of brown and tans with a thick layer of gravy seeping into everything. He shoveled his fork through the plate and brought a large mouthful to his lips. The smell was invigorating. Wilson ate quickly holding his head low and close to his plate. Martha sampled her plate much more slowly. She pulled at the meat with her fork and mixed it with a small portion of potatoes before dipping into the gravy. She ate happily, always her one hand patting her thigh in a slow rhythm as she hummed a singsong melody.

Preacher Boy helped his father from the hallway into the living room and then finally onto the couch. In the kitchen he mixed seltzer water and some lemon juice and brought it to William. His father slipped the drink slowly being careful with each swallow. Preacher Boy took the glass from his father when he was finished and returned it to the kitchen. William had slouched down low in the couch, his head resting on the back. He moved his hand to motion to Preacher Boy. His hand looked smaller than usual, and each knuckle was filled with an unrecognizable tireless effort. Preacher Boy moved toward the couch feeling the floor leave him slightly as he stepped towards his father.

"Son, what do you see?"

"People."

"What people?"

"The People on the boat."

"Show me, son."

"Yes, father." Preacher Boy had left the floor completely and was with his father.

"Let me see, son." William reached his hand for his son and found his slender wrist. He wrapped his hand around it and watched the boat stained with salty ocean push through the waves. The people were chained by their necks and wailing. There is the one with the seed. How does she keep it safe? A whip, then another, the white man with the gun and scabbard.

"Is there more, son?" His father had not opened his eyes to see Preacher Boy.

"Yes father."

"Let me see." Preacher Boy began to cry, and his father felt the sting of the ocean in his eyes. The whip cracked hard against his skin, and he watched the blood run down the deck. The man with the scabbard, laughing. William's hand was pulling hard on Preacher Boy making it difficult for him. The pain did not end on the island. Here he watched them work, toiling in fields of white gold for poor rations and shacks.

"Where is the seed, son? Show me the seed."

The tree had grown strong in the shade of one of the shacks, a large sapling now. It had made firm roots despite poor soil. She hovered over it daily, sharing her water, pruning away the dead so the living would survive. Preacher Boy began to urinate on himself, and it ran onto the rug. He emerged from the shack with only a pair of burlap trousers. His body lean and cooked in the sun's work, the skin of his back tight and scarred. Father. Grandfather. There was no longer a collar but his ankles were heavy with metal. The scabbard gone, now a long switch of ash slid into the laughing man's belt.

Come here boy

Yes Sir

Is that your woman

Where Sir

Don't get smart with me boy

Yes Sir

The one with that tree

No Sir

Don't lie to me boy

No Sir

Is that lady your momma

No Sir

Don't lie to me boy

Yes Sir

Where did that tree come from boy

Africa

I said don't lie boy

The switch came hard across his chest and then his arms. The leather straps that held him to the post bit into his wrists. His fingers were bleeding full of splinters where he had gripped the wood tightly in order not to scream. When the switch was brought down for the twentieth time, he was sobbing uncontrollably. After ten more, he no longer could lift his head to cry. His back bled for four days while they let him hang there. William vomited on himself, and Preacher Boy found the ground again. Grandfather.

Preacher Boy ran into his mother's arms and she held him hard against her breasts. He welcomed it and smiled at the smooth feeling. William began packing immediately. The rental truck arrived on a Tuesday morning, and William stuffed his family into the small cab before dawn. The look in his eyes had no call for disagreement. The truck sputtered into George's Garage just outside of Princeton, New Jersey. The repairman kindly said it would take at least two days to repair and recommended the Holiday Inn down the highway. The service man's wife was kind enough to give the Lourds a ride to the hotel and waved as she sped back towards the garage. William rented a small room and a cot for two nights. There was no television. They settled quickly, and Lydia declared that she was going to take a shower, something she always loved.

William was reading the complementary newspaper sprawled out on the bed, his shirt untucked and his shoes off. Preacher Boy was sitting in the only chair counting cars in the parking lot.

"Father?" His head was still heavy with numbers.

"Yes, son?"

"Do you think you will find the old woman's tree?"

"I have to, son, I have to."

William had slept quietly that night for the first time since the visions began and Preacher Boy was born. He knew that morning would not be easy. He called the garage early in the morning to hear the progress on the truck and to see if it would be available earlier. The garage man sighed into the phone and said no before hanging up the receiver. William hung up the phone desperately.

"Well?" Lydia had her hand at her side and a towel wrapped around her head.

"No luck. Says he can't get it ready until tomorrow." William looked desperately anxious.

"I guess we will just have to sleep all day." Preacher Boy smiled and dove into the large hotel bed. He had been watching those awful dreams all night.

"Don't be ridiculous, boy. We might as well go look around this fancy little town." William was already dressed except for his shoes.

"I don't want to walk around some stupid white town." He buried his head in the blanket.

"That's enough. Who told you to talk like that? Now get dressed. We'll get some breakfast and go see the town."

It would not be until the end of the day when they caught him with his first drink in almost five years.

Preacher Boy faked an episode while in the shower making wild gestures with his arms and banging the walls until his mother finally heard. She grabbed him from the tub and wrapped his naked body in a white hotel towel. Lydia sat on the toilet and held Preacher Boy close to her breast. He clawed at it mercilessly until she opened her shirt.

They left the hotel room at ten o'clock despite the episode. The town of Princeton was large as towns go but non-existent on a city level. It was old brick buildings crammed against new ones surrounded by the Gothic architecture of an Ivy League university. It was reunions week when alumni return from all over the nation and orange and black swarmed through the sidewalk like perverse wasps. They all had buttons, ridiculous hats, tiger tails, and suspenders. William was laughing himself into a stupor over a women with a mounted tiger tail attached to the back of her skirt. Lydia was horrified. The shops except for a few minor corporate uprisings were mainly little boutiques, little expensive boutiques. There were sundresses for 100 dollars, and a leather bag made for just a compact and lipstick for three times that.

"Isn't this just wonderful." William breathed in a heavy breath and smiled as they turned the corner by another boutique. A man with striped suspenders and an enormously large hat bumped into them and snarled slightly. William gripped the inside of his pocket and let the man pass. They ate breakfast under stares in the pancake house.

> *Daddy they have his eyes*
> *Whose eyes Preacher Boy*
> *The man with sword*
> *They have his eyes.*

William patted his son's leg under the table. He rationalized the whole town in his head. He told himself that the stares were just queer curiosity and odd looks were because of the camaraderie of the great university's reunion weekend. *They don't hate us, they just don't know us.* Preacher Boy could see it coming in the hotel room, Lydia knew it was coming ever since they got married, William had denied himself forever.

They walked carelessly through the town for hours, doing laps around certain blocks, resting on familiar benches. They enjoyed the smell of George's Ribs but decided not to eat when they saw the Asian looking owner. In the center of the town they found comfort in the anonymity of the shadow of a giant evergreen tree. The sun was beginning to disappear over the tops of the brick building and pouring past the peaks of the university. William wanted a drink despite the voices.

"I think I want to go have a drink, Lydia. You stay here with Preacher Boy while I go into that bar up there on the corner." William pointed from the deep shadow of the evergreen across the square.

"Let's just go home, Bill." Lydia pulled Preacher Boy close to her.

"Just one drink, baby."

No one could call William an alcoholic. He did have a problem though. William Lourds could never just have one drink. William could only drink until the bar was closed, or he had passed out. William hitched his pants up and took big strides. The bar was packed with hard wood supports and foolishly dressed men. William smiled at the beautiful girl at the door and felt something old stir deep inside him. He picked an unassuming stool at the end of the bar and ordered a scotch, a triple, neat with water back. William always had patience with the first drink, enjoying the flavor, the feeling in his throat. The second drink took less time and soon William would be reduced to taking shots of the bar's cheapest liquor.

Lydia was getting cold as she felt the evening chill setting in with a quick wind. She pulled Preacher Boy close to her. He felt her heart at his lips and took the sweet warmth inside him, in the dark, for the last time, a place where no one had ever seen them.

William saw them from across the bar -- two large older white men smiling and joking about old times at the university most likely. Who fucked who, who started the prank war in '76, who had a higher GPA. They moved toward William like unwieldy bowling balls, colliding with each other and knocking over bar patrons along the way. When the one opened his mouth, William knew how it would end.

"Hey jasper, me and my associate here thought we could buy you a drink." He waved towards the bartender.

"No thank you Sir, I can pay for myself."

"Don't get all uppity, son. My friend just wants to buy you a drink."

"What did you call me?" William stood up from his stool and felt the sure-footedness of being only slightly drunk.

"He said you was an uppity nigger." The two let laughter rise from their bowels and shit out their mouths. The bartender made an arresting motion with his hands, but William was alive with the buzz. The alcohol had been something he needed for months, to suffocate his brain and drown out the whippings, the blood, the screaming, and make mystery simply disappear. He felt the youth of New York Projects surging up through him. The men fell quickly, and the crowd broke into segmented fractions of frightened patrons.

William felt them pulling at his back yanking on his coat until they had his arms locked. They jammed him against the wall, five of them holding him and rubbing hands against his face. There was no need for a reason, just an excuse was enough. They pulled him from the bar dragging him face down and kicking all the way. The bar emptied, but there was nothing that could be done.

Preacher Boy already knew, Lydia had seen it since their wedding night, and William had felt it forever. They tied him to a light post with a belt and stripped him bare. There were Sirens in the distance. He only received a few strikes before the police flooded the scene with light and noise. They left him there while they shoveled the men into their cars, handcuffed and proud. A small female officer undid the belt and helped William get dressed. She noticed the sleekness of his naked body. Preacher Boy was shaking horribly, but Lydia was sore and used. They knew he would leave in the morning. Preacher Boy had known before the vision began. Lydia had seen it since the Hotbox. William had denied it forever.

William left at four in the morning with the Ryder truck. Lydia found a job as a waitress at a local diner, and Preacher Boy would not hear his own name again or of the incident that destroyed his father for eight years.

Leslie felt sick the entire ride home. The bus breaks screeched, and she winced. The tires sped over a bump, and her stomach flipped twice. She closed her eyes and tried to think of William. *Why did she tell me to do it, like that, in the field? The sun was so hot.* She opened her eyes and noticed the bus was more than half-empty. She moved across the aisle and stretched her legs across the larger seat. He was smiling at her through the window when the bus halted abruptly in front of her house. He had a simple smile and looked pleasant without his dog. His black skin sweating and showing through the light white cotton shirt. Leslie gathered her things quickly and hopped off the bus. She was running, her skirt flapping up in the back.

She slipped in the gravel at the edge of her driveway. Her knee ran along the curb as she fell and began to bleed. The asphalt was hot as Leslie laid back. She could feel it throbbing against her leg. It moved past her knee and up her thigh. She felt hot in the place that William had been. It made her sick. Leslie felt her heart leave her, the taste of blood in the back of her throat, and their pain sear the empty spot in her breast.

It crawled into her and began pushing against her insides. She spread her legs to make it easy for him. To let it pass, to help her understand. She was pulling on the chain at her neck, blood trickling down past her swollen breasts. The people were withered and crawling like snakes. He hit a guard with the back of his hand and felt it on his back for three days. The two of them watched over the poor thing, bathing it in rationed water and excrement. He almost died keeping it alive. They used him like a galley and ate all he could offer. Poor sister, poor sister with her habit stained with blood and excrement. She had lost her head-dress in the jungle when they took her hair for a comic wig. They crawled about each other black naked snakes playing with each other's limbs, dangling arms, and legs, spider's webs making nests in their chests. He pulled so hard on the chain once that he ripped the tip of his finger off. Who could blame them. With that face no one could resist her once the first had done it. Then came the sweet flavor of the sun and scorched backs that ran with crimson, all until he ended it with smiling white faces and the beast's mouth full of spite.

Leslie opened her eyes and saw it all so very clearly. She knew them all now, Larry, Sister Sarah, Martha, and Wilson. Their history was hers, her present would be their future. She picked up her books and straightened herself. The blood had dried on her knee and left a thick trail down her shin. Her mother was waiting inside the door holding her own hand.

"Leslie, are you all right?" There was an absurd urgency in her voice.

"Yes mother, I just slipped on some gravel."

"Let me clean that up for you."

"I'll take care of it, mother."

"Just make sure you don't let it get infected." Her mother was pulling hard against her own hand.

"I know, mother." Leslie stormed the stairs her heels hard and loud against the bare wood. The little chick was sleeping in the cotton nest she had left for it. Its eyes were still almost translucent. She put her bag on the end of her desk and moved to the bathroom. She ran water in the tub and let it fall over her fingers until she felt it warm. She took off her strappy sandal heel and slipped her foot into the tub. The warm water was delicious. She washed the blood until her leg was clean and felt her smooth skin. She enjoyed the sensation of teasing the invisibles on her legs. The blood swirled a circle down the drain. Leslie was fascinated at the pattern with the rhythm of the sound and began to hum a singsong melody.

Wilson had taken residence with the pretty waitress from the diner. She lived in a local apartment just a few blocks from the diner. They ate leftovers and tomato soup.

"Do you want tuna or turkey?" She smiled and held two sandwiches wrapped in cloudy plastic.

"It doesn't matter, baby." He had his back turned while he was huddled over the unassembled parts of Helen's radio. His hand was wrapped tight around the end of the screwdriver, and he stared at the sprawled guts of the transistor. The mass of red and green wires tangled and pulled about along with the black. Circuit boards laid belly up with flashing teeth of glitter chips and solder that hold so fragile the line that gives them power. Dozens of wires all independent lying together across the same plain bridging gaps that pull their lives together in a kinetic universe where things travel in nonlinear paths. It is difficult for Wilson to predict the result if he cuts just one, severs one tie, breaks one bond. How will that affect the others? Will they cease to function, no longer exist on the plane except for a stranded streak of color? Or should he tie two together, bind them under melted metal so that they can share their commonality, expose their differences for better reasons? It is a unique plane that holds all of these things, these fine electric lives, each one just as valuable as the other. All of them careening about in their own current until they collide, spanning generations of use until a cataclysmic event either brings them life or splits open their shell on the coffee table.

"Then you are having tuna."

"Lovely." He reached his hand out behind him and accepted the sandwich. It was still cool from the refrigerator.

"I made ice tea today." Wilson heard the hammer crack against the cutting board. Ice did a mad dance across the counter top before it spun and settled against the sinks edge. Helen scooped the ice into two large glasses coated with worn out sunflowers and brought them along with the pitcher to the coffee table.

"Delicious. Did you add the mint leaves?"

"Of course." She said it so matter-of-factly that it made Wilson blush and smile. She filled the two glasses and Wilson listened to the ice pop. She made a distinctive sound with her lips while she drank and put the glass on a coaster she made of hemp. Helen carefully unwrapped the sandwiches and placed the tuna in front of Wilson. He was still holding the screwdriver tightly in his one hand. The radio was a disaster.

"I don't think I can fix it, baby." Wilson used his free hand to pick up half the tuna sandwich.

"It's okay, I can get another radio." She reached out and grabbed a circuit board holding it upside down enjoying the tangle of colors. Wilson put the screwdriver down on the table and reached for his glass of ice tea. It felt cool, and he enjoyed the mint as it rolled down his throat. Helen swallowed the last mouthful of her turkey sandwich and removed a joint from her pocket. The smoke was sweet, and Wilson waited for his turn. They sunk into the couch, and Helen passed the joint to Wilson. He inhaled deeply puffing out his strong chest, and Helen watched his shirt rise and fall as the deep smoke sifted through the room.

They let the night roll in on them pulling the shadow from the back of the room until it was flushed out around them. Helen had her eyes closed and Wilson drew the points of the constellation on her body with a trail of ice. The tail of the serpent dragged across her flat white stomach, and Wilson undid the top of her jeans. He took his time with the head turned down its mouth open over her breast. He had been battling the serpent since before the jungle to the island and deep into the white fields. Wilson followed the serpent into the bedroom.

There was a weight in her head the next morning, and she denied herself about what it was. Helen pulled her uniform over her head and checked her hair in the mirror. Wilson was still lying cold and restless in the bed. He had not stopped turning in hours. She felt it stir in her too. Helen heard the toilet flush while she was scrambling eggs for his breakfast. Wilson walked out into the kitchen in his boxers. His feet made an odd slapping sound against the cool linoleum. Wilson let the smile creep slow into his face as he watched Helen make breakfast. The pan made a comforting sounds and he thought of Sister Sarah on the island, making breakfast on metal sheet over an open fire.

"Morning, honey." Helen shoveled the eggs from the pan to a plate along with two strips of bacon.

"Hey, sweetie." Wilson wrapped his arms around her from behind as she cracked another egg into the pan. It splashed the sides and the whites began to bubble. She liked them loose. The egg only fried for a matter of seconds just long enough for the whites to stiffen. Wilson reached above her for a plate and Helen slipped the egg smoothly onto it and they broke for the table. Helen always ate voraciously in the mornings. She swallowed her fried egg almost whole, and Wilson was amazed as she consumed three extra pieces of toast. He kissed her full on the mouth enjoying the flavor of coffee and eggs before she left for work. Wilson stacked the two plates and carried them from the small butcher-block table to the sink. Helen always wanted a dishwasher but told her friends she would settle for Wilson. He enjoyed the effort that went into cleaning the egg pan. It would never be completely clean, they both knew that, but he tried his best to remove the obvious.

Helen's legs were sore by the time she reached work. She cursed herself for staying up too late. It was ten before six and the cook, Billy, had already begun to cook the regulars' breakfast. Helen grabbed the filters and began to brew the enormous pot of coffee. The smell was delicious. It would take eight minutes for the coffee to be finished. The coffee machine gurgled and strangled itself forcing the hot water through the beans. Helen watched the drips, simultaneous, as both pots began to fill. Billy hollered over the cook window for her, and she pushed her hair from her face. It would be a long day.

Lilly had been staring dream-eyed out the window since the sun began to fall in late 1968. Mr. James D. Witmore was planning to visit her around seven thirty. Martha had laid out a white lace evening gown for her. When she dressed, it felt awkward on her new body. James had not seen her since he left for California in search of silicon gold. He would be surprised by her. Lilly decided that she did not need shoes. Her bare feet slapped loud as she hurdled down the stairs. She could feel her mother's disapproval.

"Martha? What are you doing in the kitchen at this hour?" Lilly pulled at the front of her dress.

"Just making preserves, Miss Lilly. Mister James coming tonight?" She had her face buried in an enormous pot. Lilly knew she was lying.

"Yes, Martha. He says he brought me some real gold from California."

"Ain't no gold but fool's gold, girl. You be careful of men with shiny things. All they want for their favors is yours." Lilly's hands played with her dress as she smiled awkwardly.

"Martha!"

"Well Miss Lilly, I know you ain't the angel you show your papa. I be seeing the way your hips look lately. You more a woman now." Martha drove a long handled ladle through the pot using both arms to stir.

"When are Sister Sarah and Larry coming?" Lilly scratched her face to help change the subject. Martha paused. Lilly felt the pain in her hand. She grabbed her wrist and Martha turned to her with a lovely wicked smile.

"You know they be here soon, girl."

"You're crazy, Martha. Sometimes I don't know what you're talking about." Lilly opened and closed her own hand before leaving the kitchen. The mark had become thick with blood and the shape that hung about Martha's neck. She could hear the car charging from over the hill.

Martha had taken the pot off the stove and let it steep full of herbs and some wheat that Wilson had brought her. It smelled awful. When the steam rose out of the pot, she barely saw them. They were working. There was a hot sun and an angry white face. The field was full, and they would not be missed. It would only be a matter of days before they arrived. She drew a long wooden spoon handle through the pot and traced a circle on the table. With her hand in the middle she could feel the serpent getting closer. The call left her, and there was a heavy sigh in the room. Wilson, sleeping in the barn, awoke suddenly with a smile.

Lilly was bored already with waiting. She had been listening to the long rumble of six horses pulling the black car over the crest and looking down on the Dupree's. The driver paused for a moment, and Lilly could see the narrow arm of James Witmore waving. The car rolled up quickly to the porch and the door swung open colliding into the side. Mr. James was half out, his foot in step before the wheels finished rolling. He hit the ground, his shoes soaking in the dew.

"Lilly." His arms were open wide as his smile. His steps were loud as he stormed up the porch. He embraced her, and Lilly could feel him swell up against her. It was an unnatural embrace. Not out of love or the longing for something lost, but almost out of necessity. It seemed to James the proper thing to do. It was not forward after all he had been friendly with her for some time. He felt her reluctance before he reached the porch. The ring had been weight in his pocket since he left California, a half carat of his parents' money waiting for Lilly's finger. It would be a difficult fit, and he knew it.

Digbee Dupree left the boat around six as the sun was bleaching the beach. The heat was unbearable and unlike anything he was accustomed to. He removed his jacket immediately and let one of the porters put it with his bags. He had come to see what his money was worth. They were sprawled out like snakes across the ground, limbs and torso exposed to insects, disease. Arms, legs, hands springing from heaving masses of night with one communal breath. Digbee grabbed his mouth and held back hard against the bitter taste. She had no clothes on, her breasts beaten raw with a cowhide as she hung on the post her arms too weak to hold. Her genitals had been mutilated. She was left to bleed with nothing behind her eyes. He untied her hands and she fell to the ground a slight swell in her stomach as she forced breath from deep inside. Digbee vomited along the side of a path that twisted towards the house.

It stood tall with lanterns burning sweet smells into the nights' heat. There were shadows moving, a couple dancing, and some with trays that sprouted glasses like sugar cane. Digbee did not knock but walked patiently around the large porch. The house doors were open wide with curtains pinned back as a sign of welcome. A young woman with fallen eyes offered to take his hat.

"You are free, beautiful one, now go spit on your masters." He smiled a bit wickedly, and she moved floating through the crowds as if she was an apparition. When she came to her master at only arm's length, she smiled full of pride and spit from her mouth a slender snake and with it, Sister Sarah would change everything.

Digbee's wife arrived several days later with their son Henry and some of the hired help they had collected. The boat made her sick. The island made her ill. Henry found his love of the field instantly. He ran through the thick crop of sugar, his hands outstretched cracking stalks, feeling their sticky insides on his skin.

"This place is horrible." Lyla began to fan herself.

"It is not that bad, Lyla."

"Are you insane, Digbee? Have you seen this place?" She rooted her hand in her hip.

"Yes dear, I have, and it could be worse."

"Worse! How could it be worse? What are we going to do with all these people?" She turned to the window and watched as the field moved in mass, hundreds of arms swinging, cutting, green stalks while others spent the entire day painfully bent collecting.

"We are going to pay them. They are workers just like in the factory."

"In the factory, the workers went home. They brought their own lunch. Had their own homes. They had clothes Digbee, most of these people don't even speak English."

"You will teach them." It was said so matter-of-factly, so perfectly that she began that very day. As the sun began to creep under the sand, she held class surrounded by torches and smoke. She screamed cat, dog, hello, dress, son, daughter, work, money, Dupree, freedom, Africa, and love all over the churning rank of insects at work.

"Father." Henry knocked lightly on the study door.

"Yes, Son." The floor squeaked as he stepped into the room. Digbee's chair creaked as he rocked back slightly.

"Have you seen it, Father?"

"Seen what?"

"The tree?"

"There are no trees for miles here, Son."

"No, Father, there is a tree."

"Where, Son?"

"Besides the shack that used to have those people."

"Get your mother and show me." Henry felt compelled. He had not felt this eager since he had heard that Mrs. Dancer, his schoolteacher, read naked in her bedroom with the light on. He had climbed up to the roof of the mill next door, keeping close to the peaks and angles. She was brilliant in the lamplight, her breasts round and slightly pointed at the end. Her hips smooth and her sex blanketed with hair. He asked her to marry him. She laughed, and he met Lillian the following Sunday. Thirty years later he discovered that her breasts were also pointed.

They moved down the house path quickly. Henry's anxiousness alarming slightly to Lyla who was in search of anything beautiful on the island. It was there as he had said. A deathly sick tree with yellow blossoms that burdened the limbs to grow. Lyla began to cry, and Henry laughed and danced a small circle around the tree, waving his hands about as if he were on fire.

"Can I help you, Sir?" She came out of from behind the shack naked except for a charm around her neck and a pail of water. He could not open his mouth. Henry stopped dancing and ran, so frightened of her boldness he did not see the sweetness of her face.

"How long has this tree been here, woman?" Lyla was the only one who could speak.

"Since the jungle, Ma'am. It came with us on the boat. It grew from the base of our spines and forked right at the heart."

"It is beautiful."

Leslie wanted the chick to live. She wanted to see it grown and have wings, maybe children. She wanted it to survive herself. It chirped warmly in its nest, but she knew it would not make it past the month. It was already waning, its chirp needy when the sun began to dip low. She dropped insects and bread from the tip of her fingers into its mouth. The beak was large and heavy, awkward, for the tiny round head. She rubbed the warm blue head and found her bed.

The sheets and the smell was a welcoming for her, but she wanted William. She reached for him in the night, desperately. She could not place her urgency, she could not understand her need, but it existed in a low part of her body. It bloomed from beneath her sex and hugged at the roundness of her new hips. It burned in her stomach, and it was what the man with the dog wanted her to see. It was the numbness in her hand. It was everything that made her special.

The morning was brilliant with a spectacle of light so daunting that she did not want to get out of bed. Leslie pulled hard on the sheets tugging them above her head. She could hear the song moving with room through her head and this time it was sweet, sweet and wanton like a complacent moon. She smiled with the melody as it rose and crept out of her mouth. She sang to the chick, her mouth barely open and it seemed to respond. She raised her voice, and the chick spread out its tiny wings and began to sing a daunting harmony that went with her delicate voice and when she had run out of old forgotten words, the chick continued happily by itself with the sweet singsong melody.

"Leslie?" There was a light knuckle tap tapping at her door.

"What?"

"Are you okay?" Her mother's voice sweeter than hers.

"Fine, Mother." The tonal change of minor to major was harsh and discordant.

"Were you singing?"

"I don't sing."

"I heard you singing."

"I don't sing, Mother."

"Open the door, Leslie. I hate talking like this." Her mother pushed hard on the knob.

"I'll be fine, mother."

"Please, come down for breakfast." Her mother was pawing at the palm of her hand.

"Yes, Mother."

Leslie fed the chick stale bread from the other night. She dressed in old clothes from two years ago that had been hiding on the bottom of her drawer. She wore lace underwear for William and enjoyed the feeling of the denim on her thighs. She slipped into a pleasant looking white t-shirt and charged down the stairs, her bare feet slapping against each step. Leslie was unusually hungry and devoured the thick southern breakfast her mother had prepared. The bus screeched to her stop just as she was coming out of the house. She ran in her white tennis shoes up the gravel drive and into the street feeling the freedom in her legs.

The bus moved before she found her seat and was around the corner before she was settled. It was a rumble she was not prepared for. The bus was louder this morning than any she could remember, and it was difficult for her to rest her head. She sat far back into the seat and tried desperately to use her bag as a pillow. The bus ride with her eyes open, made her ill. She could not stand the whistle of the slightly open window, the chatter of the incessant voices, or the smell of leftover lunches and gym clothes. She felt it pulling at her stomach, and she closed her eyes. She heard the dog barking, and they were waving from the shores, thick dark silhouettes with white smiles. She pulled her head down to her lap to try and stop them from talking. They were destroyed on the island, except for their seed. It spread throughout them urging them to keep moving. The field was wet in the morning, and the leaves cut at their skin. Martha had not eaten in days but instead made compost of her rations, gave her water to it, and it grew. It grew miraculously in those conditions. It had little attention, as much as they could survive without, but it still grew. It grew, and she cherished, feeling its tender skin and when it split at its heart, she was cleaved too. She watched them searching one hundred years apart waiting for the call. She watched them with wild eyes making love in a barn in Texas. She saw the man with the dog smile awkwardly at an elegant white woman. She saw the flames of ignorance engulf a poor wooden church. She watched her give out the call. She watched them wait, she watched them suffer.

Digbee had the tree moved from the shade of the shack to outside the house, and it grew. It grew with every lesson Lyla taught, with every crop of cane, with every birth in the field, and with all of Sister Sarah's dreams.

They were to be married under the tree. In the cool of the off-season when the blossoms of the tree were their biggest. Thick and full with enormous unusual blue flowers. They would be brilliant in the setting sun crowding about the branches haphazardly and emotionally. Someone, perhaps Martha, would wrap a large ribbon around the tree. They would kill extra pigs and perhaps a whole cow for the event. The pit would need to be expanded. The work would be done early, and the vows would be performed as the sun began to cut into the beach. It would be magnificent, full of orange smiles and truth.

Larry had been smiling since the Dupree's had arrived two months ago knowing that in due time he would have her. She had devoted her spirit to it, but her body -- that was his. He had waited since the jungle, and her promise is what kept him alive. It kept his hands from a white throat, his legs from collapsing, or his neck from the rope. He had avoided the post in order to not be broken, and she did the same. Larry, that is what the first one called him, was enormous. He arrived into this world 28 inches long and continued to grow until he was seven feet and more. His height was his enemy in the old ways. He was the easiest to spot, the first to be blamed, and the last to be saved.

The white man had stormed through the jungle with machetes and dogs burning their path with gasoline and hate. They burned the roofs of the huts chasing out the residents with smoke. They reached in with nets, ropes, and gloves pulling lovers out of their nests. They laid them on the jungle floor and bound them, but he was last. He was the last to be netted with coarse rope, or to be grabbed with a leather glove. He was the last because they argued whether there was room on the boat. They argued whether they could sell one that tall, whether there was a use for one that tall, whether they could control one that tall. With angry faces they shouted at each other, foreign gibberish, and held him against the door of his burning home. He was the first to feel the heat, the first to choke on the smoke, and the only one to run. He pushed past them and their loud mouths and ran through the jungle. He disappeared into the heat and darkness until she called for him, and he was the first to hear her voice. He heard it before the animals in the lofty branches, before the insects, before the ground rooted mammals that burrowed. He heard the sweet song before the white men and their nets, before the pistol fired, before he was separated from Africa. He was the first to hear her cry for him, her voice sweet and high-toned above the others wailing, wailing that singsong melody. He knew he would be the last.

The ceremony was beautiful and short which is what everyone wanted. They did not want long-winded speech and patient eyes. They wanted roast pork, and large cuts of beef that they could eat off the bone with their hands, and they did. They ate with smiles and songs, while musicians played instruments they made from hides and hollowed out logs. They blew into empty sugar cane and hollered from deep in their throats. The young ones ran and screamed across the front yard of the house. They did laps around the tree and felt free to swing from the porch posts. It was wonderful, and Larry never let her go. He held Sarah's hand the entire day keeping her close in order to smell her new scent, scent Lyla had given her.

The storm had rolled in with a ghastly silence. It had been born off the shores of Morocco spinning in the Atlantic with wisps of Adriatic wind. It was a conglomerate of tropical breezes and European winds. It was an improbable storm completely unfounded in the natural world. A storm that could not have traveled so quickly, so diligently from its unusual source to their island, the island they were now glad to call home. It picked up strength from the water, pushing choppy shores with it and dragging history from the coasts of the western

Atlantic. Then it changed direction whipped around the serpents' tail and traveled down the coast following the jagged line until it rolled off the tip of Florida and towards the island.

They had eaten almost everything when the wind blew out the torches. It was a quiet subtle gust, but Martha moved for Sarah immediately.

"It's come, dear child. Hurry." They all held hands tight and fast to the posts that had lain dormant for months now. The wind was the first to come howling out of the sky and ripping through the cane fields until colliding with the house. It pulled leaves from the fresh clean plants with a velocity that drew blood. Digbee felt the sting as he helped women into the house. They did their best but only so many could be helped before the howl shattered the glass. The French doors that lay open in the lazy heat were ripped from their hinges as the storm barreled through. Lyla felt the glass against her face. The sound was enormous and Henry began to scream, a sound worse than the howl. The china cabinet toppled over and the furniture began to scatter about the room. The rug picked up, and Digbee found himself on the floor. Larry's hand was raw, his body fighting against the air. Martha and Sarah were clinging to his belt. Wilson was crying in the tool shed. His eyes burned till they felt like they were bleeding, and then it stopped. It faltered and halted as it came in quietly until the rain began in a line so thick that one thought night was moving upon them. The drops were heavy and with such force that they stung and the water rose quickly.

Larry helped Martha and Sarah into the tree and watched as they disappeared upwards into the dark wet branches. The wave came over the entire island slamming into the shore with such force that it drove water three hundred feet inland. It would spare nothing. The rumble began as the flood ended. The water began to subside thick and milky with sugar. The storm was low and struck suddenly. The people who were still alive ran, ran in all directions hopelessly as if anything could save them. They scattered and were struck down fiercely by lightning, and Martha smelt human flesh burning for the first time. When the bolt cleaved the tree, Martha left her body and went to him. She went to him and told him they were not ready. When the storm finally stopped, it all ended again. The Dupree's left the island, leaving the survivors with their ruined shacks, taking only what belongings remained whole and a wayward blossom pinned to Lyla's chest.

Mr. James proffered the ring from his pocket in late 1968. Lilly held it in her hand until she could no longer see it in the dim light of dusk. She slipped it on her finger, and it was difficult just at the knuckle. She did not like the weight of it. He kissed her, and she returned the favor because she knew somewhere her mother was watching. They walked the length of the porch to the back of the house. They were facing the deep of the woods. Mr. James left his right hand trailing behind him and his suit jacket over his shoulder. Lilly straightened her dress before sliding in through the side entrance. When she saw it waiting there its mouth open and smiling with her own betrayal, her legs left her.

Wilson had her by the shoulders when she woke up. His hands felt large and soft as he shook her.

"Wake up, girl." His voice was broken. "Wake up, poor child." Wilson shook her lightly again and Lilly felt the flutter in her eyes. Her face felt flush when her lips met his. She felt her body leave the floor of the kitchen, and her heart was cleaved when he entered. Afterwards she had already felt it begin to grow and knew with its harvest would come the greatest storm they had ever seen.

Larry arrived at the Dupree Plantation two days before Sister Sarah. Mr. Dupree agreed that fixing the road would require more than just Wilson's effort, and Larry could stay until the job was finished.

"Damn road seen better days." Larry dug his shovel into the roads' edge pulling on the handle to separate the overgrown grass. It was a long sick winding dirt road overgrown and ugly. The two would need more than a month to make it right. The high grass had grown heavy and thick into the road's edge and with it came feeder roots that were pulling at the dry soil. Wilson pushed against the edge cutting the tiny roots with the end of his shovel. The sun had risen high for noon and was already burning on the back of his neck. They worked, quietly digging, prying, pushing with their flat square shovels until the edges of the path were clear. The field was almost burning in the deep orange flash of the setting sun.

"Goddamn, wheat in Alabama." Larry pulled at a stalk and bit the end in his mouth. He chewed on the dry yeast flavor and spit into the dirt path. "It must be here." They worked on the road lazily for the rest of the day enjoying the heat and humming a low sweet singsong melody.

"Lilly dear, come here please."

"Yes, Mother." Lilly climbed off the small lounge and went to her mother. Lillian was placing stemware on the table. The glasses were long and brittle looking with flutes that smiled cautiously at the chandelier.

"Help me set this table." He handed her daughter a pile of linen napkins.

"Where's Martha?" She folded the first napkin, once, then twice over into a neat triangle.

"Today is her day off." Her mother placed another glass on the table resting it in the embroidered edges of the tablecloth.

"Where is she?" Lilly folded another napkin.

"Who?"

"Martha, Mother."

"Oh, I don't know where she goes. That woman is strange. She just up and disappears. She said she'd be back in time to help with the cooking." The napkins looked comfortable enough for Lillian to begin setting the plates. It was the fine china, one of the only things to survive from the island. It was for Mr. James. Her parents had seen the ring that Lilly was carrying heavy on her finger. The Whitmore's were, of course, now expected.

"It looks just wonderful." Her mother stood back against the large fireplace that dominated the north end of the room. Lilly slid the last plate onto the table and returned to her lounge. She could hear her mother from the other room mumbling about the evening's guest list: The Whitmore's, The Johnsons, and several other families who still had their minds in the old ways.

Lilly slipped out the large French doors that dominated the entire house. The grass felt nice against her bare feet. It was soft despite the dry spell and like the field grew with an appetite. She pulled at the front of her dress and ran to the woods. She found it last week growing brilliantly and awkward among helpless rails of maple and sycamore. It was taller than the rest, and she enjoyed the comfort of its stature.

Martha did not hear her. She was not listening for the light quick steps of a young white girl. She could not hear the rustle in her dress, the heavy breath of her run, but she was ready. Wilson felt it in his stomach when she tore the flower from the branch. Larry's arms went too weak to swing the axe. *We are home again*. Martha held the bud close to her face and let the smell roll over her. It was so familiar, she began to weep. Lilly fell to her knees when the wind swept up beneath her skirt. It was uncontrolled and amazing as it whipped about her ankles, played with the back of her knees and tightened around her neck just slightly before it sang a sweet singsong melody in her ear.

Martha moved toward Lilly, the grass barely teasing the bottoms of her worn feet. It moved with them, an enclosing tangle of branches and blossoms soaked in the warm scent pressing around her. It filled Lilly with the heavy smell, and she was overcome. For the first time, she could really see them. They had existed since before the calendar or the concept of her race. They had been born from the sun and the earth in a slick ceremony that bonded water with the land, and they began to grow. It was a patient process, the two of them living their lives in an opus. They existed only in the outskirts of the world in a vast garden that reaped fruit and flowers. They lived in quick smiles and heavy sighs until there appeared a third much older than they and darker than midnight. She lived with them and filled the garden with wisdom and the storm of her temper. She warned them of evils and the whip and taught them of the horrors to come. The unavoidable storm that would try them all. Then from her came the forth, born with a destiny that grew like the tree with a wickedness running through the center that would break them all. Then more came, and they began to outgrow the garden, their lives becoming more than the fruit of the garden could support. They began to leave in pairs, two poor soldiers moving out into the jungle, into the desert and passed desperate looking mountains. They began to spread out of the entire land dividing territory among themselves in quiet quarrels and living off meager farms and narrow cows. The four stayed, stayed in the garden with the faithful ones, with hushed tones as the jungle began to creep in. Time and Civilization brought the serpent, and the garden began to disappear. They built the village around the tree. Small quaint huts with thatched roofs and stick walls. They lived in wait for what was their destiny. The four like midnight and her face as white as the African moon.

Helen tossed the plate and the food into the kitchen garbage can. The chef smiled and shook his shoulders up and down several times. She smiled plainly and returned to her tables. She took only a minute with herself, holding her hands at her waist before the next order. Wilson had left the house around noon in hopes of finding permanent work or at least a few dollars for today. The town of Princeton frightened him. There were no shop jobs for blacks, only lawn-work and labor but he did not mind the sweat of the Jersey summer. He had been making his rounds for the past month soliciting his service to offices and houses that seemed in need of maintenance. Most of the owners were smiles enough but paid as if he was a child. He could not live with Helen if he did not work. He had always worked since before he could remember the notion of his own time. Even in the garden he had worked for her, bringing fruit, making trinkets, building needless shelter just to see her smile.

They walked the entire coast of the island after Digbee and Lyla Dupree left. They followed the foaming currents, traced their way through the hot sand, and waited. After they had completed the entire island, they returned to the house. It was a disaster but more home than they had seen in almost ten years. They had begun cleaning, the ones who remained, with an odd diligence. The large pieces were removed first collecting them in buckets and old crates and carting them away to a large pile that was forming behind the rear of the house. Much of the furniture was destroyed. The fragile fine wood cabinets had been smashed like a toy under an angry boy's fist. They righted what furniture remained placing it about in unusual patterns as if they have never owned any-thing besides a table and chairs. There were no plates, stemware, or glass left in the overturned china cabinet. The kitchen appeared to have been rioted by an eggbeater. There was a smell already growing from the spoiled or wet food. It was all removed by anxious and hungry hands. They ate what was barely eatable nibbling on half-flattened tomatoes, unripe bananas, bruised fruit. They made coffee with left over rinds and tea from leaves that had been soaked by the storm.

The pile at the rear of the house was growing almost a second story. A bizarre bi-level effect began to take place as the food stuffs were balanced precariously atop the remnants of chairs, tables, china cabinets, a hutch, a four-poster bed, a rocking chair, and helpless sticks of furniture. The food hung like jungle fruits on their hand-spun limbs and a fit of laughter began to overtake them. They were full of smiles as they piled more food and shattered furniture to the enormous wreck like a ship tossed violently. The sun fell slow as the last of the debris was added to the pile. The men gathered with proud faces around their enormous pile, and the women gathered, proud of their men. In all there were 102 standing there when the fire spread. It was controlled at first, the pile burning with an awful odor and a heavy gray smoke. It was odd to see the fire with such spirit despite the wet air. It sprang with ferocity over the pile and burned so hot that the bottom had all but disappeared. The top of the pile full of rotted vegetables, stained linens, and splinters came vaulting forward. It was an instant and then the flames were over them like jelly rolling over their skin and burning the light film of body hair. They screamed like rats and Wilson, Martha, Sarah, and Larry watched them and realized they were alone.

The bus driver shook Leslie awake and, startled, she almost struck him.

"The bells already rang, sweetie." The driver seemed worried.

"Thank you." Leslie pulled her bag over her shoulder and scuttled off the bus. Her class was already settled into their desk chairs with books and note-books sprawled open for attention. The teacher did not look pleased as Leslie slid into her seat. She removed her book from her bag and opened it carefully to the middle. She had no idea what chapter they were on. Was it 1869 or 1960? Were they discussing Thackeray or Thatcher, secession or the Suez, expansion or extradition? Leslie looked down casually at the book and then to the black-board were the words spread out like a disease. Checks and scratches that formed sounds, that made up words, which composed fragments that spawned sentences, that conducted lessons on how we live and who we are. Lessons of regret or redemption but never of the ugly past that she had seen. The painful existence of poor black bodies writhing in overcrowded boats, and on the posts of southern gentlemen. They touched on it once or twice but never the brutal savagery she felt in the pit of her stomach. The feeling that made it hurt to uri-nate, that made her sick. They paraded statistics like small numerical martyrs dancing on clean white pages, easily forgotten by sex-obsessed teenagers with acne. It disappeared instantly from them as the bell rang as they passed through the door washing them clean of anything that hurt. Anything that preyed upon their fragile minds, they forgot purposely replaced it with pop song lyrics, base-ball statistics, last night's date, the cigarette they smoked. Numbers were sim-ple. They were clean that is why men obsess over them. Why men devote lives to chalkboards and dusty hands. They are relentless and totally unsolvable and that is why they disappear. That is why we forget them so easy why distance ourselves from reality with them. Distance ourselves from the blood that flows fast from history. Leslie pulled hard on the front of her T-shirt and scratched at the mark on her hand.

The garden burned quick. It smoked like an extinguished phoenix as they stormed through in English pants with French cuts. They swung at limbs freely blood mixed with leaves failing about wildly amongst the screech of animals and men. Leslie felt the sickness move up from her stomach, and she ran knocking books from her desk. The smell of the toilet made her feel worse as she vomited into the bowl. The bile leaked up past her nostrils. She buried her head under a sink of cold water enjoying the clean flavor it brought. The man with the dog was standing behind her, his face full of sadness. She could not talk, it would have killed her. He placed his hand on her shoulder. Leslie stared at the dog, sickly and wasted. He smiled calmly, and she recognized his worn face. She felt safe. She felt she could understand.

William had decided that after reading the letter there wasn't much reason for school except for her. He watched his mother leave for work, her uniform too tight around her hips. The early shift started at six, and by seven William was already back in bed enjoying the warm blankets. The large glass of milk was sinking into his stomach, and the sleep began closing his eyes. They crept into his head slowly at first, for the first time in years. The four of them standing so serenely, their own dark shadows on the shore of the godforsaken island. They were crying in the flames, their faces melting like sweet chocolate. Men made of bone and glowing eyes dancing about fires of burning refuse in cans or on the ground like holy saints from his father's old sermons. Who were they behind those masks before Grace set them free with one great blow. Wilson was their messenger with his straight angle face and long hands. A carrier of half the spirit they would need to save them. William twisted the sheets up in his sleep feeling the heat they brought. He watched spirits move through the house along with them. The four of them nurturing that poor scorched tree. When the horn sounded, the sea seemed to part and they left soaked in ash with only some soil and the sweet smell of the blossom.

William rose out of bed at nine, his head and pillow still damp with sweat. He showered with a ferocious passion scrubbing hard at his armpits and genitals until he felt sore. The towel was soft and smelled like fabric softener, and William was happy to escape the dirt he felt. He put on clean clothes from his drawer. He took the container of orange juice from the refrigerator and left towards the school. His steps were long, and he carried the juice low at his hip. He tossed his head back to drink and enjoyed the cool taste down his throat. The container was empty by the time he arrived at the school. There were kids sprawled out everywhere on the grass enjoying the sun.

He found Leslie behind the tennis courts alone, eating from a paper bag. He kissed the back of her neck and settled down into her hips on the grass.

"Where have you been?" She swallowed a grape.

"Home."

"What about class?"

"I got a letter the other day. They say that no matter what I am out. Out for good it sounds like." He leaned back on his left hand and felt the hot grass.

"I wish it would rain." Leslie swallowed another grape and held the bag open for William. He took one preciously between his two fingers and shot it into his mouth. The flavor was almost perfect. He kissed her again, and her hand slid up against his thigh. Leslie did not want to make love in the same place again. She wanted a bed at least this time.

Martha held the flower under her nose, and Lilly felt her knees begin to quiver. It was a sensation that made her feet leave the ground. She held on to Martha's shoulders for comfort and let the scent wrap around her. She saw them all, in the garden, on the boat, on the island, and now waiting here and she understood. She understood the path of the serpent. She understood his desire. She understood her place in their lives.

When they came to the garden, they sacrificed humanity in all regards. They took what they wanted from the slick dark bush and watched in humor as men ran from long nets and whips. Then she appeared hanging over them with a force that made them crawl. It was a moment in time that was completely frozen except for the desperate gasp that sucked the sound from the jungle. An inhalation that made the instant disappear from history. She was completely bare except for a small circle of red cloth around her round hips. The men with guns and whips collapsed to their knees trying to reason with it, trying to discover how she had come to be in a place they so hated. How something so incredibly beautiful was not crushed by the suffering they created. She only stood, unmoving, occupied only with her own grace. They stopped for something that was endless. The men with trousers around their ankles ceased their bodies shaking and released their prey. The men with guns dropped their barrels to the ground. The whips made only a slight crack as they went limp towards their targets. She moved towards them all as they stood frozen with fear and disbelief. Her bare feet barely touching the jungle floor. Suddenly they felt a sensation of the earth begin revolving towards her and the men with their guns, their whips, and their exposed manhood began to whimper. A flood of fear began to overtake the men as she continued to move closer a flock of birds fled for safety. No sound could be heard, the animals had ceased their symphony, not a single man's breath had left their open mouth since she appeared. The silence was enormous and then all at once an echo emanated from her with tremendous force. Her body collapsed like a flower, and she fell to the jungle floor. They watched the blood seep across the jungle floor spreading in all directions like the sea. Wilson threw himself on his Grace and looked upwards at the serpent's gaping mouth.

Sister Sarah arrived in 1965, two days after Larry, with a basket of homemade bread and a smile that crushed Henry Dupree. He had no reason for her to stay but she did anyway. He had no work for her, but she stayed anyway, and she had no love for him, but he did anyway. For the first month he was relentless in pursuing her. He moved through the house in his quiet wool slippers in the most unbearable heat. He held a hand mirror around corners and listened at the door while she bathed in the servant's quarters. He waited on her patiently with hope and slight looks when passing in the kitchen or on the porch. It was mild at first, like any crush, but Lillian saw the motives behind Henry's eyes. He was no longer a young boy in lust. He was an old man, methodical and becoming desperate. Lillian had not been able to perform since the sickness set in, and Henry was ripe with vigor. He helped Sarah put away groceries, feed the horses, and held the wash bucket when able. Lilly was blind to her father's passion. She had been overcome by Martha. The serpent was growing in her daily. Wilson could already tell, and the rest would see the signs soon enough.

Mr. James was due at noon for lunch.

"Lilly dear, mother said the strangest thing the other day." He was full with fresh ham and Sarah's homemade bread.

"What was that?" Lilly was playing with the linen napkin.

"She said that with all these black men around I had to be careful with you." He laughed harshly through his nose. "To think you would be lying with one of those field boys." He smiled and brought a glass of brandy to his lips. Her father had left cigars on the table in a cedar box, and the smell was beginning to fill the room. Lilly pulled on the front of her dress.

"Isn't that just a laugh?" He snorted through his nose again and looked to her. Lilly knew that things had to be done. She rose up from the table and took Mr. Jame's hand and kissed the large knuckle just slightly. He smiled and she led him to the field. In the hot sun of the summer afternoon, she pulled at the straps of her church clothes. There would now need to be a wedding.

There was a fear in their faces that no ship's captain could understand. They did not move much during the trip huddled at the rear of the cabin with few possessions and a tablecloth full of wet dirt. They were fed in the best of the ship's meager means and asked only to do minimal chores. Larry did most of the work that was asked of them. He cleaned the decks, sewed a torn sail, and repaired a hole that had begun to rot the ship from the inside. They spoke few words and asked no questions about their destination. The captain, a large white man with an enormous beard that seemed to swallow his head, treated them with kind words offering his pipe to the men and his wife's company to the women. There was talk of children and crops but little else was said.

They came to port 22 days after leaving the island and the captain offered a few dollars to each of them. Larry took the money and washed the deck one last time before leaving. They had arrived in 1867 in Louisiana.

Larry and Sarah left immediately following the sun towards the west. They traveled for more than three weeks in a boxcar waiting on dirty children and preparing meals for richer families in search of summer homes. There was no pay, no garden, nothing but Texas.

They found themselves at a ranch where a pasture spread like a blanket across the horizon.

"You two healthy?" The rancher had his hand on his belt.

"Yes, Sir."

"You have any bugs?"

"No, Sir."

"No diseases?"

"No, Sir."

"You can work?"

"Yes, Sir."

"What about her?"

"She can work."

"You know anything about animals?"

"Yes, Sir."

"You eat much?" He pulled at the buckle of his belt.

"No more than any other man."

"You got children?" Larry looked to Sarah and felt empty.

"No, Sir."

"You can sleep in the barn for now. We wake one hour before dawn. I'll show you how to milk."

"Yes, Sir."

He turned and tipped back slightly and looked to Sarah. She was still wearing the same plain habit that she had received from the missionaries.

"My wife, she can use some help with woman things."

Sarah smiled and nodded slightly.

Larry enjoyed the feeling the barn gave him. The horses were welcome companionship, and Sarah enjoyed talking to them. Her voice was a high little squeak and click pattern that excited them as she pulled lightly on their ears. The largest one, black and shiny, seemed to like her the least. An obvious male, he seemed too full of himself to care for a woman's sweet hand. Sarah pulled her attention to the other two, brown and smooth like chocolate. She fed them from her hand and kissed their flaring nostrils.

Larry laid out the blanket he was given over a large section of hay that seemed suitable enough. It had been long enough already since they slept in a bed of their own. It would be easy to make this their home. Larry stretched out on the blanket and rubbed his hand over the coarse cloth. He lit the lantern the rancher's wife had brought to them. It burned greasy black smoke for a few seconds before funneling into a clean crisp orange flame. Wilson sat the lantern a distance away from the hay and the horses.

Sarah fed the last of her hand between the two brown horses and moved towards the blanket. Larry had already removed his shoes, socks, shirt, trousers and was lying on his back in his underwear. They were snug around him and Sarah thought about it for a moment before slipping out of her dress. The fabric dragged across her skin and the feel of the night air was welcome. She shed the rest of her clothes quickly enthralled with the cool air that was sweeping into the barn. She lay naked next to Larry pressing her body close and pulling the blanket edge over her. She rolled on top of him and he felt her breasts against him sticky and heavy. He kissed her on the mouth lightly, and she let him inside with a heavy sigh.

They were both dressed and awake before the rancher came to fetch them. Sarah had already fed the horses out of her own happiness and Larry was sharpening the tools he found hanging in the rear of one stall.

"Morning." He tipped his hat and stuck his thumb in his belt.

"Morning, Sir." Larry put the scythe down slowly keeping focus on the ground.

"My wife needs some help in the house."

Sarah dusted her hands off on the front of her dress and disappeared into the growing light of the new day.

"I see you found the tools and the stone."

"Yes, Sir."

"Good to know."

"Yes, Sir."

"Time for milk. Then breakfast." The rancher turned on his heels leaving a heavy imprint in the sand. Larry followed his tracks out into the rising sun. The milk cows were kept in a large barn with a stone floor. The rancher's boots made an odd click on the hard surface. He pulled two stools from beneath a workbench and handed one to Larry. Larry followed the sound of his boots to the rear of the facility. There were metal pails hanging next to every stall, and Larry noticed that many of the cows were still sleeping. The rancher sat his stool next to the cow, and the bucket disappeared underneath. Then came the sound slight at first in drops a plit-plat-plit-plat ringing against the empty bucket. The rancher's arms began to move more loose now, his hands sliding freely over the animal's tits creating a rhythmic slish-sis-slish-sis in the pail. He stood up from the stool and rubbed the animal's head and back with long strokes. The rancher picked up his bucket by the handle. Larry took the bucket from the hook and slid into the stall tucking his stool between his legs, plit-plat-plit-plat. Then came the rhythm slish-sis-slish-sis, a sweet kind of syrupy singsong melody.

Wilson found himself in an enormous house surrounded by black faces with white hands. They smiled pleasantly, but he could see the panic behind their eyes. The housemistress was thin and frail with a tongue like an eager whip. Wilson held his hand against his chest.

"Well, you certainly look authentic now, don't you?" She smiled and held a cupped cigarette to her lips. Wilson smiled and fumbled over the collar of his shirt. "Well, what do you have to say for yourself?" She exhaled a long thin line of smoke that drifted up and about the room before dissipating. The men with white hands were eager to fan away the smoke. She smiled to herself slightly and then her face was stuck with an odd quirk.

"My husband has banned me from smoking." She said staring wickedly at her cigarette. Her voice was thick with contempt and she rolled the wet end of the paper in her hand.

"I love a good smoke, ma'am." Wilson smiled his mouth wide and full of helplessness. She looked at him, and he saw something drowning behind her eyes.

"Well then, you are hired." She opened a large silver box and offered a cigarette to Wilson. He took the white wrapped tobacco gently from the case rolling it, caressing it, with the ends of his fingers before slipping it into his mouth. One of the white hands stopped its incessant flip flapping and lit a match for him. Wilson inhaled deeply and threw his neck back blowing the smoke into the lofted ceilings.

"Thank you, Ma'am."

"No, no that won't do. Kristine. That is my name, and you shall use it. Your room will be the first one in the servant's hall. They will show you." She inhaled again and made a motion with her cigarette. Wilson followed the man to his room. It was simple enough. A bed, a lamp, sink, basin, rocking chair, a small chest, and a table. Wilson sat on the bed and enjoyed the comfort of the mattress. A woman burnt like the sunset knocked on his door before opening.

"She wants you to have these." The woman smiled and bowed slightly before leaving, her feet quiet and wrapped in leather. Wilson looked carefully at the pile on the bed still holding the smoldering cigarette in his one hand. The clothes were smooth and fresh with a deep heavy perfumed smell he could not recognize. There were also sheets, like glazed silk, that he spread across the bed. He dressed and studied himself in the mirror. He understood his role completely.

Martha was playing with a stray cat when they found her sitting on the steps of an abandoned storefront. She was still holding the dirt-filled sack with pride against her chest. They were all painted with reds, blues, and hues of colors she only recognized from pictures. They took her by the arms and pulled her towards them. They smiled and chatted with hopeful tones about the rise of her people. She followed them in confusion. Her spirit was not theirs. Theirs was enough for an army. She admired their enthusiasm and they were surprised by her youthfulness.

The building was white with blue banners and slogans draped over railings. The placard pronounced them proudly *Southern Women For Equal Rights*. The activity inside was sprawled out across the entire house. All women, moving with snap motions and click-clacking feet that made odd beat rhythms on the hardwood floor. In one corner they were painting signs, in another a large group was studying an enormous woman with gray hair as she spoke, and a third larger group was preparing items of publication. It was an amazing hive, two dozen maybe more, all furiously engaged in their own activity, but all with similar goals. The women who had pulled her with them had left her standing holding her bag of dirt by the doorway. There were no men, black or white, waiting for her and she wondered why they had brought her there. It was sometime before the painted ladies found her again sitting on the porch of an abolitionist's house in the heart of Alabama with her bag of dirt over her lap.

"Well there you are. We have been looking for you." She smiled and snuggled into a large wicker chair next to Martha.

"You all looked so busy. I just thought I'd stay outta that mess." She looked off towards the road where she heard some children before.

"We have a lot of work before us now."

"I understand."

"You look like you been through a lot."

"A lot for most people, just the beginning for me."

"You are just precious." The lady smiled and smacked her hand against her thigh. Her skirt was stained with dust from the road. "So are you going to remain the mystery lady or you gonna tell us your name?"

"Most, most call me Martha."

"Well, that is a pretty name. Martha."

"It was a present."

Lawrence had been fanning herself with a large slick leaf all morning. Her habit was soaked through with sweat, and she could smell herself through the fabric. The other four sisters were in similar condition each with a giant green leaf that appeared almost artificial. The four horses that they had been riding had grown so weak and malnutrition they sold them for meat at a small village and purchased the four beasts they were riding now. Annabel claimed that they were donkeys, Mary agreed, and Lena, Lena had another word for them. They were slower than the horses but seemed content to wallow in the insufferable jungle heat. The four had long since carefully and with superior respect folded their full habits into their packs in exchange for some austere pants and a more modern head habit. It was most unconventional, but under current circumstances, Mary claimed it was righteous enough.

They began in Morocco traveling quickly down the coast in boats with white traders and businessmen until they reached the Ivory Coast. At the seaport they bought their horses, supplies, a map and trail guide and moved towards the jungle. Their guide was a traditionalist in tan pants, tan shirt, a half-bent hat and some rugged old army surplus boots.

"You know, sisters, this is undiscovered territory we're headed into." His voice was proud and eager to have a trail follow his name through the jungle. The sisters were not interested in trails or undiscovered country. Their business was God. They had crossed the western coast of Africa following the slender shape of the beast. They had argued in the nunnery about the nature of the sign.

"It is a dove's wing."

"A crooked olive branch."

"The arm of Jesus."

"The hand of God."

"Undiscovered country, sisters, a great step for man." He touted it proudly as he pulled on the brim of his hat. They had been riding for several days and seen nothing of civilization in any regard. They camped slightly before nightfall and their guide built a small fire between the three tents. Lena had whined about her own tent but then whined even more when she learned who would be the one to carry it. She decided sharing with Annabel would not be horrible. The guide had eyes for Annabel. Mary and Lawrence could see it in the way he lifted her unto her animal or in how he watched her slender throat while she drank.

The tents were simple coated canvas, the same they make sails out of, with strong poles for support. They set them up in a triangle pattern with the fire in the middle and the flaps facing each other. Lena despised her own odor. She hated not to bathe. They had been eating stale bread and dried meats since they left the western coast. Their guide occasionally would snare an animal. A helpless bird or small rodent, but his poor hunting skills were far superior to his cooking skills. They had grown content with their stale bread. It had become almost an entertainment with them. Who received the hardest slice of bread, who had the most mold to scrape off, who had the least?

The sun creaked over the roof of the jungle slow and desperately. It was hot enough and only nine in the morning. The guide shook the flaps of the sister's tents. He enjoyed watching the shadows rise and dress. Annabel slipped out of the tent and flattened her modest blouse against her stomach. He enjoyed the rise in her breast. Mary and Lawrence moved out of their tent with an effort not to disturb the jungle. The mornings were Mary's favorites because in the silence she could find the beauty of her god.

"Lena!" She shook at the edge of the tent.

"She's awake. She just does not want to move." Annabel smiled and slid her eyes towards the guide.

"Lena, get up. Get up now." Lawrence shook at the tent and gave the dumpy shadow a light kick while the others were not looking. Lena growled inside the tent and rolled over. The three sisters prepared themselves and a modest breakfast while they waited for Lena. Mary was in charge of breakfast. It was made from crusts of bread and cornmeal that they had packed. It tasted almost worse than sawdust but not any better than dinner. Lawrence gave the bowls and spoons out and Lena rolled out of her tent. She was not wearing her habit yet, and her hair was long against her straight back. The guide smiled and tipped his hat. Mary pretended not to see. They ate in relative silence and smiled plainly at the guide who used his hands to eat.

The four of them had been blind about following the path of the serpent since their departure from the English countryside. It appeared to them on the seventh of July just as the night rolled over the pasture and not left them since. They followed the course of the serpent down the rough seas of the African coast and into the jungle. The guide packed up the rest of the camp and helped Annabel onto her animal. He held her thigh tightly enjoying the broad smooth feel in his hand. She smiled and thanked him as he moved to his own beast.

There was no path in the jungle, no worn trail, no inclination of the passage of men or time. The leaves and soil were undisturbed. The jungle was dark even during the hottest part of the day when the sun steamed the wet off the trees. The canopy was amazing and the sisters prayed daily for its salvation, for without it they knew they would not survive. Annabel was fascinated by the dancing stems of light that fought their way through the thick foliage and crisscrossed the jungle. The guide had been leading them into what he called the heart of Africa, a mysterious and unusual place. Lena despised him. She had grown to blame the guard for the entire trip, for their failure to see the sign, for the heat, for her smell, and for the growing hate she felt for her sisters, and for the lord.

Lawrence had plotted the course of the serpent every night before she retired to her tent. She used an old piece of cotton parchment and ink she had coveted since England. The trail of the star was long, winding and slender following the coast darting through trees and parts of the map marked black with primitives surrounded by question marks. The guide was unaware of her sketching. The sisters were unaware of their true purpose.

They came upon the village suddenly and did not realize the tall thin huts until they stood amongst them at the center of the civilization. They dismounted their beasts and watched as they struggled towards the edges of the dark village for food and rest. The guide for the first time was speechless. He ceased his spouting of unmapped territory, of new worlds, of hidden riches. Lawrence turned on her heels. They were scattered about in no likely pattern, no discernible order. Lena wiped her brow and sighed heavily.

"Is this it?" Annabel asked quietly keeping her mouth almost closed.

"I do not know. I do not know." Lawrence whispered. Lena was the first to see them. Tall and thin and moving out of the doorways of their huts with relaxed grace and serenity. There were only four at first, two men and two women. They were dressed lightly in flayed skins and cloth that none of the sisters recognized. The one man was remarkably tall with arms that reached past his waist and a well-rounded head. The other man, more compact, was strong with fierce looking features and eyes set deep against his black face. The woman was of remarkable beauty with long thin arms and round hips. Her eyes were oddly slanted, and Lena could not look away except to see the other. She was old, at least in the dim of the jungle, but her eyes shone like a young girl. Her features seemed to be in motion with lines and creases in her face appearing and reappearing as her mouth curled a slow smile. They spoke nothing but remained with their arms outstretched. Mary was weeping.

The guide held his hand fast to his hip and the thick handled knife that he kept there hidden in leather. Lena moved towards them opening her arms slowly as she approached. There was no embrace, no touch. She stood her arms open around the tall one, her face almost against his bare skin. He remained motionless and waited for her. She looked to him, her habit slipping backward as she held her head up.

"Yes."

"Yes." His voice was deep and thick.

"Lena."

"Lena."

"Women."

"Women."

"Love."

"Love."

"Thank you."

"Thank you."

Lena embraced the man and felt the ridge of his spine. She enjoyed the feel of his arms around her. They stayed, almost motionless, except for breath until Mary spoke.

"Thank you God, thank you."

It had been three weeks since the guide left them for supplies and to make himself famous. His claims would be outrageous. Mary and Lawrence were the main disciplinarians keeping their younger sisters sharp and smart while still teaching the village English. Their aptitude for repetition was spectacular, but what was more amazing was their comprehension. She had taught them, using the Bible, the English language and the meaning of words. They spent hours each day under the deep canopy learning not only language but culture.

Mary was in love with the whole experience, settling on this as the purpose of their journey. Lawrence, sidetracked by the immediate, was hoping for something grander. Annabel was ecstatic. Lena did not believe in any of it. She just wanted the tall one. They had given names to the whole village, John, Jacob, Job, Abraham, Daniel, but there were so many that names had to be made up. Lena named the tall one Larry after her father, Annabel named the strong one Wilson, and the pretty one Sarah after her servants. The old one with the mystery face Mary named Martha after herself.

It was these four that Lawrence had decided were the best of the village, the most attentive, the most astute, the most apt to take with them. They were to return with their guide, four strangers, and proof of God's message. They began spending extra time with them teaching them ways of high society. Sarah was the most interested. She began to follow the sisters around and had learned so fast that she began to teach the rest of the village wearing Lena's discarded habit. Wilson was holding an armful of plants when he found Sister Sarah.

"I understand. I will be there." Sister Sarah rolled the words off her tongue carefully taking time to enjoy each letter.

"Yes sister." Wilson disappeared into his hut with the plants. Wilson brought the plants to Martha. The two women had been waiting all morning in his hut. Her stomach had swelled large, and both Wilson & Martha worried that the child would kill her. The rest of her body was remarkably untouched by the pregnancy except for some weight around her thighs. She did not sweat. She did not breath heavy. Wilson had taken time to teach her on his own the words that the sisters were teaching him. He had Sarah bring him books and papers that the sisters had given to her. She had not left the hut since they arrived, and the village was beginning to feel awkward around Wilson and his secret. They did not know that her exposure would bring their end.

Mr. Malcolm Ginsing had left the sisters almost seven weeks before he found himself wandering around the seaport of the Ivory Coast. He spent a whole night drinking in a tavern telling tales of his trip into the jungle and the primitives he had found. He drew pictures on napkins and sketched out trails on the backs of old parchments. He had emptied an entire bottle of whiskey before he stumbled out of the bar and into the hot night air of the African coast. There was no cool ocean breeze, no gulfstream to alleviate his heat. He drank water from a pump outside a small canteen and urinated proudly in the middle of the road. There were no women in Africa besides nuns, social workers, desperately married socialites, and enterprising whores. He held himself openly in the road enjoying the feeling of it even after he had finished. He walked the road hanging out of his trousers looking in windows and banging on closed doors.

The brothel loomed large at the end of the street that was the end of the seaport. There was one found in every port, on every coast, that the Europeans had set foot in. They came with the explorers, with the maps, with the proud admiral's wives, they came with the sailors, the rats, the disease. They came loudly with drinking halls, saloons, and street fights. They came with smiles, and screams, and they came only for enough money. Malcolm had been slouched against the stripped doorjamb when she opened the door and he fell in. She had a mountain of red hair, piled like misshapen bird's nests, on top of her painted face. She puckered her lips and put her hands on her knees.

"Well Fella, I'm Sally and this is our lucky day." She cackled a little like a broken valve, and Malcolm felt himself moving. He watched as the walls went by, canvases smeared with Botticelli look-a-likes and Rubenesque naked hips full of secret folds. He watched high shined wood floors slide by lit by indecent phallic lamps that hung from the ceiling like cave architecture. They removed his boots first, then his shirt, his undershirt, his belt, his trousers and left him lying in a bed in only his underpants. Malcolm heard the door close and the sound of laughter high and full of rolls and from behind the walls. He sold the village for her and by dawn the next day was leading a pack of white men with nets, guns, and angry faces towards the sisters, the fire they had begun, and her.

She appeared to them right after the child was born, her stomach still extended and awkward looking on her slender frame. They were glowing.

"What is your name?"

"I have no name." She spoke broken words of a child.

"You must have a name."

"Grace." Lena shouted from behind Lawrence.

"Grace." Annabel agreed and looked to Mary for reassurance. There would be no more said about the name. Wilson took the child from her arms and held it close to feel its breath. The child seemed to engulf him. Its white spirit hung like a bright moon, making Wilson shine. The sisters all had spent time with the baby before they decided. Lena's beliefs had returned, and she demanded the return of her habit from Sister Sarah. Sarah did not believe in miracles. Martha knew that no good could come of so much talk. They sat in their tents at night, a small fire smoking outside, and discussed what they had seen. They had convinced themselves of what action was needed. They had convinced themselves of their place with God. The eye of the serpent shone bright ruby red the night they took the child from its crib. It was Lena who slipped her slender arm under his cherubic body supporting the head with her warm hand. She pressed the child close to her breast as she ran from the hut where the fallen mother slept.

"Did you wake them?"

"No. They were like sleeping snakes all wrapped together."

"We have what we need. Forget it little sister."

Their beasts were well rested and waiting at the mouth of the village. They disappeared into the jungle just as the sun began to burn away the bright curves of the snake, its mouth wide and smiling. The sisters had left their fire burning, and the flames snaked through the jungle canopy towards the clear sky. Malcolm Ginsing pointed to the sky with his hand and the men with their guns, and nets ran to fan the flames.

In the morning the village gathered in the center around the tree. Martha had severed a single blossom and Wilson kept it close to his heart. They spoke their thoughts in a new language. Wilson looked to Grace. He had never seen her sad before. Wilson felt for her hand.

When she first appeared to him, at night, he had thought he was dreaming. Her skin was white as she was torn away from the moon. A miracle ripped from the sky by the serpent's coil. He had a great struggle in rescuing her. He battled with sharpened spears and shield made of animal skin. He had severed its body in half and watched it reform. He broke one fang with a rock and watched poison drip from its mouth. Only after he had squeezed its heart did the beast rest. She fell to him tangled about in stars. He slept for six days. When he woke, she was there waiting with her wings spread around him. Their time had been momentarily altered, but their lives still remained unchanged.

Helen came home from work remarkably tired and Wilson was worried. She began dinner clanking pots in the kitchen loud enough that the neighbors could hear. Wilson stared at the dissected radio that still lay on the coffee table with creeping wires. The kitchen was not large enough for two whole people at the same time, especially this evening. Helen was making a mess, something she rarely did.

"Bad day at work?" Wilson stood at the sink filling a heavy metal pot.

"Not now."

"Why not?"

"Not in the mood for that."

"For pasta?" Wilson smiled to himself and shut the water off. The pot was heavier now.

"You know what I mean." Helen was moving quickly, her hand doing a rhythmic number on several unpeeled carrots. Wilson watched her hand move.

"Sorry."

They ate dinner rather quietly under the buzzing of the fluorescent light. Wilson did most of the talking with or without food in his mouth. Helen forced a smile between mouthfuls. They did the dishes slowly running them under the hot water repeatedly before using the sponge, then the steel wool, then the sponge again, then another rinse. Wilson dried, holding the towel with one hand and wrapping each plate carefully. He applied an unusual amount of pressure for drying and rubbed each plate until the dishes were completely dry. They returned them all to their cabinets, drawers, cupboards, shelves and stacks making sure each was straight. When they were done Wilson took a cigarette from the pack beside the bed and moved to the porch.

He enjoyed the night hot or cold, warm or cool. It was the sky that comforted him. Wilson exhaled a deep stream of smoke and followed the trail as it curved and melted into the stars. The sleek body was unusually bright. Wilson had been watching it ever since the island and waiting, its eye carrying a red hue that he had not seen since the garden. He inhaled deeply from the cigarette and closed his eyes. She startled him when she appeared on the porch. He did not hear her creak the old boards, just before the screen door, that needed mending. He did not hear her skirt rustle. He did not hear her heavy breath, always through the nose. He could not see her eyes past her face. She was white, a white he had forgotten. A white he did not want to remember. Her arms were spread before him, soft and full of Grace. Wilson let the smoke roll out of his mouth and over her.

"Boy or girl?"

"Boy baby, it's a boy."

Wilson kissed her stomach and she pulled him towards her.

Grace.

In the morning Helen felt ill for the first time. She spent most of the morning making time with the toilet while Wilson made breakfast. Toast. Helen ate slowly and carefully with only a small amount of jelly on her one piece. Wilson ate the remaining seven enjoying each one with a different combination of jelly, butter and cream cheese. Wilson pleaded with Helen not to work, to relax but he knew it was just play. Her check is what kept the apartment. Wilson's work was merely his own distraction.

"I'll be fine."

"You're sick."

"I am fine." She was gripping hard against the end of the counter.

"You are not."

"I am going to work, and that is it." She grabbed her apron from the coat rack beside the door. "I'll see you later honey." Helen disappeared. Wilson would wait.

Sister Sarah was a whirlwind in the kitchen while Larry finished in the barn. The rancher's wife was a plump woman with a hand like a claw hammer. She chirped incessantly and Sarah smiled plainly not trying to look too happy or too awkward.

"I want to have all of these preserves ready by the end of the morning."

"Yes, Ma'am."

"The fruit will be no good if it lasts longer than that."

"Yes, Ma'am."

"We only get fruit once, maybe twice a year out here, and it has to count. My husband loves jam in the morning."

"Yes, Ma'am." Sarah was preparing the wax.

"So no time to dawdle."

"Yes, Ma'am."

"We moved to this ranch almost ten years ago before anybody would even think to live out here. My husband said it would be nice to live rugged on our own. He wanted just to have a small place, just for us. To grow enough for us. To live just for us. I can't have children. Then all of a sudden people wanted our cows, our milk. The more we had, the more they wanted and that is where we are now. Well, where you are now."

"Yes, Ma'am." Sarah was pulling the stems from the strawberries with her sharp fingers. The smell of the fruit was intoxicating and spread over the entire house. Sarah had seen the house on her way in. The walls were crowded with tapestries and needlework. She only could see the hallways narrow, dark and hypnotizing as they seemed to spread in both directions. Sarah was amazed at the amount of light that filled the kitchen. There were windows everywhere decorated with curtains that bounced colors across the plain stonewalls. The ceiling fascinated her the most.

It was unlike anything she had ever experienced. It spun upwards with a series of supports that looked painstakingly measured and assembled until they formed a miraculous dome-like structure. At the pinnacle of the dome was a fabulous pane of glass that allowed the sun to filter down into the kitchen and the stars to shine.

The preserves were done before the noon sun. Larry enjoyed milking the cows and the repetition of the rhythm. After the milking there was mending. An enormous stock fence surrounded the rancher's property made of neglected boards and posts that he had accumulated along the way.

"You start there just past the barn." The rancher pointed his hand casting a long shadow.

"Yes, Sir."

"You work till sundown, then cleanup for dinner. My wife will give your woman supper to take to the barn at sundown. The water pump is behind the house."

"Yes, Sir." Larry watched the rancher jam his hands into his pockets and turn into the sun.

Larry enjoyed the work. He had become comfortable with his hands on the island and settled himself in his mind that his calling was in the field. He had taken a wheelbarrow and filled it with tools from the barn. He worked removing, replacing, repairing the long slats of the fence until sunset. When he returned to the barn, Sarah was waiting for him with a pot and some bread spread across a crate. It would be their table for the next eight years until she got the call.

Wilson understood what Kristine wanted. He understood that he wouldn't be the first. He had dressed both himself and his bed as he was instructed and tried to arrange the room the best he could. He did not work. He did not set the table or serve the dinner. Wilson only waited. He waited at the edge of his bed sitting with both feet flat and pointed toward the door. He waited with his hands smoothed out on his thighs and tried not to sweat. He did not want to make his new clothes damp. When she finally came, it was like a cannonball. The door swung open so hard that it crashed against the small bureau. It was closed with the same vengeance. She was already half-undressed before Wilson could stand up and as soon as he was up, she wanted to go down. Wilson could not tell if she was beautiful. He had only seen one other white woman naked. Kristine was a flurry. She was on top of him before he removed his shoes, and she did not care. She only spoke to him once.

"Don't say anything." She threw her dress over the back of the rocking chair. Wilson watched her move in the mirror. Her hips were narrow. She unbuckled his belt and it all began. He bit his lip not to make a sound and followed the singsong rhythm of the old bed. She gripped his shoulders hard enough to make his body ache for the next eight years until he got the call.

Leslie was tired of school. In the mornings she was usually sick, and by the middle of the day, she could no longer pay attention to her teachers. Her grades were falling, her mother was beginning to become a nuisance, and the chick was dying. It started subtly at first. She noticed that the feathers that were barely new had begun to turn brown and some black. Its eyes had begun to slope shut and the quiet singing that she loved was nothing more than a desperate whisper. Leslie had given her new bedding and increased the amount of food but, it went uneaten or was vomited while she was away at school. William told her that birds need to be in the outdoors but Leslie knew that there was something else wrong, something she knew from the beginning.

"So Leslie, I hear you been playing more than tennis on the courts lately?" Amanda had an upturned face and high breasts that made boy's eyes wander.

"What?"

"You know what I am talking about." She said it so slickly that Leslie felt guilty.

"I have no idea what you are talking about." Leslie began to pull at the front of her shirt. The hallways were full of ears.

"Oh, it's okay. Honey, we all need a little sometime." Amanda put her hand on Leslie's shoulder and the weight seemed tremendous. She wondered if William had been talking.

"Don't touch me." She shrugged her shoulder away.

"No reason to be so sensitive." Amanda had her locker next to Leslie's. Amanda's was open. She looked at herself in the small mounted mirror and smiled rubbing her finger along her gum line. She pouted her lips and applied a coat of lipstick. "Do you like my breasts?" She did not turn away from the mirror.

"What?" Leslie's head was aching.

"Jesus, what's up with you? I just asked if you think I have nice tits." Amanda turned from the mirror and faced Leslie. She was pulling down on the collar of her shirt so Leslie could see the tops of her breasts.

"I don't know."

"Just tell me."

"They're fine, I guess."

"You guess? Are they nice or not?"

"Compared to what?"

"Compared to yours. Look at yours, they're like perfect. Not too big, not too small, just in the right place. Do you wear a bra?"

"Why do you care?"

"Just wondering. Diane says you do but I think you don't." She looked back to her mirror staring down her chest. "Well, do you?"

"Do I what?"

"Wear a bra."

"I gotta go."

"Oh, come on it's no big deal. I mean if you got it, flaunt it. With tits like that, it is no wonder William likes fucking you." Leslie was down the hall. Amanda was preparing her breasts for fourth period.

Leslie felt the remarks trailing after as she moved down the hall. She knew he could not talk about her to other girls. Her head was pounding. At the vending machine, he was standing with his hands in his pockets like he was waiting for her. He did not look up when she walked by. William fell into step with her quickly, and the fresh air was welcome. The tennis courts were littered with leaves and debris from last night's storm. They leaned against the storage shed and slid down. The grass was cool in the shadows and William lets his hand rest in her lap. The man with the dog was leaning against a large oak tree. His face was obscure under the tangled shadows of the tree. The dog looked sick, its tail was still. Its coat too slick. Leslie looked to William. She never felt his hand leave her lap. His feet glided through the grass smoothly like floodwater. Leslie did not dare move. She stayed, her lap empty, watching. Their faces reflecting each other like mirrors.

"I know." William was very still while he spoke.

"That's good." The man knelt down next to his dog.

"What do we do?"

"Wait, he will come."

"I am not sure."

"She will understand."

"How?"

"I have shown her." The dog licked at the man's hand.

"She knows?"

"She knows, but she does not understand."

"Then what?"

"She will, don't worry."

"I love her."

"I know."

"When?"

"You will know."

"How?"

"Trust yourself."

"But how will I recognize him, Grandfather?" William put his hand on the man's shoulder.

"He is your father, Preacher Boy. You will know."

"I am not ready."

"You will be ready. She will be ready for you."

When William returned to Leslie, he was already naked, his clothes fluttering amongst the leaves. Afterward they enjoyed the smell of smoke as it sifted past their heads. Leslie woke up half-dressed spread across the grass. William was standing a few feet away, his chest bare and shiny with sweat. The school was quiet except for lingering group voices. She rolled onto her back and squinted up at the sun. William's shadow was tremendous in the sun. It stretched like a snake in a thick wave behind him. Leslie crawled toward, him following the dark line. She traced her way past the bulge of his head and down the long twist in the neck. She followed the sleek body, its slight wave comforting. When she reached the end of the beast she could no longer separate them. Preacher Boy.

Helen died in labor. Wilson would have died if Martha had not called him again when the orphanage took his son away.

It is time.
I do not understand.
You will.
I cannot leave my son.
You must come to us.
I cannot leave my son.
She would understand.
I cannot leave my son.
You must come for us, for Grace.

William enjoyed his time at the orphanage and followed the righteous path until he was eighteen and the visions began. The nuns at first thought the visions to be ecclesiastical in nature but soon decided that his torment was due to sins committed despite them. The nuns told him his influence over the other children was too dangerous and sent him on a train to New York to live with a retired priest. The man was old, older than anyone William had ever known and it frightened him. The proposition of being so close to death did not agree well with William.

The old man's daughter was a much more comforting presence to William. Lydia smelled of flowers and spring at all times and by the end of the year they were married. William had begun working at a local nightclub to make ends meet and despite the old man's warning, he gladly took over the business when the time came. On Sundays he would preach at the local chapter of the southern Baptists always casually instituting his Catholic upbringing. In 1978 William Jr. was born, Lydia no longer needed to work, and the nightclub was big business. Then disco died.

William loved to dress the part in flashy suits made of new age synthetics and shiny boots of imitation leather. He was famous in the lower Queens neighborhood and out past Valley Stream, Long Island. The Hot Box originally started as a jazz club, then a rock club, and when Led Zeppelin gave way to John Travolta and the Gibb Brothers, William bought a mirror ball and polished the parquet floor. William Sr. had learned to master his visions taking deep breaths and trace amounts of morphine had helped to calm the episodes. Episodes that is what Lydia called them. William Jr. was born in a storm. In February of 1978, the East

Coast was sent headlong into a devastating Nor'easter. The snow rode up to Williams's hip as he tried to shovel the driveway. The car, a Lincoln, was completely buried except for a small patch of metallic gray on the roof. The National Guard had been deployed by Carter, and William Jr. was born in the back of half-track along with three others by an army surgeon and an infantry driver.

William Sr. saw it as a sign. He sold the nightclub to a local promoter at the height of the craze and opened his own ministry. The loyalists that had seen him preach on Sundays at the Baptist chapter were easy converts, and their friends soon followed. William preached every day and Jr. grew up under the vengeful eye of a new lord and his father. A preacher's boy from birth, the prodigal son. William Jr. loved music from the start, playing in the church choir at age four, and then acting came later when his father's church began producing short plays based on the Bible but translated to modern slang. Preacher Boy had the visions from the start. In the beginning before he could speak, he would simply scream, cry, and kick till Lydia soothed him with her breast. When it came time for school, his attendance didn't last past a month before the teacher began to ask too many questions. Lydia began to teach him at home.

William Sr.'s passion and visions grew worse with every year until his addiction to morphine forced him to close the church and sell the upright baby grand. The graffiti began when Preacher Boy was five, after the church closed, and William's addiction became common knowledge. He still preached occasionally on street corners and brownstone steps, but his reputation as a morphine addict spread faster than his good words. They were subtle at first with crudely drawn needles and heavy black lines against their white garage. Then simple quick one word insults like addict and junkie. They sprayed for almost two whole years. One morning in June, William Sr. went for the paper and saw heavy red letters dripping down his brick front. *Preacher Boy Junkie Son.* That night William waited with a gun he bought at a pawnshop during the days of the Hot Box. When they came in the night with rattling cans and hushed laughter, he fired two shots clear over their heads and they ran leaving a trail of spray cans and whispers. Then for eleven years that was all William would hear.

The servants had been setting up chairs all day. Sister Sarah had strung white lace across the new gazebo and tacked the posts with tangles of baby's breath and wildflowers. There would be too many chairs to count when Larry and Wilson were done. Martha had been making favors and food all day enjoying the time in the kitchen to herself. Lilly had been dressed in her slip for hours and was waiting in the light spring air for her mother to finish with the dress. It had to be let out. Her mother did not want her to show. There was one large table draped in a beautiful cloth at the end of the yard decorated with wonderful silver serving dishes and carefully placed flowers. Martha had prepared her stew, a roast, two whole chickens, a turkey, a ham, and more than four dozen homemade biscuits. She had spent all night skinning and slicing potatoes for her famous mash, and Sister Sarah had gathered fresh herbs from the small garden they kept along the rear of the house.

Lilly gathered the bouquet herself the night before when the sun was setting dark with dew and fresh smells. It was simple wildflowers that had run ragged lines around the property. Wilson had gathered one blossom for her from the tree. There was no doubt in her stomach about her love for Wilson. When Mr. James arrived, he had a beautiful brown dog with him. He was keeping it in oversized wicker basket with an enormous handle and a bow that looked like an afterthought. Lillian took it from him with a polite smile, and they let the animal loose at the rear of the house. Wilson enjoyed watching the pup run. His legs were awkward with paws too large and a head that swung about hazardously.

The chairs had been finished for several hours, and Mr. James had taken to one of the spare rooms to dress and prepare himself. Lilly's brothers would be ushers, her father would give her away, her mother the maiden of honor. Mr. James' sisters would be there and his only brother would be the best man although Lilly had never seen him before. There were constant stories about his affairs with heroism. Mr. James had selected rather simple but elegant attire for the affair, a fine clean well cut suit in a deep charcoal gray. Lillian had finished letting out her own dress in order to make it Lilly's and Lilly was waiting rather uncomfortably on the toilet for her mother. Her stomach had been ill all morning and there had been some unexpected bleeding. Her mother tried to comfort her with tea and old wives tales. Martha had prepared a thick green soup for her, which tasted slightly of dirt. She could not stomach to deal with either.

Wilson and Larry were to bathe and shave before the affair and dress in the clothes provided by Mrs. Dupree. The heat was unbearable, and the field would need to be cut by the end of next month. The crop would be twice as large this year. The field seemed more alive than ever. Wilson had first noticed it when he was walking through the field at night back to the main house. The rows had grown twice as thick, and stalks had sprouted almost overnight to clog the neat tilled pathways. There was no longer the calm organization of the field, but a tangle of wheat that sprawled out in all direction past the edge of field and into the thick grass plain. It had grown more than waist height and drooped limply under its own weight without a stiff breeze. Martha had made bread with a small harvest she gathered herself and the loaves yielded were unusually large. Henry Dupree had not noticed the new life in the wheat field. He did not see the furrows of wheat intertwined amongst each other. He did not see the tangle of stalks knotted amongst each other. Only Wilson understood.

Henry Dupree had been chasing Sister Sarah since her arrival and twice placed his hands upon the flat of her stomach with motions to make more. Sarah did her best to quiet his intentions, but she knew a storm was brewing inside him. Lillian had moved her bed into another room of the house, and her time away from the plantation had grown increasingly obvious. She would take trips north to New York or Chicago, and when she returned, her face always looked younger. Mr. Dupree did not notice his daughter's pregnancy. He did not see her sickness in the morning, her pale face, or her tired eyes. He did not see how Wilson smiled at Lilly, or how Martha whispered quiet things under her breath. He did not see Larry sharpening tools.

Sarah had finished the decorations for the wedding early and was enjoying time in the breeze on the rear of the house as the pup ran madly about. She set water down in a large bowl and the dog's tongue made loud noises. There would be leftover roast and chicken for him later. In an hour the James family would arrive. She had laid a simple dress out for herself, one that Lillian would not mind. She bathed and used a sweet perfume that Martha had prepared. She pinned a small blossom to her breast.

"Martha?"

"Yes, child."

"I'm scared."

"No reason to be scared, child."

"What if he finds out."

"No man gonna find out. Men only know what we tell them."

"It don't feel right."

"Of course, it don't feel right."

"Then , I shouldn't."

"Well it's a little late for that now, Lilly dear. You just do this one thing, and Martha will take care of the rest."

"How are you going to do that?"

"Oh, child you might have seen some things in your life. Think you are worldly now that you can read the stars, but there's a whole lotta things you poor angels don't know."

"Oh, Martha I don't know."

"Don't you worry a feather over this, girl. You just do what I tell you."

"And it will all be all right?"

"Of course, child."

In the kitchen Martha stirred the stew once and bit her lip.

The James family arrived in several cars each gradually longer than the previous. Mr. James' mother and father arrived in separate cars each with their own drivers. The James sister arrived in her own car, which she drove proudly. Brother James arrived last in the longest car and waited for his driver to open the shiny black doors. They gathered on the front porch around Lillian and Henry Dupree. Sister Sarah was serving drinks and small shrimp stuffed with meat and breading. Mr. Dupree watched her narrow arms with the silver tray.

"So this is the famous hero we have heard so much about?" Lillian motioned with her glass and a smile towards Edgar James. He was dressed well enough to be a hero in a thick blue suit regardless of the heat and his shoes carried a high polish.

"Oh, nothing more than a good man would do." Edgar James swallowed the rest of his champagne and moved towards Sarah and the shrimp.

"Really Edgar, we've heard some pretty tall tales about burning buildings." Mr. Dupree laughed lightly, stuffing two whole shrimp into his mouth.

"Nothing more than an honest man's work."

"Really?" Henry Dupree swallowed hard as his wife shuffled her heels.

"Yes, really."

"I would say saving a family of five from a burning dormitory is more than just an honest man's work. Sounds rather extraordinary."

"It, it, it was just what had to be done."

"Was it a large fire, four alarm perhaps?"

Edgar James carefully wiped his forehead with the cuff of his suit jacket. His eyes, searching, found Sarah.

"Oh Mr. Dupree you know stories like that always get blown out of proportion. It's your daughter's wedding. There be no need to start a feud already." Sarah smiled and held the tray cautiously in front of her.

"Well I, for one, just don't care, Edgar. As long as my son in law is a good man that will be good enough for the Dupree's." Lillian chuckled slightly, her breasts moving artificially. "Isn't that right, Henry?" She looked sideways at him.

"Yes dear, just fun, that's all. You know boys will be boys." Henry's eyes ran like rain from his wife. Edgar smiled slightly at Sister Sarah and moved towards the edge of the porch. Sarah waited patiently while the five some emptied her tray. Martha was a fury in the kitchen. She had all the pots simmering, boiling, stewing, and cooking on every burner and a pan bubbling quietly over the old wood stove. The room was sweating like the jungle. The walls were shiny with moisture and steam made thin translucent clouds. Sister Sarah put her tray down on the butcher-block table and fell back against the wall. Martha looked for only a glance and then filled the tray. It would be a long day.

Martha enjoyed the cause. She liked watching the white women in their large hats with protest signs and loud voices. There were no white men even when they would need them the most. The signs looked used by Saturday morning. They had painted them fresh on Thursday, but a riot full of garbage and stones had scarred their red-letter surface. The women had all gathered on the steps of their white house by mid-morning and drawn a route on a piece of paper. It was a short straight march that moved through the center of town. In the past the routes had curved about town staying closer to the black neighborhoods. Today the march would move through the center of town. They would hold their signs in front of the feed store, the general store, the hardware store, the dress shop, the leather maker, the bank, the schoolhouse, and end at the church with the wooden cross. It was not even noon and already dangerously hot. The black men had marched on their own from their houses on the east and north sides of town singing old gospels brought from the farms. They came with uneasy smiles and restless hands. The women were glad to see them. Martha squinted against the sun.

They began the march slowly with little noise except their feet shuffling and a stray cough. One young man was smoking cigarettes, and a lady with a large hat frowned. There were boys lingering in the back kicking spare stones. The workday had begun at dawn for most. Shop doors had already been propped open with shaved sticks and half-full mop buckets. Men had swept their shops into the street and washed their glass windows with hand soap and old rags.

The march had gathered steam at the beginning of the main street and the men in the back had soon moved to the front of the group sharing duties with the women shouting slogans and carrying signs. There was awe at first. A gaping jaw look from storeowners and passersby at the group stomping down the center of town.

A boy threw the first stone out of curiosity. He had never seen a black man without chains. The second stone was from a shop owner. The third stone brought a hail of violence that the Sisters of Freedom had never seen. The men who had sang their freedom song so bravely now hurled rocks at shop windows and white men. The stones ricocheted off the signs and one woman was struck in the head. Her hat fell off, and she collapsed to the ground. Her skirt was a puddle around her. The men charged from the sidewalks with tools in their hands. The man who owned the feed store could be blamed for the whole thing in Martha's eyes. He struck a young black man with a garden hoe and blood surged from his scalp quickly. The women were horrified and began to run. The stampede triggered an unusual reaction in the young black men. They began to chase after the women, out of their own fear, seeking protection behind their skirts. The whites in fear and ignorance brought a rage that was uncontrollable. Some had guns, one an old sword from the war, and the rest used hammers, axes, shovels, stones, and hatchets.

It was a massacre in the end just outside of the church. The blacks on the outskirts of town who had heard rumors of the riot arrived with a makeshift militia armed with pitchforks, sticks, and liquor bottles. The fire started in the feed store first. The bottle crashed through the window and spread like a snake until the timbers of the building caught, and the swell of heat made the corn pop. The flames jumped like flies from one building to the next until the roof of the brick schoolhouse turned into a hot carpet. There were at least a dozen dead or lying bleeding with ugly wounds from crude tools when the church started to burn. It was subtle at first with wisps of smoke fluttering from behind closed shutters until a serpent of flame chased its way up the steeple to the gilded cross wrapping seductively around the wooden structure. Martha grabbed the pendant around her neck and felt its heat in the palm of her hand. She looked into the beast's eyes as the fire grew hot, and when she let go the mark was in the palm of her hand. She fell to her knees, and it felt as if the ground shook. The steeple collapsed and, for a second, the serpent remained coiled tightly in flame. Then the cross came down, and Martha called Wilson first.

It would not be until 1960 when he would find himself at the courthouse waiting for her.

The ceremony was beautiful, and the rain was burnt away by a late afternoon sun. Martha smiled. Wilson was at ease. Larry was weary. Sarah had become cautious. The Dupree's, except for the oldest son, cried and the James smiled while Edgar slipped away into the kitchen. He enjoyed the heat of the whole thing. The smell and the way it made him feel. His suit was becoming wet, and he removed his jacket. There were herbs on the table and a spare wooden spoon. He ate from the largest stew pot that was simmering over the heat. He found an open bottle of red wine on the table and was pleased to help himself.

The justice of the peace rambled only slightly but only Lilly really cared. She closed her eyes when she felt it move. The rings were simple but sufficient by Mrs. Dupree's standards. She would have liked something more but Lilly had settled, and there was no more to be said. Mr. James slipped the gold band across her finger pausing only slightly at the knuckle. Lilly would not sleep in her own bed ever again. Henry Dupree paid the minister in cash after the service and invited him to eat. Wilson left the dog to help serve with Martha. The dog was a flurry of ambition all day. His shiny coat got underfoot of long dresses and squirmed against the legs of light summer suits.

There was a tremendous amount of laughter throughout the day as the young couple's mothers talked of children, cradles, and brand names. Lilly found Martha waiting for her at the tree. The blossom she had slipped into her bouquet had opened with a heavy scent.

"You hear me call?"

"Yes."

"I knew you would."

"I don't know what to do."

"Let me see your hand."

Lilly offered her hand to Martha her fingers train-track straight.

"The mark is strong now."

"I can feel it stirring."

"Don't worry, Miss Lilly."

"I see bad things when I sleep."

"That's just nerves, girl. It will be right in the end."

"I'm worried, Martha."

"No worries, Miss Lilly. Now you go back to that party before they come looking."

"Yes, Ma'am." Martha let go of her hand and watched Lilly wander away from the tree towards the guests. Wilson had been playing with the puppy all afternoon. There was a storm coming from the west.

When the baby was coming due, Lilly convinced Mr. James to let her return home to be with her mother. Martha had prepared her room with flowers and new sheets. Sister Sarah began coaching her for the pain of labor, and Wilson had taught the puppy to sit and roll over. The harvest was due, and the wheat was very dry.

Henry Dupree stood over his crop from the top of the hill with his two sons, each one dressed in ragged jeans and a sloppy t-shirt. They would be gone before the end of the day. The oldest was headed towards California in order to work in the wine valley. The youngest was moving towards Tennessee to become a country singer. Wilson was to take them to the bus station after they harvested the crop. The sun was still hot as it began to sink towards the west. The thresher had been bought at the beginning of the season when Lilly was only several months pregnant. Now that she had come to full term, almost ten months, it would get its first use. The brothers had taken care in oiling and greasing the engine and double-checking the pressure of the tires. Henry Dupree was proud of his new machine. When Digbee turned over the engine, it ripped a marvelous sound over the quiet field. The thresher began to turn slowly at first with a creaking sound that almost worried Henry, but when the blades began to spin, he felt at ease. They moved so quickly they whistled, and Wilson watched calmly with Larry. The new thresher did all their work including the bailing and tying. The only work that was left for Wilson and Larry was to stack the square bales on one end of the field.

They used an old field truck with a wide flat back driving with the wheels straddling rows. Larry drove, and Wilson, using two massive farm hooks, lifted the heavy bales onto the bed of the truck. It would take over two hours to do the enormous field. Wilson would drive the second half. The sun was almost gone when the first half was finished. The thresher was cooling at the edge of the barn.

Martha had held over a pot for the boys on the stove. Sister Sarah was busy with Lilly. Her entire body had become drenched in a heavy sweat. Her mother had left for Chicago for two days. She had told Lilly that she was not feeling well. Those two days would not make a difference. That in two days nothing could happen. That in two days she would be back to normal. The women were gathered in the living room. The men were admiring the thresher.

> *It is time.*
> *I understand.*
> *Keep those men from this house.*
> *I understand.*
> *I hope you do.*

Wilson placed his hand on the cooling engine of the giant thresher and began to discuss the complicated machinery with the Dupree boys. Sister Sarah had laid a cool smooth cloth across Lilly's forehead and into the palm of her hand. Martha removed the short stool from the sewing table and brought it to the living room. The child had already begun to push, and Lilly was screaming. Sister Sarah closed the French doors.

"This is an incredible machine," Henry Dupree rested his hand close to Wilson's. "The best investment I ever made. Right, boys?" Henry looked to his sons who had become infatuated with the chicks in the barn. They had multiplied since their arrival. One mother hen and a stray rooster from another farm had produced an odd crop of chicks almost blue in color. Digbee was gathering them in a stray milk crate that he found in the barn. There was talk for another few minutes until Sarah closed the French doors, and Henry's ears pricked up. He began his stride across the field with long steps, letting the tall grass whip at his bare legs. The boys followed, Digbee carrying the milk crate out in front of his small stomach. Larry waited behind for the storm.

It came from the west like a beast rolling across the empty ranches of Texas and barreling across the southern cities. It had a ferocious head on it coiled and sharp. When it hit the edge of Alabama, it exploded with a rabid bite sending strikes of lighting haphazardly across the state. The wheat burned easily with only one strike smoking at the edges first before igniting into a blaze that leaped across the empty field. It scorched the empty half and darted like a tongue through the rest of the harvest and into the woods. The heaviest part leaped upon the barn, and the roof almost collapsed before Larry could run.

Henry Dupree barely heard the rumble that was rolling across the field. His daughter's screams were rattling his ears. The French doors opened, and the storm would come flooding in. Digbee dropped the milk crate, and the chicks began to scatter across the hardwood floor like marbles. The baby was already born and crying in Martha's arms, the cord uncut. Larry was running now as the flames found the forest. The tree began to burn quickly, and flames wrapped about the thick branches. With a knife from the barn, he cut loose a fresh green shaft with an unopened blossom and tucked the sweet smelling bud into his shirt. As it burned, the smell began to drift towards the house.

"Mr. Dupree, don't be getting violent." Henry could not look past the black baby in Martha's arms. Sarah was pleading her hands on the man's chest. Henry never looked before he struck her. His hand was closed tight and Sarah fell feeling a yellow chick against her belly. Daniel pried the baby from Martha's arms and blood began to spill out across the floor as the cord ripped away from his sister. Lilly grabbed her stomach and screamed. Digbee was standing, painfully still in the corner. Wilson grabbed Henry from behind, wheeling him around and sinking his teeth into the side of Mr. Dupree's neck. Henry Dupree let out a gasp of hot air and pulled Wilson from him. The blood ran quickly over his white shirt. Wilson struck him in the face once before he was met with a heavy blow to the stomach.

"Mr. Dupree, she be your daughter, your only daughter. Think about what you be doing." Martha was holding fast to Lilly's hand. Lilly could feel the mark burning. Henry raised his hand to her and held his fist over her head. The fire had crept up the front porch. Digbee began to cry as the small chicks began to burn, their voices pained and frightened. Lilly struggled to her feet and felt the blood run down her leg. She stumbled towards Wilson still holding her stomach. He had been coughing and blood was on his lips. Henry Dupree's fist was shaking.

"No!" Sister Sarah had crawled her way up to the man's feet. The blow struck Martha square on the head, and she slumped to the floor her body looking odd and too still. Wilson could hear the puppy screaming from the back room. Its wail high and pained. He opened the door to the porch, and the puppy was standing, his body hot and stinking from the fire. The flames had moved through the front half of the house, and smoke was slipping thickly into the room. Henry shook Sister Sarah from his legs. His belt was unbuckled even before he was on top of her.

"You like fucking Edgar! Didn't you? Didn't you!!" Mr. Dupree pulled at the back of her dress.

"I didn't touch that man!!"

"You lying bitch I saw you. I saw that look he gave you."

"Please, please Mr. Dupree." Sarah was sobbing wildly.

"You think I didn't see him. Didn't see him sneak into the kitchen, to find you." Sarah could feel heat between her legs.

"Henry, I never touched that man."

"I loved you." His fist was closed when it pushed her head into the floor.

Larry came heated with more than anger. He drove the knife deep into Henry Dupree's side and watched him fall from his wife. Sarah had stopped sobbing. The blood was spreading over the carpet. Wilson was holding the dog like a baby, and Lilly was still bleeding. When Larry saw their eyes past the thick smoke and felt them, her last words, before he burst from the steps of the burning house.

Run

Run

Run

Run

Run

Lilly picked up a chick from the floor and watched as it tried to move its wings. After she would leave, Digbee would pull the knife from his father and find his wrist easily. Daniel watched them burn, until the smoke filled his eyes, his hands clutching the baby. Lilly took the chick and held it in her hand facing towards Wilson. The dog was no longer moving. Wilson could feel it in his head despite the swelling pain and looked to where Martha lay as he felt the serpent bite his shoulder. *Grace. Her Grace will return us all.*

Lilly walked from the house until her bare feet felt the dirt of the road. She was still bleeding slightly. She began to follow the road away from the house looking back only once to see smoke. The house was a skeleton, just old timber and memories wrapped, a neat package coiled in the tale of flame and smoke. The mark on her hand stung as it began to fade. When the dirt road that led to the Dupree farm met the concrete of local highway 24, the sun had begun to disappear past the horizon. She could smell the diesel of trucks. The chick was no longer chirping. Lilly pulled away the scarred feathers from the tiny bird. After the sun had set, she pulled at the soft part of the flesh.

Daryl Walker had been driving since Texas and followed the storm most of the way. He would have never stopped except for the speeding ticket and Lilly, of course. The local cops picked him off only two miles off from the interchange and cut in at least twenty minutes to his route. Lilly would pull him off the road and take the next eighteen years.

"Going somewhere, miss?" Walker was laid out across the cab of his truck, his head in just reaching the passenger window. The air brakes made a terrible hissing sound. Lilly climbed up the heavy sideboard lifting her dress and slid into the truck. They did not talk until the truck had reached Florida.

"Thank you."

Lilly married Daryl by the end of the month when his truck had reached Lawrenceville, New Jersey. Daryl's mother did not like Lilly. After the honeymoon, Daryl began driving again on the cross-country circuit making it home twice a month at the most but that would be enough. Leslie would be born and Daryl would drive his truck off the Trenton Bridge two days later. Lilly worked as a secretary for the shipping company when they first got married. When Leslie was born, Lilly was already the head of the northeast district, an area that spanned from Maine to the Carolinas and as far west as Virginia. The salary was more than adequate for her modest living. The mark had almost let her forget completely, but the pain in her hand still lingered.

Leslie was born in Robert Wood Johnson Hospital in Princeton, New Jersey during the spring and Lilly moved shortly after into the area in order to send her daughter to a better school. Lilly changed her name for the third time just before Leslie was one. They would live comfortably as the Dulins for the next 17 years.

It was an enormous story for the local town. When Lillian Dupree had returned from Chicago, the local police met her at the airport. When she received the news that her daughter's body was still missing, she wept. When they told her it was most likely destroyed, she finally lost her mind. She would not last more than two months in the hospital.

Larry found work on another farm several miles from the ashes of the Dupree's. The work on the farm was easy enough for him. He still felt young enough to work in the field. He planted the switch from the tree behind the guesthouse in a modest pot and waited.

When William left Princeton after the incident, he looked as if he was dead. His face had lost most of its color, and his right eye was swollen tremendously. He walked until Atlantic City, following the railroad tracks and sleeping in makeshift tents with other vagrants. In Atlantic City he found a wallet under the boardwalk. The driver's license said the owner was twenty-three. There were several credit cards and two hundred dollars. William imagined his hand wrapped around the red dice playing craps in the back alleys of the Hotbox. He bought a bus ticket with the money that took him all the way to Alabama. The man at the greyhound terminal gave him complete directions on how to get to Route 24 including a little story about the great fire.

"Such a shame, that poor family. Never even had a chance." William took the map he offered with the highlighted line and left the bus terminal. The heat was oppressive, but William was grateful for the breeze that whistled past his ears. William carried the tune all the way to Larry enjoying the sweet singsong melody.

When he found Larry, he was still working the same farm. The family that he had worked for after the fire had moved to California after buying a vineyard. Larry worked for the new owners, a black family with few questions about his life or stories of the great fire. Larry was working in the rear garden. It was a small plot of land full of vegetables and herbs that would grow in the unforgiving soil of Alabama. In the rear of the small garden it grew luxuriously. The trunk was thick and squat and the branches sprawled in all directions tangling with themselves over and over again. It was heavy and green, full of leaves and small brambles, but only the single unopened blossom remained.

"We've been waiting for you."

"It has been a long trip." William wiped his head clean with the back of his sleeve.

"It has been very lonely." Larry placed his trowel on the ground.

"I know."

"I could not make it grow any more."

"I understand."

"They will make it grow."

"I know."

"Is he ready for you?"

"I don't know."

"Are you ready for him?"

"I think so. I know he will understand."

"Of course."

"I am worried about her."

"She is ready. She just resists."

"It is in her nature."

"What will happen to you?"

"We will be fine."

"You can come with me."

"No, we will all be together soon enough."

"Then what?"

"Don't worry."

"All of us?"

"Yes, all of us. The time has come." Larry placed his thumb against the stem of the blossom and it snapped off easily. William watched as he packed it with wet leaves into a small wooden box that had been resting beneath the squat bush.

"Thank you." William held the box carefully in front of him.

"This is for you return." Larry handed William several bills rolled together.

"Thank you."

"To be the last is to be cursed."

When William left the garden, he kept the box close to him and moved towards the road. When he looked back Larry was already gone. The road was steaming, and William was thirsty. She picked him up just after the farm in a green convertible.

"You're not some sort of psycho, are you?" Her lips were bright red against the fair skin of her face.

"No, just some guy who needs a ride."

"What's in the box?" Her gum popped and Wilson opened the box.

"That's pretty. I have never seen a flower like that before. What is your name?"

"William."

"William, I am Kris."

"It is nice to meet you."

"Same here. Where you headed?"

"The bus station."

"The bus, where you really headed."

"Well I was taking the bus back north to New Jersey."

"Well I'm headed upstate towards New York. I can take you."

"Are you sure?"

"Not a problem." She shifted the car into gear and pulled it onto the road. "Besides I feel like I know you."

Preachers Boy waited in an empty booth for his mother to finish her shift. The cook had brought him a hamburger and a glass of soda. He had spent the day with Leslie in the park at the center of town. Leslie had not been to school in over two weeks. They spent nearly every hour together and made love in the laziness of late afternoons before midday traffic and the schools emptied out. William had not seen the man with the dog since that day. Leslie had not told her mother about William when she found the condoms in her desk drawer.

"What are these for?" Her mother was waiting at the top of the stairs holding the blue Trojan box in her left hand. Leslie looked at the box. "Are you going to explain this to me?"

"No."

"No. Who do you think you are, young lady?"

"Oh god, mother you are so stupid."

"Leslie Dulin, you will not talk to me that way." Her mother tightened her hold over the condom box.

"Fine then, mother, you want to know what they are for. I'll tell you. They're for sex. I have been having sex for months."

"With who?"

"That is none of your business."

"Damn well is my business."

"You never cared this much about what I did before."

"That is because I trusted you."

"That is such bullshit."

"Don't use that language with me."

"Just leave me alone."

Leslie pushed past her mother using her arm. Her mother grabbed Leslie's hand tightly, and Leslie screamed. When her mother pulled apart her daughters fingers to see the mark, she began to cry. When she was done, they shared everything.

William left the diner with his mother's hand in his. He was happy to walk with her and the street was rather empty, except for some children playing catch between two parked cars. His mother lingered slightly in her observation, and William smiled when she looked fondly at him.

"How come I don't see you with any boys your age?"

"I don't know, mom."

"It's not healthy not to play with the other boys."

"I do, I do. I am just not too into sports."

"Why don't I ever meet your friends?"

"I don't know. Just don't come over, I guess."

"I would like to meet your girlfriend." William let go of his mother's hand. When he looked to her, she was smiling. "You didn't think I knew, did you?"

"I don't have girlfriend."

"Oh William, I found the rubbers in your draw."

"I just bought those because I wanted to be like the other guys."

"William, I don't understand why you are always hiding from me. You're just like your father."

"Don't say that, don't ever say that. I would never leave you."

"I know honey, I know."

When they reached the front step of their house, there was a letter from the school in the mailbox. After his mother opened it she cried. Then William told her everything. He told her about the visions, about the island, about the fire, about Leslie. He told her his father was coming.

They had planned a dinner with William's family for the evening despite the televisions storm forecast. The weatherman had called it an odd beast moving up the coast in an unusual pattern. Lilly had been cooking since three o'clock preparing a roast and an assortment of side dishes. William was wearing his best slacks when he arrived, and his mother looked remarkable but tired. The house was lit with candles and wonderfully complex hurricane lamps.

"Dinner will be ready in a few minutes. Can I get anyone something to drink?" Lilly had a small white apron with frills around the corners. "Perhaps a glass of wine?"

"I would love that."

"Red or white?"

"Red." William's mother was looking over the mantle at the timeline of pictures. "You were such an adorable baby, Leslie."

"William?" Leslie was standing in the doorway of the living room.

"What?" He moved to her after a moment of silence.

"I love you."

"I love you, too." His voice sounded scared.

Leslie slid her hand against his slender fingers and rested them on her stomach.

Dinner was enormous and quiet. He was soaking wet when he appeared in the doorway clutching a wooden box. His face casting long shadows, Lydia almost did not recognize him. Preacher Boy knew immediately.

"How did you find me?"

"I followed the storm."

Lydia felt the pain in her breast.

"Where is she?"

William turned to face Leslie.

"Is she ready?"

"Yes."

"Then this, this is for her."

He handed Preacher Boy the rain soaked box as if the weight was tremendous.

"The storm is upon us."

"I know."

"It will arrive soon."

"I know."

"They are waiting."

Leslie could hear a dog barking from outside the back of the house. She moved to be by Preacher Boy's side. Her hand was burning in his palm. When Preacher Boy opened the box the shutters rattled, and the wind scratched loudly at the siding.

"They are waiting for us."

"I don't understand."

"You do. Inside you. You understand."

"Help me, William."

"She will be beautiful. Just as the moon."

Preacher Boy placed his hand to Leslie's stomach, and she felt it move. When he placed the blossom in the palm of her hand, it seared to the mark, and she could see it. She could feel everything. The jungle, the island, the plantation, her mother, four faces like midnight and Grace rising like the moon above them. When he kissed her, she understood. Her mother was crying.

When Leslie opened the door the wind rattled the pictures off the mantle. The lantern wicks jumped flames scorching her mother's white curtains. They were all gathered in the yard. Four faces now familiar ready and returned. Leslie knew all of their names, all four faces, she knew everything. Preacher Boy moved towards his grandfather. Martha moved towards Leslie and took her hand pressing the blossom tight into her palm.

"Your child will be full with Grace."

The serpent had coiled itself tight around the house with spit, wind, and hail. When they planted the blossom deep in the earth, the serpent shook the shutters from the house. Leslie covered over the blossom with earth, the serpent ripped the shingles from the roof. When she gave birth to their spirit, Preacher Boy began to sob. When he held it up to the beast, it hissed. Then he let it guide his hand, together they struck down the best.

When the beast finally lay dormant, they walked to the garden. Wilson collected the dog in his arms. Lilly was sobbing. Sister Sarah began to hum a low melody, then Larry. Then they all began to sing. It was quiet and surrounding, a long melodic combination of voices. They were only four at first but the chorus began to return. As the storm began dying another member joined fitting there voice into the complex fabric of memory. The blossom began to grow, the garden grew around it and with it an endless rhythmic pattern of harmony seeping out into the night calling out for its chorus in an endless singsong melody. When they all arrived Leslie could still see their four faces black as midnight, beautiful, and their child pale as the moon. Grace.

and building something

A bird. Blue, with a light red in its chest waited patiently on a mailbox. There was nothing much else for it to do. There was no song. No whistle. And when the sun creaked out of the clouds it flew. Wings desperate for air leaving nothing, but everything, behind.

There is no town east of West Medford. At the edge of the road that turned into dust before it turned into the highway, Yusef leaned against a gas pump, his arm throbbing.

Kyla tied her shoes carefully.

She knew that, in the walls, these things were waiting.

The sun was a thin line burning ochre across the flat land of West Medford. Leone was at the sink when she saw her mother in the yard. She was just beyond the flowerbeds, drifting.

Willie pulled the truck into his spot. It would be hot across the whole state, but West Medford had nothing but slanted roofs and dust.

One

Sunday

Yusef

Yusef

Yusef

Yusef

Yusef

Yusef

The woman had a low slender voice. He slept there with his arm laid bare. She was pushing gently at his shoulder. Yusef was still holding tightly to the length of rubber hose.

Yusef

Yusef

Yusef

     She pulled herself out of the bed, wrapping the blanket around her shoulders. Her voice trailed after her. It was still early even for Sunday morning. The light came spilling into the room as she pulled the shade up. The light was brilliant and full of morning dust. Yusef clung to the sweetness in his arm. Even Sunday had a hard time waking him. She waited by the window for him. Her breasts were pale. Yusef struggled, then sat up. He smiled at her as she began to dress. There were his photographs lying around, lazy, like leaves on the ground. He was still wearing everything but his shoes. It was almost 6.

The farm was awake. It did not take much to stir animals that slept standing up. Yusef listened, as he lay in bed, to his mother make breakfast. The large metal skillet was sizzling with butter, eggs, bacon. The time before the farm, when Yusef did not know his mother, she would have screamed. Lectures about cholesterol and fatty foods. That was California. That was 1966. When his grandmother, his mother's mother whom he would never be able to meet, died, the farm was left to her. It was a rolling expanse of dusty brown earth. There was a creaking barn plus a house that was flat and pushed out on all its edges. It was all wood made light by summer suns and bleached by the heart of winter. Yusef had seen the snowfall in heavy wet blankets sometimes heavy enough to push in windswept banks past the kitchen windows. He watched the summer keep the ground dry, a pale and gritty yellow dust, for months at a time. The only salvation was the sound of a wheezing pump and desperate irrigation. Yusef had watched this cycle for fourteen years and this was all he had known. His father, had hands once made for music, now made stiff by the unrelenting seasons of self-discovery. It was an idea at first. The both of them, musicians and new parents, would work this small farm. They would learn to use the tractors, the milking machine, the hand tools. She would learn to raise her child, her home, her husband. He would learn to be a man.

Yusef waited in front of the mirror for her to finish on the toilet. He always thought that the sound of it was relaxing. He always wanted to see an ocean. Yusef brushed his teeth. He could hear the pipes working inside the walls. The rattle it made for the neighbor's shower, or when their downstairs toilet flushed. He lived in two houses pushed together and the difference was made up of poor carpentry and worse plumbing. His aunt, from his mother's family, lived below him. The other home had a family with two children and a spare room with a newlywed couple. This was a place of very few secrets. Things that hid between wet walls, and behind fixtures, whispers that rang inside stained porcelain. Yusef played with his face in the mirror for a minute, pulling at his chin and pushing up against his cheeks. He was aware of how thin he'd become. The farm had always kept him lean but now he was losing the roundness of his muscles. Yusef quickly pulled his shirt on and turned towards the toilet. She had left the room, it could have been ten minutes since, and he was happy to be alone. He brushed his teeth and urinated at the same time. The sun had crept all the way across the floor. It was getting late for Sunday.

He walked to the service, the same way he walked every Sunday, along the smooth sidewalk of West Medford. The town was remarkably clean. There were was no litter, no trash, no cigarette butts. People in West Medford washed their driveways. People in West Medford swept the sidewalk in front of the coffee shop, the general store, the farm store, and the hardware store. Everything in this town appeared clean. Yusef felt the warm air embracing him; he still thought it sweet this early in the season. Everything in West Medford was about the season. Even the man that ran the car dealership, 50 miles outside of town, knew this. A good season means good money. Good money means more dollars for the church, for the coffee shop, the farm store, the hardware store. Everyone prays for a good season. Everyone prays for rain.

Amanda made fresh bread, something his mother never did before moving to the farm, and the smell was a blanket that filled the farmhouse. Yusef was still washing the sleep from his face. His mother always stressed good hygiene. She always said that it was important to start the day clean. Yusef finished washing and listened to the drain for a minute. It had a distinct desperate notion of swallowing. He smiled and dried his hands on the small set of towels that hung next to the sink. Yusef always felt they should be hung higher. His father, Joshua, was a tall man. He looked thin in early pictures holding the baby with the tall hands, tall fingers. In that photograph they had already found god. Since then, they'd always looked like good christians. Yusef had attended his first tent revival meeting at age six.

The tent was the thing he could remember the clearest. It was an enormous billowing white structure strapped down to a patch of land between West Medford and the edge of everything he knew. As they approached, from the distance, it appeared as if the wind could whistle and carry it away wrapped in its melody. The line of pickup trucks, cars, even tractors, prodded along that dirt road with eager hope. Yusef had never since been so excited. Everyone was there.

In the kitchen the smell of the bread beat everything past his nose. He loved the smell of honey-wheat, fresh and full of yeast, on Saturday mornings. This was simple. His father always told him, be good, be simple. Bread. This was simple, at least to him, and good. The butter was fresh. Today slept late. Yusef, Amanda, Joshua all of them were lazy on Saturdays and enjoying how easy it felt. They ate breakfast from thick porcelain plates, the grandmother's, and drank from cups full of fresh milk. Yusef watched as his father ran his bread through the yolk that broke open on his plate. Amanda settled down to her own plate, no longer thin. She ate with the only men in her life. Yusef drank a long swallow of milk before starting at his plate. On Saturdays he enjoyed stacking his eggs and bacon with a slice of cheese on his mother's bread. There was little work for the men on Saturdays. The chicken coop, the milking, which his father had done earlier, and some fence mending. Yusef enjoyed mending the fence, riding in the tractor along the edge of the farm, and talking with his father. The sun was shy and quiet today, changing its face between the clouds.

The service was to begin soon. Yusef wanted to boot once before the service. He pulled his bag with his kit tight over his shoulder and looked carefully at the church doors. They were tall black, classic, oak doors weathered by sharp winds. Yusef thought perhaps once they were not coated in layer upon layer of black paint. They might have stood taller then. The church was, most certainly, the tallest building in West Medford. The bells of the steeple still operated for weddings, funerals, holiday mass, and other special occasions. Yusef once pulled the ropes on Christmas, two years ago, before he left his mother and father on the farm. The minister was a large man, fed on sacraments and donations, who preached with red-faced hand gestures. There were still a few people talking outside on the expanse of steps that led up to the doors. The church never quite seemed part of this town after it was rebuilt. Yusef was only five when the fire had swept through the pews burning a thousand gilded pages. They said that the creaking was the most desperate sound they heard. Everyone just waited for it to fall, watching the quick hand of god.

It did not take long to rebuild, but too much concrete had been used out of fear. The doors and the bells were the only hope that remained from that honest building. Yusef always preferred the suddenness of the revival. He could not forget that he first saw her there, blonde hair, sleeping casually with her back against an old post, a white cotton dress cascading out past her feet. She had a peaceful smile and when she touched his hand, it was warm. The reassurance of faith was astounding. Yusef found a seat near the middle of the room, where it was easier, and slipped his bag underneath the pew. He brought his own book. It was a small slender volume with a worn cover and his mother's name neatly written on the inside cover. Yusef waited to pray. He did not like when others watched him.

He rode tucked tightly next to his father in the cab of the tractor with the wagon pulling supplies.

Yusef enjoyed the rattle of the tools as the tractor humped its way over ruts and small ditches. The fence that lingered at the edge of the property sagged and was always desperate for attention. It, the fence, was not that important to the farm. They did not keep many animals and the cows had their own corral. It was a matter of principal for Joshua, and a reason to enjoy the sun on Saturday afternoons. They worked slowly, taking time between posts to talk and listen to the quiet of the crops shiver in the wind. Yusef stood with his back into a fence post, his head rolling to one side. They both knew there was not much work to be done. The fence took little abuse now, and kept itself well enough. This--this thing, this ritual--was an excuse.

"Yusef, we best move on to the next section."

"Yes. Dad?"

"Yes?"

"Can I ask you something?"

"Of course."

"You have to promise not to be angry."

"I can't make that promise, Yusef."

"Why not?"

"Because what if the thing you say makes me angry?"

"I don't know."

"I can't swear here, in front of God, that I will not be angry."

"What if you promise to try and not be angry?"

"I think, that He would accept that. I will promise to try and not be angry."

"Good."

Yusef rolled away from the fence post. He pulled at his gloves and tucked them into the back pocket of his jeans. His father placed the sledgehammer back into the wagon. They climbed into the tractor and settled into place. The space between posts, and repairs, was filled only with the shake of the tools and the throaty rattle of the tractor. It was enough to fill a year of Saturday afternoons.

After the service Yusef was desperate to push off. He knew that he could not wait until he was home again. He watched as the pews emptied and people flooded out the front doors, fanning themselves, talking about brunch and the spring bulbs. The morning in West Medford was just beginning, even for a Sunday. Yusef used the stairs nestled between offices and storage at the back of the church. The basement was mostly for Sunday school, daycare, meetings. This was his favorite place to push off and where he felt the most comfortable. He placed his bag on a small children's table beneath a basement window. The room smelled of shoes worn only on Sunday mornings and Kool-Aid orange punch. Yusef used a candle when there was enough time. He took his kit from inside the bag that he carried. He pulled one of the small chairs, made for children, to the edge of the table. Yusef rolled up his sleeve turning it over several times to make sure it would not interfere.

The day had started while Yusef was in the church basement. The sun had done away with the morning clouds and the heat was coaxing the birds to sing. The rhythm had started to move West Medford and Yusef felt the rush of the sun grab at the back of his neck. He had been working every weekend at the café since he moved into town. It was still early for Sunday. The regulars and a few others has just begun to fill the booths or crowd about the counter. Yusef always enjoyed Sunday, the heat from grill, the smell of the coffee brewing, the sound of the register, the quiet melody of the radio, the humming from the freezer, the soft lilt from the fan, the click-clank of ice in a glass, the chime of the bell above the door, the payphone calling, and the metal ring of utensils on plates of satisfied men.

Yusef was full and he moved behind the counter with light smiles to the customers, the cook, and the waitress with the low slender voice. It was still early and his favorites had not come in yet. He looked above the grill for the clock, a balking rooster, 7:30am. He had two hours before his break. Two hours before he could push off. After thirty minutes Yusef moved in his sleep, filling napkin holders, salt and peppershakers, old ketchup bottles, and emptying the oversized ashtrays that crowded the counter.

The sheriff was out of uniform on Sundays only but he still wore that oversized black belt. Not once since his arrival in West Medford had Yusef seen the sheriff without his gun. There are some things that have to be expected. He brought him coffee, a bowl of flakes, and a hard-boiled egg. Yusef always kept his arms in close when he was around the sheriff. He looked up, 8:30am.

The sun was too hot for an early May morning on the farm. Yusef did not want to get out of bed. He did not want to feel the start of the day across his bare back. The smell of breakfast pushed against his door. His father's razor was tapping against the edge of the sink. Today, the birthdays, 12 and 40, but there was work to be done on this farm. Too much was dying all around them. They ate in silence that weighed enough to break any humble man. The skillet barely had enough grease to keep talking and his mother had been mourning because the bread did not rise. The summer was pressing in on all four walls. Yusef's father was mumbling.

"It is only May, it is only May, Please, Christ, it is only May."

The sun looked inviting to Yusef now that his shift was over. He lay down on his back in the small park. The shift had ended with almost nothing to say. The businesswoman ate her two eggs over-easy as usual. Yusef pushed off, twice, before noon. He rubbed daisies into his hands and enjoyed the smell. The warmth was pulling at every part of his body. Yusef felt his heart, a distinct un-patterned rhythm, pushing the blood and junk through his body. His hands stretched out across to the Red Mud River, up past the rich peaks of the mountains and desperately grasped at the sand that was rattled by the ocean. There were birds singing, wings fluttering, desperately inside him. They had been there forever longing to sing, crying for escape.

He placed the pot on the stove. The electric burner a brilliant fake orange. He waited for the water. When she was not in the apartment he always played the stereo. The sound of gospel choirs and songs folded out of the field tripping harmonies with the secrets that hummed inside the walls. Yusef stood in the kitchen barefoot, listening, and waiting for water. There was nothing else to do.

They came in vans, cars, and even on motorcycles with sidecars and saddlebags. The dust would not settle for days. They came with guitars, groceries and cameras with flashbulbs. They had long hair and dresses that tumbled from their bodies like maple leaves from fall trees, all in colors matched by birds he had seen in picture books. They came with books, music, records, phonographs, tambourines, stories, trumpets, snare drums, and smiles plastered on like church flyers. Yusef loved them all.

They unloaded their cars in a joyous stampede of chatter, greetings, and open arms that held invitations to possibilities. Yusef ran to them, dragging back suitcases and bags to the house, piling them up on the porch one after another. The sun was pulling its way down, and a bath of burnt orange turned them all into silhouettes. The smell of his mother's baking filled they house. They had been making the pilgrimage since the beginning. Yusef could not count the seasons without them.

Everyone was thinking about food. The sun had set and the smell of cooking was everywhere now. The table, one of his father's first projects, was large enough for everyone. Yusef was enthralled, watching them at the table, drinking glasses of deep red wine and devouring his mother's food. He always thought they must not eat in California. There was always one turkey, one ham, potatoes, bread with sweet butter, fresh greens and pea pods from the garden. Then afterwards there were pies. The crusts generous and thick, browned and made crisp like turning leaves of sycamore trees. Yusef knew that with their stomachs full they would begin talking. This, this, was what he loved the most.

Their mouths moved independent of consequences. They had ideas and stories wrapped in a language that seemed like code. He could not stop himself from laughing, smiling, singing at the top of his lungs to records he had only just heard. Yusef had never known his parents to be so happy. There was no room for silence and for these moments he was grateful not to be so close to god. This was the first time Yusef had been awake to see the sunrise spread out across the field and it did in magnificent strands of sharp color flooding the house with the warmth of new days as they sang. Sang playing guitars, used and loved, cascaded with innocence as they let folk songs, Evangeline, run up the stairs through the dining room and spill out over the front porch railing. Yusef took his first photograph and cried at what beauty he could capture.

The next morning Yusef did not wake until the call for lunch. He pulled the blankets tighter around his body, trying to remain asleep. Their voices echoed in the house, humming songs, and talking about the ocean. He listened, still drifting and waiting for nothing to happen. Downstairs, the house was all activity. They were making blankets, breakfast, bread, candy, and his father was smoking a pipe, while leaning in the frame of the open screen door. He saw the camera sitting comfortably on a shelf mixed with terracotta bowls and plates. It began, simply, just like this. Yusef picked up the camera and placed the strap, braided with native colors, over his neck. The sound of the shutter made him ecstatic. He saw everything as it was in those simple moments. A man and woman holding hands over coffee and homemade biscuits. The lean outline of his father perched and sunning in the doorway. His mother's round body washing vegetables in the sink. A guitar left alone in the corner to enjoy the echoes. Two men sitting comfortably with each other with only silence between them. A woman brushing her long hair. The field whispering in the summer breeze. Stories of past seasons with leaves thin as bible pages. When Yusef had used all of the film, he felt an enormous sadness. He knew he would never feel so full again. He would try everything to find this feeling again. A man with a slender body, flannel shirt, and small hat took the camera from him. He promised.

"I will show you, and then everything will never look the same."

Yusef lie on the floor in his apartment and felt the hard cold subtleties of the entire building. He held his photographs against his chest the smell of developer, still working. The windowsill was clinging desperately to the edge of Sunday.

Monday

There was candy in the drawer of the nightstand. Yusef liked to hold the chocolate in his mouth after he pushed off. Hershey bars with almonds. The sun was still finding itself behind a small stream of white clouds, burning them off with each passing moment. He fumbled over his works with small slit eyes. The taste of chocolate on his tongue. He took his morning prayers at the edge of the bed in only his underwear. The words came from his mouth like water and he rested his head on the bed, hands still clasped together. He could feel, with his whole body, the light pining through the window. It was warm on his bare chest. With a slow heavy breath she placed her hand against his face. It felt small with little determination but to hold him and wait.

When Yusef's eyes opened the sun was the only thing holding the sky together and she was gone. He dressed, listening to the building begin. Running in the hall, water against steel sinks, the tumbling locks and the sway of wooden stairs. In West Medford everyone was getting ready. He found clothes, clean enough, from the bottom of the closet and dressed while the toast was browning. He knew he could eat more at the café. Yusef took spare sheets from the dresser. He draped them over the stereo, the television. He placed a piece of electrical tape over the digital alarm clock and the timer on the microwave. He placed his electric shaver in the bathroom drawer. Tape over the light-switch. He left candles on dinner plates near the door and the bed.

Yusef's mouth was dry. He could feel it. The corners at the edges of his lips pasted together and thirsty. He tried not to sweat on his several blocks to the West Medford Social Club and Café. He hated the feeling of his clothing. The sheriff's truck was parked outside the café, neatly tucked up against the curb with the keys shining on the dashboard. Yusef looked into the cab, clipboards, nightstick, newspapers, candy wrappers, and a motel pamphlet.

The café was full. The counter was tight with men, waiting and talking. The four booths that hugged the long narrow wall held a teenage couple, the sheriff, the man who owned the tractor repair, and a man with a long face. Yusef smiled, slightly, and found his way behind the counter. The men smoked at the counter between mouthfuls of eggs and Yusef tied his apron. He served plates and poured coffee. The woman who owned the West Medford Café and Social Club, had worked the grill for the last four years. The girl with the low slender voice would not look at him while she worked. She held empty plates and wore rubber gloves because of the scalding water. She brought glasses of water to the tables and utensils wrapped in paper napkins. She held the door open for the older customers, and handled hot plates with a difficult smile.

Yusef barely could be next to her in the café. He pressed the hard plastic buttons of the register and rang the handle, enjoying the rhythm. The sound of the griddle and the smell of grease kept things moving quickly. Eggs, scrapple, home fries, toast, bacon, sausage, hotcakes, and the occasional piece of French toast. The cook was a large woman and looked even larger in white, the apron snug around her waist, and grease smeared across her thighs.

The sun was a hard line in the early morning. The farmhouse burned full on with orange and lavenders. The season had set in. Yusef could feel work in his bones. He picked up the camera from the small desk, eyes still contemplating morning. There was little time for this. He found film, still in the package, and opened the camera. Yusef sat at the edge of the bed, working with his eyes closed. He loaded the camera, feeling the small line of felt at the edge of the film canister. He stood in the yard, in his thin boxers, and began. The shutter moved fluidly, his thumb winding quickly after each shot, one after one casting his lens steep full of color. There was nothing else but her. He could see her clearly in the warm embrace. Her white dress, like an ocean, cascaded onto the worn wood bedroom floor. She disappeared easily in the early morning.

The animals were talking. Stilted conversations about cold hands and the rusted handle of the feed bucket. They mused on lazy sons, the creases in a farmer's face, the smell of fresh bread, and the disappearing chickens. Then there was the heat, they always were talking about the heat in the morning. Yusef dressed in his room. His jeans, still dirty but broken and comfortable. T-shirts and sneakers from neighbors whose children had grown larger. Yusef placed a watch without a band inside his front pocket like his father showed him. The day had just begun to fill the barn with shadows. Yusef inhaled the dry air and scent of straw that littered the floor. He picked up the bucket and listened to the sigh of animals and rusty handles. There was work, but there was no reason to any of it anymore. He saw that clearly now.

The grill sizzled with what was left of the lunch: BLTs, fried egg sandwiches, hot pastrami, buttered rolls, and grilled cheese. Yusef leaned against the counter, littered with rumpled napkins, plates, and coffee cups. He stared out the window between the posted menus, local classifieds, and the hand written flyers about tractor or feed sales. The street looked lazy, empty at the edges, and Yusef wanted desperately to run. He took his kit.

There was nothing else for him except to push off. He did it quickly and waited for the release. The sun, sagging low, was warm on his thin face. Yusef closed his eyes and could feel her small hand. It was the same as always. Warm and full of faith. Her eyes blue hard and deep like the untouched oceans. She did not speak but waited, as warm as the summer, for him to rise up. Her white billowing dress folded around him as she called to him. Everything about her was endless light, and that was all that Yusef wanted. Then, once it had passed through him, he saw everything so clearly that he turned and threw up in the sink. She had left him without even a scar.

Tuesday

Yusef woke up naked with a shiver that ran deep into his muscles. He twitched like a spring set loose and could not keep his eyes closed. The room was spinning and everything was photographs. The light switch did not work. The lamp was left broken, neck open and gaping. The wire pulled out, rabid and frayed. The whole thing heaping on the floor. It was still too early to be all the way light. He fought his own head to keep his eyes from closing. His movements sped up, then cut up, then slowed down, sped up, slowed down, and shown back to him. Yusef could not get his hands around it. The microwave was a deliberate pile of plastic and catastrophe, left burned, and mutilated wires melted to the floor and leaked blood into the tile. He could not see enough to hold himself to take a piss, hearing the ring of the tile and the back of the toilet. When his head met the cold and ripe edge of the sink, there was never a single photograph that had developed so clearly.

He woke up with heavy smell of urine and a little blood dried to his skin. His mouth was aching, and his muscles were so sore, it felt like hot razors under his skin. He itched. He itched badly enough that the thought of touching himself made him feel sick. He climbed from the bathroom floor, his apartment stagnant with thick afternoon light. Yusef shook his head violently, pulling and pulling at his hair to try and hold things still. The switch in the bathroom bled light out of the fluorescent halo. It crushed him to his knees. He could not even crawl. His body converted to thick syrup, he slowed his way across the room until the coolness of the kitchen linoleum grabbed at his legs, pulling him down. His face found the cold tile like a pillow.

There was nothing but the pale white of the bathroom light to guide him. Yusef had his hands folded between his thighs and felt the heat from his crotch. He had vomited more than once and could still taste it, dry and burning in his nose. He found his legs like two desperate tree stumps. He moved them and each step echoed in his skull like a bible closing. At the sink he drank the hot water until it turned cold enough to make him bite back on his teeth. He could see now. Eyes brilliantly still. Slow and languid moving with such ease, steady and purposeful. Yusef climbed onto the kitchen counter, his muscles burning and pleading. His camera and film were hidden beneath the false ledge. He loaded the camera balanced at the edge of the Formica countertop. He stuffed four extra rolls of film into his underwear.

Yusef had no idea of what time it was in West Medford. The streets that had limp lamps glowing complacently along the street. His bare feet began to shake against the concrete and his fingers worked over the shutter and the f-stop with speed and patience. He began to fill negatives with West Medford. Long and winding, and fluid strips of time and place flushed against each other, numbered, and subtly categorized with the ease of modern machinery. He took the lamps apart with a lazy smile and shattered plate glass windows, pushed down dry mortar and red brick walls. He found his way through pipes and wires, into bedrooms and living rooms. He saw kitchen tables with lace tablecloths and wilting flowers. He blew the dry dust and grit of the street into whirlwinds and then dissipating into the flood of warm nights. The town was littered with memories.

Mrs. Brown's two boys left like martyrs in the field, blood on a plow, mud on their boots. George Smith's old Buick wrapped around a lamppost, Tennessee whiskey on the passenger seat. The processional of 532 graduating classes marched like chess pieces across the high-school fields. Fourteen good seasons followed by seven years of tough times, two droughts, another good season and then more of the same. Halloween costumes, candy corn, Thanksgiving turkeys, and local parades, homecoming, Christmas, window dressings, and lampposts wrapped in garland. The smell of ash from the rapture as they watched the church burn like matchsticks and dry leaves. The heavy smell of concrete dust from the new construction. All the joy and heartache brought with the rain. The rain in endless cycles, tempting and full of redemption. Coming down fast and hard, slow and long in lazy fat drops with screaming winds. Sweeping in sheets of grey across town squares. All this rain. All this heartache, and Yusef waited with arms dying like hickory branches. Rain was coming.

Two

Sunday

Yusef

Yusef

Yusef

Yusef

Yusef

Yusef

Kyla had a low slender voice as she tried to wake him while he slept there with his arm laid bare. She pushed gently at his shoulder. Yusef was still holding tightly to a length of rubber hose.

Yusef

Yusef

Yusef

Kyla pulled herself out of the bed wrapping the blanket around her naked body. Her voice trailed after her. It was still early even for Sunday morning. The light came spilling into the room as she pulled the shade up. It was brilliant and full of morning dust. She watches as Yusef clung to the sweetness in his arm. Even for Sunday she had a hard time waking him. She waited by the window for him. The blanket fell away slightly. Her breasts looked pale. Yusef struggled, then sat up. Kyla began to dress. His photographs were spilled out across the floor. When he got out of bed she noticed he was still wearing everything but his shoes. It was almost 6. Kyla stood in the kitchen, still almost naked trying desperately to remain silent while Yusef got dressed. Yusef left her there, nearly bare with her skin crawling.

She could hear them in the walls. All those whispers. Always talking about her. The remainder of her clothes were piled near the door. She had undressed immediately and found her way to the bed with her eyes closed. When her head was buried under the warm blankets, the hot air of her own breath, she felt safe enough. After she could smell the sulfur of the first match Kyla would crawl out from under the blankets.

She looked at the bed and the space he claimed, left neatly but not quite comfortable. She went back the bathroom and stood in the bathtub. In the mirror across from her, she stared at her body. Kyla ran the water, feeling it on her feet and waiting until it was warm. She washed herself carefully with a soft cloth. The scar on the back of her leg was still tender and left her with a small limp, especially when she was tired. Her bush was full and her skin so pale it was almost past white. Kyla sat down at the edge of the tub, her body cool, and spread her legs. With her hand she felt for his name. It could not wait much longer. She could not wait at all.

There was nothing to do until church was over. She looked around the small apartment. It was dead. Everything covered in sheets, blankets, and old t-shirts. Yusef had his photographs scattered on the floor, heavy and honest. She sat at the edge of the bed, feeling the warm sheets on her bare skin and held a stack of glossy prints with both hands. Mothers, fathers, sons, daughters, cooks, farmers, nieces, nephews, aunts, uncles, houses, homes, cafés, pool halls, streetlamps, Buicks, Fords, Chevrolets, pickup trucks and tractors. Sacks of grain, worried hands, empty skies, cracked sidewalks, the church concrete and self-assured. The pastor and his uneasy smile, the sycamores that shade the park laughing with the setting sun. The rattled wire fence of the baseball cage, candy wrappers and paper napkins. The burning pure point of another dry summer. The painful sight of waiting. A white tent exposed and naked set out against a bone broken field. A young girl with hair like the ache of the sun. The grey expanse of fields waiting for harvest. The setting sun a hard dime at the edge of frame. The history of West Medford stacked, spilled, framed, left on the floor of the apartment, sad and dying.

Kyla finished dressing, humming to herself in a low slender voice. There was a comfort to the orange sunrise on the splintered wood floor. Knives in the kitchen. Knives in the kitchen. She looked away and toward the window, her breasts still exposed, waiting for the warm sun to fill her up.

After the sun, she found herself dressed and running from those walls. Those merciless voices plunging in and out of corridors, running along the baseboard. They were perched with hot breath at the small refuge where a door sweep should have been. The air outside hit her in a cascade and she went spilling into the summer with her eyes closed. The sun was ripe and high even for early Sunday, a few cars left baking outside the town hall. Everyone would be hungry whether it rained or not. The West Medford Café was all they had. It was the town hall, the jury and the court. It was the banquet hall and the coffee shop. Everything in this town ran through the café, no one could change that now. The trip to work had left her hot and the sweat kept her hair to the back of her neck.

Kyla washed dishes. She washed tables. She washed the counter, the windows, the chairs, the bathroom, the grill after it cooled, the walls sick with grease and nicotine, the cups, the saucers, she washed. Kyla never touched the register. The sound of it, of all of it, if she really listened, if she could not stop herself from hearing, made her sick. It was all around her and she never could forget.

The apartment on the sixth floor on Martin Luther King Boulevard, on the cross streets of Broad and Avenue 6, on the rotten foundation of an Oscar Myer plant, on any day even Thanksgiving, smelled. Kyla would never forget that smell.

It was in the cement. In every porous inch poured sixty years ago and soaked in with the smears of hog casings, grease and intestine. All this despite garlic, onions, butter, banana bread, cranberry mold, orange rinds, coriander, apple cores, raisins, nutmeg, sweet potatoes, thyme, green beans, squash, and department store perfume.

Kyla set the table, placing the candlesticks in the middle because she had pleaded all month for them. Her mother pressed her to be calm. They had only just moved a few weeks since her fourteenth birthday and were still without incident. The other residents of the factory had their ears pressed to the worn wooden walls, bleeding with stories. Kyla could feel the twinge in her leg and held herself for a minute from breathing. It was clawing at her to speak.

After the rush, when the West Medford café was quiet, she watched Yusef move slowly to the bathroom. This type of silence was the worst. The lights hummed to themselves quietly, and the fan circled endlessly in conversations about nothing, but she heard it all- the murmurs that were in her body, the rumors in her hips, the lies at her feet. Kyla closed her eyes and things moved around her. The sun rose and fell, the sky stayed dry, people moved in and out of their lives, farms, homes, cars, and tractors piled up like bones left for vultures in empty fields drying, desperate and bleached. Then Willie Huff. Willie Huff with his belt full of black leather and history. Kyla looked at him as his body settled into the chair. Yusef was still floating when she looked to him for salvation. Her hand shook while she grabbed the bright orange handle of the coffee pot. She was grateful the day was in the middle, the coffee pot, barely half-full, click clacking against the side of the cup. Coffee spilling into the saucer. Yusef had sun in his eyes. She would have done anything to be next to him when he was this warm but now there was so much space between them. She left the coffee pot on the counter and walked the cup towards Willie Huff. She thought her body would tear itself apart. She had made up her mind.

The light pitched left and right and when she turned, Kyla could see nothing- not the naked swinging string of a basement light bulb, or the kerosene sent skidding across the floor. The electrical wire nearly killed her, the fire almost destroyed her. The house was burning, quick and cheap. She was kindling at age 16 not quite strong enough to push through the steel heavy storm doors. She could not scream, her throat choked with wires.

When Willie Huff left his seat for the second time that day, discarding his newspaper alongside the empty plate, Kyla's day was over. There would be no customers on her shift, and Kyla could not work at night. She cleaned the dishes with scalding water in the metal sink and wiped the tables, counter, and moved the grease streaks from left to right on the window. She looked for Yusef. He had pushed off twice, even before noon, and now with the evening drawing fine lines on the face of the town. She could not find him. She was not sure she wanted to. Kyla stood outside as the café, keeping her distance from the windows, and watched the sun. The heavy heart that came with night setting itself down at the edge of barns, and in the corners between buildings. The wires beginning to hum, to whisper, to murmur, and talk with eyes alive and looking. She felt a twinge in her leg and stopped her hand from clawing at it. There were no cars left on Main Street.

Kyla found herself at the gas station again. The pumps, on the south end of time, had long been abandoned and the station left to rats, owls, and anything else with a desperate appetite. She had long ago removed anything offensive to her. This gas station was the last thing between West Medford and nothing. After the rotten metal pumps and the stripped and peeled sign for cigarettes, the road turned into dirt, the dirt turned into dust, and the dust consumed everything.

In the office there was a desk, a chair, the open walls, and piles of broken drywall. Kyla had candles, matches, and magazines. Books, paper, pencils, ink, paint, canvas, charcoals, crayons, brushes and rags. She had brought it all over the last years since the fire. Nothing else felt safe after that. They could get her almost anywhere now. She had stolen an old rug from the dumpster of the hardware store. It was only 9 x 9 in various colors and it lay out like a quilt spotted with paint and wax but still soft enough for her bare feet. Kyla took off her shoes and sat in the chair. Her leg was aching. She knew they were still left crawling inside her. She had not rid herself of all of it, of any of them. She would wait for the sun.

Monday

The light came through the front windows of the gas station with an intensity West Medford had not seen yet this summer. They would be praying for rain. All of them in whispers, small closed fists, tired eyes and mouths pulled into tight curls and stories of the last season when the hand smiled upon them. Kyla kept her eyes closed as long as she could, feeling the warmth on her skin. Everything was wanting her but she was only wanting to remain. She could hear the power lines running and alive along the spotted road from West Medford. Her feet were tired and with blisters. She could not use the phone anyway. Kyla picked up her shoes from the desk. She almost wretched when she saw the letters there. All of them. Each one postmarked. Each envelope carefully written. Each time the same address. Each time her father's names printed over and over again. Each time Kinshasa, Africa. Each time return to sender. The whispers were laughing like jackals. She found her way into her shoes and began to walk back towards all that was left for her. West Medford.

The sun was killing her. Every day, in this town with this sun, was killing her. They were laughing at her with every step. There were no trucks. No cars. Nothing but the sweat on her skin and the taste of heat in her mouth. Through the dry dust and the pain in her leg, she could see the top of the steeple. A wrought iron lance rammed into a pillar of concrete with fear. Kyla picked up her leg with each step and began to walk faster, the sweat beginning to stream from her. Her body was wet all over, but she could not stop herself. She knew something was coming. She knew something was building now. She could see it swirling in the thick dusk column burning in the sun. There was so much heat. Something would have to change.

Just past the edge of town she took a ride from a young man in an old pickup truck. It was a short ride and she was grateful for that. She had not been to her home in two days. Her body was thick with dirt and sweat. Kyla walked around to use the backdoor. She did not want to walk through the living room past the television, the VCR, and the sounds of them laughing. The boy had followed her around to the back of the house. Kyla held the door open for him and watched as his worn boots worked over the kitchen tile.

"do you want something"
"wouldn't mind something cold to drink"
"the fridge is over there"

Kyla did not take her face from his eyes. She barely lifted her arm to point. They were pressing in on her. His eyes were an easy grey that nearly made her cry.

"thanks"
"there are glasses in the cabinet above the sink"
"thanks"
"i am going to shower. you can sit at the table"
"all right"

Kyla left all the doors open between rooms in the house since the fire. In the small second bathroom there was only a sink and a shower. The light fixture had been removed, abruptly, from the wall. Kyla lit two candles that were resting on a small plastic table just out of reach from the open door. She lingered on the smell of the matches. The water was more than hot when she climbed over the edge of the high tub. She closed her eyes and felt the heat in her chest. She felt it running down the roundness of her breasts and slippery past her hips. She felt it between her thighs. She felt it running down the damage she had left in her leg. In her eyes she could see the ocean. A fine beach sprouted with a few dry shrubs, an outcrop of rocks and a weathered dock like a well-rested arm lingering in the water. He should have been standing there, his shoes tied around his neck, and his pants rolled up just below the knee. Sunglasses and a dry smile. Kyla opened the eyes and grabbed the razor from the edge of the tub.

The young man was standing in the doorway of the kitchen. He had heard about this house with no doors. This house with tape on every switch. This house with dust gathered on the television. He stood in the open doorway and looked through the kitchen, through the hall, through the frame of the bathroom doorway until he saw her. The razor in her hand, a slight line of blood running the inside of her thigh. She was laid bare for him. He knew she was the most beauti-ful thing he would ever see and he had to do all he could.

Kyla waited for him to move. She was watching the razor in her hand, her skin still stinging. She had removed every hair and never once opened her eyes. Her hands knew every inch of that map. The slender roads, the thick line of the muddy river. The heavy dot of the destination. She covered thousands of miles in less than 5 inches. She touched herself following the exacting details the dusty trails and the jungle outcropping that she had painstakingly made six years ago. This was where she was to go. This is where she wanted to be in order to make something. He was there, left alone from all these whispers and lies, breathing comfortably on the shores of a lake in Africa.

The boy still had the long glass of lemonade dangling from the edges of his fingers when he reached the bathroom. The room was sweating and anxious. The house had not seen so much chaos since the incident. He drank from the glass and placed it down on the top of the toilet tank, a tissue pasting itself to the side. He opened and closed his hand a few times at his side. There was no reason to stop but he could not move, more frightened now than when the storm ripped down, god's quaking finger.

Kyla saw his hand open and close. She waited for him to strike her. The shower was now silent as she stepped onto the warm bath mat. She waited for him to unleash everything that had been burning inside him since the day he learned this town was nothing but dust and prayers. She waited to feel the hard angry dry skin of a young man already used. She clutched the edge of the sink the razor waiting helplessly at the edge. It was of no recourse at the moment. Her other hand desperate to hide the only thing she had left to be ashamed of. She welcomed him to bring an end to it all.

He closed his hand and took one-step towards her, the toe of his dirty boots finding the soft edge of the bathroom mat. His eyes opened wide and he looked down as if something had crept up to him. He stared at the mat damp with her slender footprints, his hand a trembling ball of force it made his heart race. This thing that has been with him since his eyes first saw inside his father's bedroom. There, though, her slender feet looked like peaceful roots taken hold of some desperate patch of wet soil. He felt the heaviness of time. He could not do this thing she wanted.

Kyla looked at him as he stood there, his boot on the edge of the bath mat, threatening her slender footprints. She looked down to his hand and saw it ready to take revenge for everything that West Medford had taken from him. So she turned from him. She turned from him and placed her hands at the edge of the sink. She knew he could not help her, so she gave herself to him.

He watched her move like a broken stalk of corn and collapse against the edge of the sink. His hand was this force. He pressed it against the small of her back with such effort that he felt her knees buckle. He was ready. Every inch of his body was ready. He stood behind her and pressed his body against her skin. He tried to turn her around. With all that force that had been scorched inside him he tried to turn her. He wanted her to see past him.

Kyla held the edge of the sink with strong enough that she could feel the fixtures shaking. She could hear the whispers behind the mirror. She could hear them all with snide lips and laughter. They were begging her to turn. They were shouting at her to give in. They wanted her to turn. To look away so they could find their way inside her. They wanted her to turn. They wanted it more than they wanted her that day when she was too weak to open the steel heavy doors. They wanted her to look away from her vigil. Her heart 14 inches from collapse.

He could not turn her. He tried with all that force that had been building for years. He could not turn her. He would not have it like this. He would not be like his father, like that thing he had seen, and all of the force that was heat in his arm left him and he fell against her. He fell against her still damp body and laid there. His weight on her like dirt. He knew he was this and nothing else.

Kyla was still water as she laid with all that pain on her. Her arms tired and her leg aching, those few whispers left burning at the back of her skin. There was a brief moment in her that she could have anything. She could not turn to this boy and allow him to see what was left to her. It was her only secret. The only place they had not found. The long ride along the muddy river. In the quiet of the continent, surrounded by the never-ending expanse of land giving birth to life. His arms open. The father. A ghost. A lie.

The young man, this stranger, lifted himself from her beautiful naked body. All he had left now was the breath in his chest. He had given the rest away to her.

Kyla walked from the bathroom to her bedroom naked. She took clothes from the drawers and dressed calmly. Her mother would be home soon flipping switches and turning on appliances. Blenders, microwaves, starters for gas stoves, lamps, VCRs, digital clocks. She grabbed her bag from the floor and left towards the kitchen. She was almost surprised to still see him there sitting, an empty glass of lemonade with a wet ring on the kitchen table. He had taken off his boots and placed them on a chair adjacent. Kyla looked directly at him but he did not have enough left in him to pick up his head. She took his hand in hers, boots in the other and pulled him up from the table. They followed their way through the house, empty doors and hardwood floors. She let go of his hand and took the cigarette lighter from her jeans. In the dim light the flash made him jump and when Kyla looked back, he had just disappeared. His boots held tightly in her right hand.

She noticed her mouth was dry. Kyla left the house the way that she entered. There were wheel marks in the dust; not all of it had settled yet. Kyla walked, an itch in her own skin. The bag that was always packed waited for her. The streetlights were lazy but ready. Kyla stayed to the middle. She could hear the Café: plates and utensils, and coffee cups on the counter. There was nothing but the empty face of buildings between the Café and the Church. Yusef would be working. In the stairwell with the sagging steps and the wallpaper that crept towards you inch, by inch Kyla could hear them whispering. The door to his apartment was open. She tried her best.

The apartment was full of ghosts. Ghosts with electric eyes hanging on every corner, off every counter, lingering in the closet, teetering at the edge of the sink, crouched on the nightstand with anger so fierce, it had burned her before. She left the bag on the floor by the door. Her leg was aching from walking, clawing at her. Kyla stood still amongst all those ghosts, her skin alive and feeling like a thousand pins had been lit on fire. Then she saw them. On the floor, on the bed, on the windowsill, on the nightstand, hiding in shadows and all like bright eyes. All those photographs, lives remembered with precision, budding romance, the desperate dry breaths of prayer, the grease from the stove, the grease from a plate. The history of dirt, dust, rust, and mud. The field. A girl with hair like the ache of the sun.

The season turned and turned year after year in rain, or the dry sun, the tall green majesty of corn and the humble pride of soybean. The desperate empty fields fed with government subsidy. Yusef's father had a straight line for a jaw. Kyla had seen him once in town, after Yusef had left that long sprawling porch for the rattling pipes of this spiteful building. His father looked worn in this picture. A coffee cup slipping in his hand. The sun was a burning reminder behind him. He looked older here and Kyla knew from his face he would not carry on much longer. Yusef had only mentioned his father to her once. It was only a memory of a look that she knew of him.

Kyla laid the photos on the floor, reconstructing everything she wanted to know about Yusef. His eager young hand snapping pictures of chickens, and bugs stretching out in long lines of soldiers across the kitchen floor. The window-sill at dawn, his mother's bread rising in the oven. A dusty guitar lonely in the corner. His hand, guided by time and patience, coaxing images of stripped corned husks. The season turning on him and Yusef growing older with each crop cycle, every long soft furrow of the plow. She watched the shadows grow long across the flat ugly face of the farmhouse. His line of sight growing stronger and taller. His father's smile no longer making heavy creases of his tough skin.

Kyla looked at the last photograph of his parents. They stood so still she thought any whisper would kill them. His mother was holding a loaf of bread. His father was barely holding himself. Kyle began to feel her lungs swelling. She tried desperately to steady herself on the floor, lying down amongst all those memories.

The room began to fill quickly. Kyla could feel the heat in her leg burning at her. They were making motions in the dark. Clawing at the walls, turning the tumblers quietly from the hallway. Tapping the pipes underneath the sink. They were patient. They were always patient. She closed her eyes and saw New Jersey.

The building stank with grease. They were so very patient that day. Kyla could not stop herself. She begged them but she could not stop herself. The building was aching for her. Even mother could not stop herself from screaming on that day.

The ghosts were pulling at the edges of her now, their hands hot and full of needles. She bit her lips to keep them from her mouth. Her body was soaked in sweat. She could only run. Run. Her legs burned, her steps uncontrolled. The steps of the building were unkind to her. She used the railing to pull herself up from the landing. The night came upon her with a piercing sound. Run. She screamed out his name into the stillness of a dry night. Father. Father she begged him to take her from this place.

At the other side of West Medford was almost nothing. Kyla tried to hold her breath in her lungs. She sat at the precipice holding her hands to herself, her feet hanging over the ledge of the concrete wall. The state was going to give West Medford a river. A long shallow snake with a tail somewhere up near Ohio and a body that stretched an endless lazy swallow way past what she knew of this place. There were jobs and trucks, smiles and farmers with greedy hands. The river would bring money and when the rain came, it could flood the banks and no one would care. Then things stopped. The workers stopped. The sound of trucks pushing diesel disappeared, replaced with idle tractors and dusty boots. The state had taken a hand from the federal government and left the river for subsidies. That is when the white tents began to appear, pulling in people from everywhere who were paid not to work. Kyla could not stand the lights. The speakers and the cables running across the empty thigh-high grass waiting, and whispering. Even her mother could be a fool sometimes. They all thought with this river, they were building something. They all thought they could save West Medford. Her body was aching. The long muddy river along her thigh had finally convinced her.

Tuesday

The sun was just barely at the edge of it all. Kyla kept her arms close to her body. A flat feeling was inside her. There was not much else. She had left her bag with Yusef. His apartment. Those whispers. Kyla liked this thing right before dawn. When the light was just an idea that crept out of the edges and corners of what she saw. It felt safe. Yusef's building was beginning to wake. A few lonely windows with the shades drawn back and the slick stained glass showing its teeth.

The door was open. The door was open. The door was open. There he was there he was. Body on the floor on the floor with all those faces. In that photograph. She stood there with hair that ached like the sun. That girl. What are they saying. That girl. Stop talking to me. Stop. Stop. Stop. That girl had taken him. Yusef yusef yusef yusef yusef. Wake up. This thing this thing it eats you from the inside. There are ghosts ghosts ghosts everywhere. Help me. That girl she deceives you. Please please please please please. Wake up wake up. Stop whispering. Stop. I can save you. Only you. Not them. Not her. I would have taken you with me. I made you a part of me. The ghosts the ghosts they will eat us from the inside. You see this you see it here on my leg this is where they turned me and I burned them out. Open your eyes look at them. She deceives you with hair like the sun. I would have taken you. I would have changed everything for you. Please. We would have saved you.

The sun was full up. Kyla's hands stung from the burn marks. Black and scarred, hurt and dry. The photographs were like fat fallen petals in beautiful shades of grey. The insides of the apartment were spread out like a thick black mess. The smell made her feel ill. She had torn at her clothes. Yusef was just barely there. His arm bruised and consumed. She did her best. Her bag was near the door.

"you are here"

Her mother had a fist balled up against her thigh. This is how she usually stood since Kyla was 8.

"yes i think so for a while"

"it is nice to see"

"i am glad you didn't put the doors back up"

"i am trying to get used to it"

"thank you"

"are you still working"

"yes at the cafe"

"would you like some breakfast"

"are you going to cook"

"if you like"

"yes then"

"is this all going to be okay"

"we will see how it goes"

"are you sure"

"for now"

"ok then"

"i love you"

Kyla had her fist balled up in her lap while she sat at the table. She looked down at the table. Her mother was opening the refrigerator. All that yellow light came spilling out across the linoleum floor.

"don't worry kyla"

They ate breakfast and Kyla felt very good. She had not had waffles with her mother since Chicago, the morning that the buildings came crashing down. Her mother had warmed the syrup carefully over the stove making sure not to burn it. She added a little extra sugar. Kyla ate slowly because she did not know what else to do.

The building in Chicago was enormous. Floor after floor after floor after floor of hallways and doors all, same railings, the same hard fluorescent lights. The only thing that separated the lives of strangers behind each muddy wooden door was a number. She was the new girl in 414. Everything about her was new. Her furniture, the carpet, her hair, her breasts, the hair between her legs. The only thing she remembered from before was the sickly whine of those whispers. She was never alone anymore.

Her mother had found a new job, in a new city, in a brand new building, with an old company. They moved with only two suitcases each and a few boxes of things they liked to have. It was an empty room but she knew. She knew they would find her. Kyla was still dizzy from the drive. Valium, barbiturates, and a long island ice tea had left her feeling sick inside herself. She knew she could never have lasted so long in a car. There were no reasons left after the incident. The marks on her back. The sound of a lit match was a comfort to her.

It felt like there was no reason to unpack. The window held a greasy spot of the sun to the worn out floor. Kyla slipped her shoes off and left them near the middle of the room. The floor was smooth and warm. Kyla felt very good with this. She had always liked the easy way of the sun. In Africa, his house, still close enough to smell ocean air, would catch the sun in the afternoon. Her father would make sure of it.

They washed dishes slowly together, her mother handing each plate and cup to her. Kyla's hands were draped with the blue-checkered towel. She could feel the hot water coming through the worn fabric. This towel had been with them since before the incident. She did not speak to her mother at all while drying. Her hands memorized patterns from working behind that long greasy counter. She thought for a minute about Yusef. His body a perfect straight line when she left running from the apartment. Her heart was louder then than she had heard in so many years. Kyla was lazy in the house, watching her mother move from room to room through the empty doors. She was busy in her mind, keeping her hands in front of her, in order to keep Kyla still. The house, in the bright afternoon sun felt good for Kyla. They were quieter during the day. She had to work.

Three

Sunday

Leone was already sweating under her blazer. It was hot for Sunday morning and she had an entire afternoon to keep herself together. Two boys from the church had set up the tables and attached the white pasteboard sign. *West Medford Business Association*. She sat in the folding chair with her legs close together but not crossed. It would be too hot today.

Leone had whipped herself for the first time while her father was haggling over the price of an old hickory stick. A man in a long white hat said his grandfather was honored enough to receive it as a commendation from Abraham Lincoln and it was more than suitable for walking. Leone did it while lying on her small bed in the rear of the Winnebago. The leather strap originated from a historic barbershop chair that her father sold two weeks ago for a Winchester that was fired by Jessie James.

The little bed had grown especially small in the last two years as curves filled out her form and her father increasingly spent more time alone in the driver's seat. Leone kept her body completely rigid, toes pointed and planted at the fake wood panels of the Winnebago's walls. The first few strikes were soft and subtle. The wide leather strap did not crack; it did not make that sound she would begin to crave with each passing year, as her body grew in shape and her appetites grew thirsty and ravenous. Still five years before college and she was already shaving between her legs. It was with the third and fourth strikes she grew more impatient and more adventurous. The fifth and sixth, the strap started to snap like she had been salivating over. Seven, eight, nine, ten. The skin on her thighs beginning to glow a nice warm red. Eleven, twelve, thirteen, fourteen, fifteen. Her hand was aching and her arm was burning from the repetition. The sheets were pulling her down. The man with the long white hat walked into the Winnebago to use the bathroom and get a glass of water. Leone would have ridden his body for hours if her father had not had a heart attack at the sight of it.

It would be very hot today. There were no other woman in the West Medford Business association. It was always the men who elected for rattling fan blades and recycled air, rather than plow lines and oil pans. The cycle was the same. They all prayed for rain. It made the money run.

The doors would be splayed open soon and the congregation would slowly seep out from the church into the rising sun. It was all orange and angry this morning. One of the wives had made coffee rolls and the icing was turning into slippery grease. There were pamphlets and business cards. The tables next to her would be filled with visiting suppliers for tractor parts, feed supply, tires, machinist, grain supplies, lumber, hardware and refurbished equipment. The men would smile, the women would try desperately at gossip and Leone would push the association as a place to converge on better ways to save their money. Leone had been in charge of the association for 3 years since she took control of the West Medford Grain and Supply. It was a tight office at the back edge of town. She sold every farm within 200 miles. Her father's Winnebago stood rusted out behind the building.

Leone was starving. The sweat was holding her blouse tight to her back underneath that navy blue blazer. She did her best to hold in every drop of perspiration from penetrating into the deep dyed blue of the blazer. She watched the men and their handkerchiefs like white flags flapping about their foreheads. Their mouths barely moved when they spoke of costs rising and prices falling. They had their suit jackets slung over their shoulders and white shirt cuffs rolled to their elbows. They were not afraid to sweat. Cigarettes were still cheap enough. Smoke seemed to seep from all their pores and hang in the air, swarming and finding its way into the creases of their collars. Leone listened, smiling occasionally, and never hesitating to speak. All those voices were whispering the same thing. Rain.

The Winnebago was a dust covered tin can with four used tires and a roof rack strapped full. Leone had lived in it with her father since her 6th birthday. She had lived with him and with the all the smallness that was his life. The pocket watch that Abraham Lincoln once gave as a gift to the boy who watched his horses. The bullets supposedly taken from the body of William Bonny. An envelope full of negatives showing Marilyn Monroe sun bathing naked near a hotel pool two days before she died. One of Macarthur's medals. Watches, rings, photographs, bullets, earrings, pendants, necklaces, handkerchiefs, videotapes, photographs, trinkets, baubles, hand-me-downs, toys, windups, pins, buttons, broaches, hairpins, hatpins, stickpins. All this kept rattling in Tupper wear, Ziploc bags, tucked into crates, drawers, and bins in every open space that was not being used for food, clothes, or toilet paper. Then there was the roof. The roof that had outgrown the long hot flat metal surface and found its way down the back, hanging off the small steel ladder and into a trailer that whistled going over 45 miles per hour. This is where he kept tables, chairs, walking sticks, pictures and frames, poster tubes, weather vanes, steering wheels, the grill of the first Model T from the assembly line. The center headlight from a tucker. A stained glass window wrapped in several blankets that once rested in the Notre Dame cathedral, still perfect except for a 2" hole left from a small rock thrown by a very young and rebellious Princess Di. A wheelbarrow used by Thoreau to move firewood from his woodpile to the small building he called home at the edge of a very unassuming lake. All this small history was piled upon Leone in her small bed no wider than her hips would grow, and no longer than 5'4" so that her toes touched the edge of the sink if she stretched full in the morning.

All this small history piled upon the back of an aching metal rickshaw pulled ahead on every mile by unleaded gasoline and an old widower, his wife a bleached out smile in a wooden frame on the dashboard. Leone never sat in the passenger seat. She had seen every state at least twice from the dirty window above the kitchen.

Leone stood in her bathroom wearing nothing but stockings and admired her breasts. She had always admired her body. Through the window she could see that the sun was beginning to fall. The hot orange glow beginning to creep into her house. She promised herself tonight. In the bathroom everything was white. This made Leone happy. It was her first bathroom. Her first oversized tub. Her first standalone shower with a door, not a curtain. Her first pedestal sink. Her first bathroom independent of any another. Her first bathroom. Leone stood in her bathroom. With her eyes closed, she could still feel the lingering drops of sweat at the edges of her skin, some just staggering to hold onto the fine hair that grouped itself in the small of her back, the edge of her forearm, and in the small loam that was between her thighs.

The house was full of color now, brilliant and burning at every exposed inch that was not being held captive by shadows. Leone felt with her hand for the edge of the bathroom sink, trying to keep her eyes closed. She searched for the cool rim of the sink, her legs feeling slightly weak. She thought about sitting down. To pick her feet from the cold floor in order to make sure that the heavy light of the end of the day did not reach her. That the night would come up quick and overtake her and she could forget what she knew she would see. She had seen her. Walking through the backyard, just past the short hedges. She had seen her every night for more than two months. She had run out into the yard, in her bare feet sometimes, only to find herself alone and her heart pumping painfully. She had seen her walking with minimal effort across the grass, at the edge of dark. Tall slender, her face was nothing more than oval held at bay by shadows. She knew that she had to look away. Leone knew all of this in her reasonable mind, but it did not matter. She found herself at the window, just to the left of the sink in the kitchen. She was there. She was there. Walking smoothly and Leone could only tremble.

Now, in the bathroom clutching the edge of the sink in her stockings, her body trembling, hiding from the light pouring into her house at every open mouth with vicious aggression. There was no explanation for why the water glass at the edge of the sink tumbled onto the tile. The sound of it so startling, Leone jolted slightly and found her feet again with slender glass underneath. Sitting on the toilet Leone still would not open her eyes, pulling small pieces of glass from her tender heel. Walking blindly, she found her way to the kitchen. Her chest heaved in huge waves. She could feel the light on her back, the subtle burn of the sunset crawling between her thighs. Searching blindly at the edges of cabinets for handles and dustpans, her eyes closed so hard that tears were pouring down the roundness of her face.

When the phone rang, it startled her so that her eyes bolted open and it all came flooding in. She saw everything in one quick flash. She saw her father buried in his first suit. She saw the rusted frame of the Winnebago. Her boyfriend in college, so frightened after she nearly died from asphyxiation. Her therapist brandishing his pencil and pad. Then every face of every man she had met in the Colonnade Motel. And her mother, her beautiful mother, who smiled only in the evening while walking in the garden.

Walking. Slowly. Walking. Never turning. Leone was unconsciously holding the phone.

Leone. Leone. Leone.

In that space where she heard her name, distant, she was all too aware that her body was completely and utterly bare.

Monday

Leone woke up cold and slightly damp with sweat. It was nothing unusual. She talked to herself while she dressed. It was an efficient and direct conversation. While she drank coffee. While she ate toast and cereal. While she put on her makeup. While she watered her plants. While she waited for seven am. Analog. Digital. There was safety in the numbers that rolled around the clock. These things kept with her and their predictability was comforting. Leone looked at her watch. This was at least something. Something she could build on.

You have to keep telling yourself things. You have to keep ahead of everything. Keep telling yourself things. Moving and telling. Telling yourself what these things are that you are working for. Keeping it right on the shelf. Keeping it right on the shelf.

The lights at the West Medford Feed Grain and Supply were a flittering jumble of electricity. Leone made coffee. She had been making coffee for men since she was seven. The smell almost always made her ill but she drank it any-way. It was 5:35 am. She knew that there were men all ready with their hands in the soil. Engines turning over. Spreading chicken feed. They rarely used the telephone. These are men who built their lives with handshakes.

Leone had to work. Leone had to work to get to them. To get to them while wearing her men's suit ordered and tailored from Chicago. She had to work to get to them over the counter at the West Medford Social Club. At the West Medford Business Association. Church fundraisers. Town Planning Meetings. She had to work to get to them. To sell them feed, parts, seed, tractors, equipment. The right shovel could buy her an entire farm. She had to keep telling herself that she had to work to get to them.

Leone's father worked over an old man in Atlanta, who was dressed in an all-white three-piece suit under the sun of 99 degrees. He was sweating, blotting his forehead with a red handkerchief but the old man in his suit smiled calmly.

He was trying to convince him to part with a musket fired during the Spanish American War that was later a gift to Robert E. Lee from Jefferson Davis. That is what has been said anyway. Leone was 8 on this day. Eight for three days and seven hours. Three days ago her father was bargaining over a rocking chair just outside of El Paso, Texas. They ate birthday cake bought from a grocery store. The old man in the white suit just smiled.

Leone would be thirty in two days and 9 hours. Her employees had arrived mostly before 8, but not much before 8. There were seventeen. Jeff and Henry. Sidney, Ethan, Danielle, Nancy, Susan, Walter, David, Robyn, Henry, Robert, Matt, Andrew, Kristine, Lisa, and Nick. She knew all their names. It was important. Leone had worked at the West Medford Grain and Supply for three years. She had owned it for almost two and had hired all but two of the current employees. Susan and Walter were the previous owners whom she kept on. In truth she did not need their services and they were quite aware of this. Their presence, however, made people feel comfortable and Leone was well aware of this. They mostly did small things. Leone had very little time for small things.

Most of the employees did not spend much time at the office but instead made their desks out of glove boxes and passenger seats. Papers and radios recommended from a trucking outfit that hauled supplies for Leone. She had tried to purchase cellular phones but quickly realized that it was impossible to obtain a reliable signal in West Medford. Instead she hired Lisa. Lisa's job was to coordinate all incoming calls or requests to the proper representative over the CB radio. Leone admitted once to her telephone therapist that she enjoyed listening to Lisa's voice because it was the sound of business and that occasionally it made her sexually excited. Leone had never once met with her telephone therapist. A device, her therapists had told her, she uses in order to remain in control of the situation.

The middle of the day. The middle of the day was this lazy thing where the sun hung right in the middle of the sky like a ripe fruit. She watched her men wrangling over the park benches out back, drinking ice tea and eating sandwiches their wives made. The women, with their hands folded in their laps, talked about everything in circles, round and round lazy as the afternoon. Leone watched them from the window, or hanging in the doorway before she went across the street. The West Medford Café was packed with sun bleached shoulders and caps, heavy and soiled. She knew every one of them just by the worn out lines on the back of their necks. They were all building something. Twenty years of dirt, twenty years of rebuilt engines and crop cycles, twenty years of children leaving home, twenty years of homemade bread, twenty years of the sun soaking into their bones.

"See this, Leone. See this, this is something special. This right here was once worn by the wife of Peter the Great. This right here is a piece of history." Leone watched her father's hand holding the brooch like a skipping stone. His fingers looked enormous next to hers. She watched him pin it on her. Her t-shirt was thin and sagged under its weight. "You can wear it while we drive." He smiled. "Do you want to ride in the front today." She looked away. "No, why not?" Leone turned from him and climbed into the Winnebago. It was near dark and most of the people in the camp had folding tables and chairs outside their movable homes. There were small grills, the smell of charcoal, and plastic Tupperware full of salads, pasta and chips. Leone had made two bologna sandwiches without cheese and left them on paper plates in the kitchenette.

"I think we should go north. We never go north. I think it is time we go north." Leone smiled with a mouth full of bread and meat. "You have never seen Lake Michigan. Well you have never seen it that you can remember. With your mother, we spent some time there. I mean when you were little. You were too young to remember." Leone could not even look at him when he talked about her. The way his eyes stayed closed too long. He always kept his hands in his lap. He drove them north. He drove them north in a long curving line that wound around mountains and followed the quiet sensations of rivers ignoring highway recommendations and most onramps. Sometimes they drove for hours without a street lamp. Leone slept with the light from the bathroom creeping out across the floor. In her sleep she took her mother's hand and felt the wonderful empty warmness.

Leone lingered at lunch. She held for a third cup of coffee from the pot that was growing thick at the bottom. The boy who poured it for her had eyes that went with moonless nights and riverbeds. His arms desperate to be steady. She had watched him before. At the register, at the coffee urn, at the counter, emptying ashtrays, and listening to the grill. He might of know of her. People in a town this small can do nothing but talk. She had seen him in the park under the sun. She had seen him in the street under the lamps, almost glowing. Leone thought about him. Thought about his thin body. His smile shining like a reaper's beacon. There was no end like the light that could come from him. There was no end like him. She had to stop herself from destroying it all for him. The coffee had gone cold in her cup but she drank it anyway. The middle of the day was a slow time for her, lying listlessly under the high hot noon sun. West Medford.

When she stepped away from the counter she could feel the sweat that had gone cold along her back. She walked to the office, feeling the heat through her shoes. The buildings gave off shade but that was an illusion. Even inside it seemed you could not escape the sun, now, in West Medford. Leone looked back through the large plate glass window to see him. Behind the counter cleaning away everything she had might have left for him. His face looked up to hers. It was a photograph.

There was a radio playing in a window, in an old home, in a town called West Medford. A woman on a porch with her hair pulled back into a grey bun. Rocking chair and satisfied smile. Leone stared at her with a hard face. She wanted to move her like a domino. Tumbling out of her chair and her porch. Away from the safe picket railing that had been painted once a year every year for every year that she lived there. Her husband sitting inside with the newspaper and a glass of iced tea. His overalls still the most comfortable skin he has. The Ford was a good truck. The roof had no leaks. The floorboard had a slight wave but it was smooth and cool in the summer mornings. Fireplace, hearth, kettle black. Leone did everything she could to move her from that porch. To shake the limb so hard apples would come off the branch. A woman, just a woman, waved. Leone had accomplished nothing.

Tuesday

Leone was full right up with pain in the morning. Her legs ached. Her back was straight and stiff, her hands tired and tender, her lips dry. The drives were beginning to cook on her. One hundred miles is a long drive in a silent car. Nothing past the headlights. Nothing but her father's voice. When she was 14, he got sick. When she was 20, he got real sick.

You have to keep telling yourself things. You have to keep ahead of everything. Keep telling yourself things. Moving and telling. Telling yourself what these things are that you are working for. Keeping it right on the shelf. Keeping it right on the shelf. Just keep telling yourself. Everything in this world is understandable if you can keep it on the shelf. Quiet and on the shelf. Your mother knew about it. She would have told you. Keep it on the shelf. Keep ahead and keep telling yourself. Moving and telling. Don't get dragged down by the incidentals in this world. Keep it on the shelf.

Leone could not bear seeing the black part of her eyes in the mirror. Her whole life was in the rapture that reflected there. She brushed her teeth with her eyes closed. With one simple look it could all so easily become unraveled. Leone was desperate. She was building something. The sunlight was pouring out of every window and into her home. It was in these brief moments before the day took hold that Leone could really breathe. Her shoulders unfettered and her body fresh and naked, nothing pulling at her, at her empty hands.

Nothing lasted long in West Medford except the dirt and the sun. Everything else was simply there. The seasons turned and turned and everything was interred with earth and sweat. Leone was no different, always thirsty with weak roots. Dry and desperate, thirsty and full of longing. Leone could see it on every face sitting through the plate glass of the Social Club, across the table at the West Medford Business Association, hanging at the coffee counter before the first phone call at work. In every aching memory of her father. The only thing she was sure of was the shake in her hand and her mother's smile. It was all about to break. To her, it seemed, it had no other choice.

She dressed quickly with the house warming at her back. Business suit. Shoulders straight, arms at her side. This was the easiest way for her to do things. She drove there fast. She always drove fast because nothing got in the way in West Medford. Her house wound out around the side roads and backroads of a town with only one main drag. Sometimes she drove flat out across the open plain in the dry season just to challenge the dust. She dreamed that it would consume her completely.

At work. There was work and nothing else. She did everything exactly. There was chatter in the morning. There was small talk after lunch. There was carousing at the end of the day. It was all just a perimeter to Leone. She did not exist in the town of West Medford. Leone did her best to keep her secret. She did not find herself in the folds of town gossip, despite her presence on community boards. Leone was not privileged to information. She was on the edge of everything and her hands were trembling.

"Leone, Remember that time we were outside of Trenton? Trenton New Jersey? 30 minutes at least in that little town with the bookstore and all the houses had plaques on them. 1892. 1907. 1899. 1912. And that one 1796. Wasn't it simply perfect. I think your mother would have liked it there. Those rows and rows of houses. Each one a sparkling shade of white. The one just on the corner had magnificent columns. There were people walking and dogs walking with them. It was simply ... I think we should try and get back there. Maybe after we sell the Chippendale chair to that writer in Utica. Maybe. Maybe." They could drive for two days and not say a word, just barely breathing in their own time. Leone had counted the sunsets on all the 48 states more than once around and the sunrise on just as many. There was no clock on the road. No hours, no minutes, no seconds, everything was calculated in miles. Miles and landmarks. Landmarks and truck stops. Truck stops and diners. Diners and state lines. State lines and county markers. County markers and town lines. Town lines and boroughs. Boroughs and street signs. Street signs and rural routes. In the warm months, every story was told with the smell of summer. "It was probably late August when I found your mother sitting in a row boat on Lake Superior with only one oar. She was just moving in circles. Rowing and rowing in circles, each one a little further from the shore. She looked ridiculous out there in her giant parasol hat and a bikini top. You should have seen her face as I started wading out towards her. Splashing like a fool in my shorts and polo shirt. Then trying to swim with all those clothes on. I don't know what I was thinking going in there in my Sunday best. It must have been quite a sight for your mother. She was just spinning around and around in that little boat going nowhere and not getting any closer to that lost oar."

The work was slow today. Leone was thinking past everything. The drive would be almost unbearable tonight. The road just a long stretch between the two ends of everything she knew about herself anymore. It would feel good. She knew that much but things like this are temporary. The feeling of skin. The smell of aftershave. The hot and sudden weight of a man against her body.

Leone walked to lunch. To the counter at the West Medford Social Club. She wanted something that would fill her up. The place was full of voices. She saw them all. The girl with the low slender voice, shy and curled away as she washed steaming dishes in water that frightened Leone, it looked so hot. He was there, always in long sleeves, his eyes poured open like the summer moon. Leone could not look at him. She could barely look around him, past him. She just needed to keep it on the shelf. The lady at the grill smiled at her and wiped her forehead with a rag from her shoulder. Hot turkey on a roll. Melted Swiss cheese. Two slices of bacon. Served open. Potatoes. Water. Coffee. Donut. Leone tried to hide behind her newspaper, kept carefully folded in order not to bother the other men at the counter. She was not even reading. She was only staring at the type, watching it. It did not offer anything to Leone. She knew she could not hide behind these things forever.

The boy was standing there in front of her. The coffee pot was steaming. He just stood there, his mouth a smooth thin line when he spoke, his eyes a camera. She studied every word that had been inscribed on his face. The long psalm that told his story. She wanted to see his entire book. To discover him page by page. To wait and consider each period, each comma, each well placed hyphen. To relive him through every phrase, sentence and paragraph. That this endless rapture could finally set her free.

After work she was afraid to go home. She had been afraid for four months and thirteen days. Sometimes she waited at work. Keeping the light on in her office until the sun lost itself over the edge of the fields. Leone could not wait today. She could not. There were men in the parking lot drinking soda from cans and pointing towards the edge of town. Their hands just barely touching the edge of nothing. Their arms weak and tired from work.

Leone drove carefully through town. She passed the brick front buildings with plain sad faces. She would have not blinked, even with the sun setting thick in her eyes, if it was not for him. He was just standing, barely holding his body together. His eyes a camera. His memory a negative. Arms like the stems of a broken kite pushing through his clothing. Pale blue eyes. He looked right past her. Past the business suit mail ordered and tailored. Past the lipstick and mascara. Past the evenly applied layer of foundation. Past the crumbling wall of her age and pulled out of her the truth in one look so simple that Leone felt tears welling up in her. She cursed herself for not driving faster. Her brakes squelched when she halted her car in the driveway.

Keep it on the shelf. Right on the shelf. That goddamn sun. That goddamn sun.

The house was bleeding orange from every corner that could not hold a shadow. It was a rush. Leone looked at her feet and saw her ankles swimming in color. She could barely breathe. The kitchen. The kitchen window. The sink. The kitchen window just over the sink. Her legs were splintering. She argued with her jacket before tossing it across the back of the couch. Leone was almost on her knees before she found herself clutching to the kitchen sink.

You have to keep telling yourself things. You have to keep ahead of everything. Keep telling yourself things. Moving and telling. Telling yourself what these things are that you are working for. Keeping it right on the shelf. Keeping it right on the shelf. Just keep telling yourself. Everything in this world is understandable if you can keep it on the shelf. Quiet and on the shelf. Your mother knew about it. She would have told you.

Leone could not stop it. It was all building towards something. She could not help herself from desperately peering out the window. It should have been nothing. It was nothing. It was nothing. It was everything. Leone just waited. There was nothing she could do. She could not stop it. She had tried desperately. She had a stockade fence installed. She had the landscapers bring in a thick hedge with sharp edges that pricked at her legs in the garden. An irrigation system to water them. She could not stop it.

That goddamn sun. Look at you. Look at you just an edge at the end of your world. Can't you see what happens here. You have to keep ahead of everything. Keep telling yourself things. Moving and telling. Telling yourself to keep it right on the shelf.

The sun was a thin line burning ochre across the flat land of West Medford. Leone was at the sink when she saw her in the yard. She was just beyond the flowerbeds, drifting. Everything was going to change. This was building to something.

Blood was the only thing that kept Leone breathing. The feeling of it hot and alive inside her body. She felt thirsty. She felt like she was dying. She felt the last piece of the sun at her throat. Then it was gone. Leone had opened her eyes. All that blood and heat left her body as soon as the sun slipped from her throat and dipped below the windowsill. The faucet had been running cold the entire time. Leone could not remember turning the handle. Every time the sink was running cold. Leone always looked away and then she was gone. Her mother's thin frame simply a spot left blurred from the sun in Leone's eye.

Leone had to get ready. She had packed most of her things immediately after she returned the last time. There was only some clothing and toiletries to put in the bag. Aspirin, Vicodin, medical tape, bandages, aloe, Neosporin, gauze, and surgical thread. All things were precautionary.

Leone dear it never hurts to be prepared. You have to know your situation. That is part of being prepared. It doesn't matter if it is a test in English class or a fistfight. You have to be prepared. Your mother always loved that about me you know. Always prepared. Like the time she fell in Yellowstone National Park. I had a splint, bandages, a complete first aid kit. She was better than new in less than a week because we were prepared. Or how about when we were in South Carolina and we saw R. E. Lee's scabbard case. I wasn't even hunting that weekend but I was ready to deal. I always had cash, and something to trade with me. You have to be prepared. Be prepared Leone. It will keep your mother happy.

She drove at a reasonable speed but in the dark it was difficult to move slow. There was nothing but space to pass the time. 100 miles. It was far enough to be in Africa. The hotel was a long flat succession of two L shaped buildings that seemed to be loosely interrelated. She had used it before. The desk clerk recognized her but only with a minor nod. That was sufficient and Leone would have not been prepared for anything more. She always arrived first. Dressed the bed. Got ice. Made two drinks. Found something neutral on the television. Laid out each item. The whip. The mask. The corset. The gag. The iron rod. The candle. The knife.

She changed, hanging her clothes carefully in the closet. She wore the same outfit each time. Stockings. Garter. Panties. Push up bra. Leather gloves. The corset. He was exactly ten minutes late which is what she expected. Leone was sitting on the end of the corner of the bed when he opened the door. Her legs straddling over each side. He was quiet but friendly as he undressed, laying his clothes over the back of the chair. He undressed completely. He wore surgical gloves. Leone laid on the bed face down her arms and legs spread out towards the edges. He placed the gag around her mouth and began. She could not wait to feel the cold blade slide carefully inside her.

Four

Sunday

Willie Huff hated Sundays. The sun was always too hot. Even the bugs moved slower on Sunday. Sunday was everything in West Medford. His boots had to be polished. His uniform had to be clean. His face was to be shaven and he had to smile at every frail and weathered resident who slid by. It made his stomach sick to pin his badge to his pocket on Sunday. Sheriff Willie Huff. West Medford. He never once passed beneath the cross that hung like a tortured weight above that door. The year he arrived in West Medford was the year the original church was destroyed and he was glad he had seen it.

Every five years, the town of West Medford bought a new truck for the Sheriff. This year Willie chose blue. The last three had been red. He knew everything about this town. The secrets that ran between wooden walls. The girl with wires for veins. The boy with sad eyes who wore long sleeves in the hottest summer. The woman with the scars on her back and the strange things in her flower garden. There was nothing in West Medford that Willie Huff did not know even if they tried. He kept it all together. Tied tightly like a bundle of twigs. It kept together that way. It kept going. The whole town. The farmers, the storeowners, the schools, even the church kept going that way. Tight and rigid but still breathing. Willie was the first to feel something building, to feel the knot slip between his fingers.

He was outside of the church at 7 am. Service was for eight. Even the preacher knew that despite the good book, there is always work to do on a farm. He directed traffic. Kept the farmers from running their trucks into the townsfolk. Willie watched their eyes. He saw the small amount of hate that gathered at the corners. They were tired of the sun. The taste of dirt in their mouths. The smell of shit on their boots. They were tired of wearing the same suit every Sunday. They were tired of not being answered. They were tired of the dust. It was hot. It was too hot for the morning. It was too hot for Sunday. They began filling into the pews, their bodies burdened and slouched over from the weight.

They sat quietly holding the book in their hands. Even trying their best was not enough for them anymore. Willie had seen the seasons turn in West Medford. The growing and the harvest. The shortfall as well as the muddy ruts. This was the end of it. This season would break them. This sun was a bright light he had never seen before.

He watched that boy with the long sleeves hustle towards the church. He walked with a long irregular gait that was full of questions. He did not talk like the rest of them. Open mouths on the hot sidewalk. Their white collars damp with sweat. He felt his own shirt soaking through. Willie looked through tight eyes at everything. It was something he had not been able to give up. His mother was the first to notice it despite the nest of brambles in her heart. Her voice was nearly broken when she said it. He watched the tiny blue sky through her window. Those girls of hers had nearly killed her. It did not take long for her to finish the rest.

Willie Huff had never felt so very still. The men were always the last to find their way amongst the pews. They held their breath while waiting and talking. Handkerchiefs unanimously surrendering and the organ began to moan. The woman had hats. They were small, shapely and well tuned to their Sunday hairstyles. The men kept combs in their pockets. The boy with the long sleeves was restless looking. They kept their eyes from him now more than ever. She was not there. He had not heard her low slender voice for more than a week. Willie had seen her coming from the old filling station. He hoped it would not be another problem. He closed his eyes and listened. The whiskey breath of a dry season. The service was usual and with its final vows Willie knew the white tents would be arriving. The trucks would fill the town with dust and shallow whispers. He remembered clearly the first time.

Everything was bleached and painful. His skin was bleeding at the corners. There had been three fights in one week. Broken windows. A dozen heated arguments. Two cases of heatstroke. One suicide. Then they came. They came in a glorious shining chrome streak. They came in a long, winding snake with a flat jailbreak face. Willie watched them run down his town. The businesswoman's head snapped around like a lawn sprinkler. It was still early in her career and things like this were a threat. They stopped their line at the Griggs Farm and then it happened. They spread out from their buses, their trucks, their vans and brought with them an endless supply. It was an operation that reminded Willie of his regiment. A sergeant barking orders from the top of idling van. A corporal for each company. A supply master shuffling equipment from the back of trailers. Then there were the soldiers. One after another working their bodies in a blistering sun. The mindless repetition. They had seen it before. Done it all a hundred times, for a hundred towns. The General sat in the shade, with a drink, and his dogs.

They worked quickly despite the sun. The white cloth stretched far enough that it disappeared in the heat. A burning line on the horizon. They sent a man into town. He was casual. Willie watched him from behind his glasses. He was shifting between doorways, small papers in his hands. He was the announcement but everyone was already well aware. Willie watched him work. He had a perfect smiling face. A well-chosen soldier. Recruitment officer. The people were different then. They kept themselves closer together. There was not so much to talk between them. About them. The perfect smile made his place carefully but their faces showed him everything he needed. They would all try to find their way under that white tent.

After services they came down the steps in a tumble. The young over the old and the elderly barely standing behind them both. Willie watched them cross the street and snake away towards the usual. The businessmen's group had their tables. The café grill was hot. The boy with the long sleeves looked especially unkempt. They were all talking but everyone was too numb to really move their mouths. The walk to the West Medford Social Club was crowded. Willie kept his head low. He was hungry. The eggs hit the flat slab of iron with a wonderful sound. There was bacon, griddlecakes, coffee, extra butter, warm syrup, two wet pieces of toast, and orange juice. He ate with large mouthfuls, reading a week old newspaper. He had gotten used to the world taking its time with West Medford. She was there before he was, her sinewy arms soft with hot water and soap. He looked to her. She turned her head with a disastrous consequence. They all saw it. The weak-kneed farmers. The dry mouthed children. The women still with spit curls and their husbands with church collars. It was only a second but her hair was a whip smart razor. Willie's mouth was full of bread so he could only choke. She nearly collapsed, but the boy with long sleeves kept her steady. Willie left his plate and the money. His stomach was full and the day had become unbearable with sun. People were still on the sidewalk waiting for something. It would not take long for things to change. The nickels were ready to turn over.

The sheriff had simple accommodations. One office, one waiting area, one desk, one chair, a filing cabinet, and one cell which was currently empty. All of it just one cut up room. Willie opened the top button on his shirt. He was sweating through his undershirt. There were some papers to be looked over. Willie leaned back in his chair and felt his eyes closing. She was right there waiting in the black part of his eye. If he could, he would pray to god she didn't burn the whole damn town.

William, my husband, you can't see me anymore. i know you have these things in you to say. things men must do. i am not that dead yet. let me have your hand. it isn't much william. we can still hear music can't we? the old songs. i had a figure then. like that girl. whispers make their ways to me still. there was a fire. let me see your hand. can you sing. all with sweet lilies. let me see your hand. where is your ring?

Willie opened his eyes and took in a wet breath. He worked over the papers on his desk, trying to make the clock move. The letters were in his desk drawer. He kept them bundled carefully together in a portfolio, since the beginning, clipped carefully with the envelope, each clearly marked return to sender, undeliverable, no forwarding address left. He read them all, each one a meticulous crafted map, the language chosen carefully and pressed into the paper. A subtle, but clear, dark blue line from the edge of the paper into the heart of the continent. It was all very, very clear to him. What he had done was unforgivable.

If he could have avoided, it he would have went anywhere else for lunch. There would be murmurs and whispered words. The heat hit him like a leather strap. The sweat was almost immediate. The bell sang as he opened the door. It was hot. The grill has been driving the place all day. The sound of hamburger and the smell of onions was stronger than usual. They had filled the booths and were hanging at the edge of the counter. They were leaning against the walls and crouched along the baseboard. The plates were working towards the ceiling and her hair was spilling out gloriously down her wet back.

The men, despite the crowd, still had respect for position and cleared their way for the sheriff. His space at the counter was cleaned and coffee found its way to him quickly. The only thing he could hear was hot water and the sound of dishes. Willie looked out through his tight face. She was keeping her back to him. The boy with the long sleeves was keeping his distance. Willie felt it all unusual. He finished and left the counter for the second time. It was early but the day was already over. The men behind him began to speak about the tent, about trying, about how this would change everything.

Willie had to work to get the engine to turn over. It was a comfort to hear once the motor started. The houses moved by slowly in the dark. Streetlights kept to themselves while the brick buildings with worn white painted fronts showed their tired faces. Then the straight framed wood homes. Front porches with hand hewn benches and metal pails. Then after a moment of beautiful bleak emptiness came the farms. The fields stretched out, each a desperate oasis with a barn and a small sturdy house jutting up out of the middle of it all. There were some larger than others. The barns with rotting slats and weather vanes spinning aimlessly. There were few stories left to tell in those spaces. He had heard them all and kept his tongue. Then West Medford spilled out in small puddles. The Grigg's farm. The Canter's. The Hillsford's. They kept to themselves with sporadic ragged fences and thinning livestock. The last was the long sleeves. The barn barely standing now burnt by the summer, washed out and left alone. The home, he had been there before, did not hold itself up well anymore. There were no more visitors. No more rumors. No more fresh bread.

The filling station was a mud spot on the horizon. He parked behind the building. She had made changes, the carpet, the candles, a gas lantern and extra blankets. She had spent time sleeping there. There were two coolers piled on top of one another. The easel was leaning awkwardly against the old desk. Her work was turning ambitious. Willie bit his bottom lip and rested his hand on his gun. The doorway was full of strange light. She was the beginning and he was building something. He had brought the letters with him. How could he explain to her what he had done? He took his watch off and stuffed it into his pocket. The building was still cooking. He could hear her low-slung voice singing just inside the office door.

Willie watched his mother wash her hair. It was a long black snake running slipstream down her breast. The beautiful shiny black beast. She squeezed the water into the sink. Willie kept close to the door and watched the muscles in her bare shoulders. The sway of her breasts. It was a quiet moment for her.

He listened to her careful breathing. She wrapped a towel around the hair and stood, hands on hips, proudly with her breasts holding up the moonlight. Willie let the door close softly. He stood there, his face against warn warm wood, and listened. His mother kept a clean knife near the edge of the sink. A nest of birds was living in her chest.

The filling station was sweating. Willie undressed Kyla slowly. Her body warm and flush with the heat. She had gotten lean in the summer. The heat working over her muscles. Willie felt enormous with the shadows filling out around him. Kyla was keeping time. An index finger with an irregular heartbeat. Willie did his best to hold her still. She was rapture. Her body the flood waiting to change it all. Willie knew he could not keep her still much longer. He laid her down. His body a mountain next to her. Her skin the snow. Willie wanted her now but Kyla was filled up and anxious.

Willie worked the needle into her bare skin. Kyla kept his hand steady with her low slender voice. A song, melody, with a harmony that could bring down a mountain. Kyla barely made a whisper as the needle wrote its rhythm across her body. She was frighteningly still while needled the heavy lines into her skin. Kyla looked at him and Willie pushed himself inside her. Then, as if surprised by the suddenness of something new, she gasped. She stared at his sweating face. Afterwards he knew she had everything she needed. It was written across her body in stark black lines. A map of a life he had never known leading to her beautiful dark continent. He had no idea how much her heart held. She had no idea what he had done.

Willie woke up with the very thin edge of the sun. He had no reason to stay. He dressed quietly. It was still warm in the small space of the station office. He looked down to her. Her body, a glorious tablet. Her mouth was a novel. Willie would follow it to the end. He left the letters at the edge of the desk.

Monday

Willie drove the road back to West Medford. The truck was ripping up a swell of thick dust. It was early, still early even for a plough.

william you haven't got eyes anymore my poor husband you lost em all together. william you won't see me anymore. i know you have these things in you to say. i am not that dead yet. we can still hear music can't we. the old things. i had a figure then. like that girl. are you tired william. lay down with me. close your eyes. i am so very tired william. all this time lying down and i never sleep. i know everything. they are here. those brilliant white hills. such smiles. all that singing. they are building something there.

Willie undressed in the bathroom. He laid his clothes carefully over the edge of the tub. The day was slow to begin. It was getting ready; by Wednesday it would be hot enough to burn it all. Willie stood running the shower. The light was eating up the hallway. The water was cool and he let himself forget things for a while. The sharp streams hitting his chest. The thin rivers crisscrossing the open plain of his back. Taking a diversion at the thick skin of old scars. He felt the water between the roundness of his buttocks. The sensitive space at the top of his thighs. The cold water stunning his manhood. It was the least he could do now. He knew, so well, he had started something that could no longer be undone.

He took the clean uniform from the closet and dressed. His body was tired. Coffee and English muffins. An old newspaper. Hank Williams on the small kitchen radio. The truck was still feeling lazy about starting. It did not have far to go. There was a heavy feeling on him now. The Social Club was already a beehive. He took his seat. She was not there and it was obvious. The long sleeves were working hard to fill the space. His face sweating and anxious. Willie had seen it before. It was of little consequence to him without the violence. A dish broke and everyone was about to panic but the door came flying open and a dozen strangers filled the awkwardness. They had been working hard setting up for salvation.

The door had a long moan when he opened it. The office was stagnant, stiff and hot with dust. Willie fell into the chair. There were papers that needed his attention but he had his mind all over her. She was wearing his jacket now. He had inscribed it so cautiously across her tender flesh. A full-length coat. All of those subtle mysteries working their way through the subtle curves. The scar on her leg the only aberration in her story. It was a finely detailed and a brutal memoir. She worked hard for that. It was her story but Willie was now the Epilogue.

He looked out the dirty window. He could feel it already, two days left to finish everything. The West Medford River would stay dry another ten years. Willie promised himself he would not see the calendar for that long. He turned his head down and let the sun roll up the sidewalk outside. It was all a matter of patience now. The whole thing was going to break, but then the door came open and the story began.

"Leone."

"Willie."

"How is the feed business?"

"It doesn't matter much now."

"Nope. Guess not now."

"I know you told me."

"Things change, Leone."

"What are you saying?"

"Things change."

"What are you saying?"

"Leone. I am saying things change."

"Willie I can't. . ."

"You don't have to."

"What now?"

"We wait"

"Wait."

"Yes."

"What are we waiting for, Willie?"

"We?"

"Yes."

"When did that happen?"

"Things change, Willie."

"I can agree with it."

"I can't take much more of it."

"It is all building to something."

"I am tired, Willie."

"Leone?"

"Yes?"

"Look at my eyes. I haven't slept in years."

He watched her leave the office, her body well contained in her phone ordered, tailored, business suit. She would have let him do anything to her, instead she left a white envelope on the file cabinet. Willie watched her settle back into her car while he counted the money. It was long drive and they were killing him, but his wife's death was becoming very expensive.

Willie climbed into his truck. Leone had left him a thermos hot with coffee and two sandwiches in a plain brown bag. He waited ten minutes and then left watching West Medford turn, and disappear, into the heat behind him.

The sun was burning up the thin dirt road like a matchstick. Willie turned hard into the motel parking lot. The black sedan was parked in its usual position. He did not recognize the car parked adjacent. The entire thing felt odd, but nothing unusual at least. The light went on and Willie settled back into his seat. The coffee was very strong. He ate the tuna sandwich first. Leone would be all night. Willie kept his service revolver loaded on the passenger seat.

His mother had been sitting in the dark all night, her dress spread out, an ocean of satin on the living room floor. His sisters were feeding on the body like hungry gulls with razors in their mouths. Willie watched them tear her apart, his pajama bottoms barely able to hold themselves up. It was a massacre and his mother was left barely breathing. They had taken everything from her and left him with the bones. She had not slept in days. He watched her, eyes like big black marbles as they swarmed about her with vicious demands and their sex swinging in her face. They bribed her with guilt and pills now. The oldest had left a baby in her arms two years ago before the state came for her. The youngest had burned her thigh with a cup of hot coffee. The twins in between turned her second husband into a criminal. She was swimming in pills. Headlights came in from the street and lit up the place with a sick light and they disappeared out the door, smelling of blood and willingness. Willie went to her. She opened herself up and he found a soft place still left close to her breast. She pressed him hard into her body. The smell was strong, thick, and her voice cracked like ice. Love me. Love me. Love me. Love me. Love me. Love me. Love me. Love me. And Willie found his mother's slender lips and promised.

Willie was half in a sleep when the motel door opened cautiously. Leone looked worse than usual. She rested for a moment against her car and he saw her lips move. She knew now, after this time, that everything was changing. Leone started the car and turned onto the road. The sun was just a thin line competing with the morning moon.

Tuesday

Willie let his truck idle and watched those men work. The tent lines, exposed nerve ready to be plucked out of the ground. The men moved with purpose and the women always remained smiling. The town would come rolling in on a steam engine. West Medford was tired of waiting. The talk over the counter. They were tired of waiting. The murmur in the church. The chatter in the market. The vibrations in the soil. The dust was filling their ears with hope. The sun kept laughing at them and the heat, this heat, it was all building something. Willie knew, to himself, that if it did not change soon, something would have to break.

Willie drove past Leone's house. It was still not quite dark. Still not quite light. Her car was comfortable in the driveway. The rest of town was sleepwalking. The morning was still too grey. Willie turned off his ignition and stared at his front door.

The house gave off the smell of heat. He opened the windows in the living room, the dining room, still enough evening air left for a difference. He ran the water in the kitchen sink and looked at the back window. He drank a tall cold glass and went to the bedroom. There was a desperate rhythm to that room. Those hospital machines were mechanical vultures. How much was there left for her to give? He looked again at the slippers, well worn and shivering now. He undid the large black belt and hung it over the back of chair. He felt so unbalanced without it, he steadied himself against the foot of the bed.

william you haven't got eyes anymore my poor husband you lost em all together. william you can't see me anymore. i know you have these things in you to say. i am not that dead yet. we can still hear music can't we. the old things. i had a figure then. like that girl. whispers make their ways to me still. there was a fire. let me see your hand. can you sing? let me see your hand. are you tired william. lay down with me. close your eyes. i am so very tired william? all this time lying down and i never sleep. i know everything. those brilliant white hills. such smiles. they are building something there. a song is going to come and rattle this town. turn it like a dime.

William was weeping.

He had watched them work her over. Standing behind the thick plastic glass of the operating theater, they turned her out like a butcher. When it was all finished, he had lost them both and his heart nearly quit. The baby looked so small underneath the blanket. He lay in the bed next to her for three months until he found his feet again. The black belt was waiting for him when he returned. There was no other way now. It was a perfect fit.

Willie showered. It felt glorious. He let it wash over him and listened to the sound as it sputtered out helplessly against the tile. This entire act was coming to a close. Standing in front of the mirror, he looked at the only words Kyla had written for him. The handwriting on his chest was ragged but beautiful. *And this is building something.* He reached down and after a few short moments, came in the sink.

It was the last Tuesday of the month. There were flyers now. It seemed, one in every window that West Medford had. They were simple sketches drawn by hand. A rough outline of the cross, the tent, and the cradled palms of jesus himself. Everyone was convinced they were full of rain. Willie had not allowed a flyer to be hung in the municipal office. They were clear though in the social club, the feed store, the church, the meeting hall. It kept a fine vigil over him. A strong black iris pressing down.

He worked. There was nothing left for him to do. There were permit requests. The Parkers wanted to build an addition to their barn, more livestock, more milking machines. The Rose family needed a new roof. The sun leaking through bleaching their floor. Leone wanted a larger storeroom. Willie signed them all. There was a request from a Chicago hospital for a birth certificate. There was a memo from the State Police concerning two brothers who had robbed several small banks and a convenient store. Willie tacked it to the bulletin board, circling their descriptions with a marker. He filled out reports and watched the clock. Those hands were a real son of a bitch.

His mother was desperate now. She moved like a rope tethered at the end. She felt safe enough in the kitchen. He watched her with the carving knife drawing long thin slices from the roast. They ate like beasts with their hands and faces. All four of them bleeding and driving her crazy. Willie waited with his empty plate. The glass of water running into the tablecloth. She could see through her eyelids now. Lucid panels of lithium and amphetamines kept her head rolling and her stomach distended. Her body had become a stranger to him. Willie no longer recognized her embrace as he waited beneath the covers each night. Tobacco and milk of magnesia on her lips. The four of them left the table rattling with glasses overturned. Willie cleared the table. He stacked the dishes in the sink and stripped the tablecloth. He used a wet rag and wiped the old oak clean, cupping the scraps in his hand. He made their plates and brought it to the living room. They ate, cross-legged, on the floor near the hearth. His mother smoked afterwards, her hands awkward, but still able to work the papers. Willie took two long drags and returned the joint between her fingers. She would be steady afterwards and they would wash the dishes. Willie felt a bit sick with the hot water steaming his face. His mother started singing, her voice choked with ghosts.

Willie woke up with his head snapped back and his mouth wide open. The sun was spying on him from its high hot spot. His throat was aching and arid. He kept a few beers in the small office fridge. He drank two greedily, the head running into his mustache. He wanted to eat. He had not been so hungry in months. His stomach was clawing at him. Willie hit the pavement in a sweat already damp along his back and underarms. The Social Club was a hotbox. The grill setting off sparks as they all crowded around counters and hugged the walls. There was no space for him. They left no path. No small line to weave. The boy with long sleeves was a catastrophe. His face a sunken pale mess. He was soaked. She was barely there. No long quiet glances. They all had seen him. His gold badge. His thick black belt. The heavy boots. The plain brown uniform. The oiled 9mm strapped to his hip. Everything about this was about to turn and Willie felt empty trying to stop it. Willie did not eat. He could not stay in the West Medford Social Club. The hunched backs heaving over counters of hot plates. The grill making a wonderful sound of grease and meat. He wanted all of her. Her entire body. He wanted to read every inch of her story. To write his own apology across her back in an unbearable prose. To show her the pain that he had been writing since he found his mother broken on the kitchen floor. He drank two more beers from the fridge in the office and two packages of crackers from his desk drawer. Then, before he could take a breath, the sun was going low and orange. The streetlights were coming up.

The truck was rumbling as he drove back towards his wife and their machines. He drove past Leone's house and watched her place that bag in the back seat. She was going. He had no time for this game now. Willie knew that it would not end well with so much urgency. The sun was nipping at the roof peaks across the street when he fell in through the front door, his body suddenly unwieldy. He grabbed the throbbing in his chest. Not a heart attack. This felt too unnatural. She was there in the bed. His wife. The machines keeping time. Willie looked at her. Her face still before she spoke to him.

william you haven't got eyes anymore my poor husband you lost em all together. william you can't see me anymore. i know you have these things in you to say. i am not that dead yet. let me have your hand. it isn't much william. we can still hear music can't we. the old things. i had a figure then. like that girl. whispers make their ways to me still. there was a fire. i know everything. they are here. those brilliant white hills. such smiles. all that singing. they are building something there. time was short. give me your hand william. you need to run from this place before it breaks you. william.

He held her hand as she trembled, the machine's rhythm becoming an endless line.

Five

Wednesday

The morning was a goddamn furnace but there was rain. Yusef was exhausted, his body aching and rigid inside his skin. He worked the counter, feeling the heat, the stale ashtrays, and watched every look she made. Kyla's low slender voice a confession, if nothing else than a whisper. He could barely hear her above the rain. It was all anyone wanted to know. They sat smiling, eating fried eggs and bacon, and laughing like children. All those men with tired arms and worn out boots. The rain was a matter of pride. The laughed like children when they could not think of anything to say. Kyla looked like she could disappear. The men from the white tent poured into the West Medford Social club to a round of applause. Hand clapped backs, tall men looking like children. They smiled, asked for coffee, and a place was made for them. That white canvas mountain would be a hive tonight. West Medford would be a flood tonight and Yusef was ready for everything to be washed clean. He knew nothing could hide from this disaster.

Kyla felt the sting in her back. The bandages were wet with blood and sweat. She had been with him last night in the dark surrounded by the smell of kerosene. There were no words left to write now. His story was complete. A story she had been told too many times. Only the epilogue remained and love like this never ends easily. A lie like this, like fire, consumes everything.

Kyla kept her face in the steam of the sink. She listened to the men with their hearty voices. The sound of it kept things quiet in her head. Her leg was throbbing. The scar, a burning interruption in her story. She could not stop talking to herself. The whispers were bringing the fight down to her. Still, she prayed for Willie Huff to keep his promise.

Leone woke up and was surprised. She had stayed the night in that room for the first time. Her body was a ruin. The marks on her breasts fresh and still red. The bruises on her stomach, her thighs, her wrists a deep purple color. The rest of her had been split wide open. The smell of blood was everywhere.

Willie did not sleep. He lay next to his wife all night. A somber and quiet vigil. He dressed calmly in front of her. Willie, before leaving the house, made sure he had loaded his revolver. The rain had already started.

There were no umbrellas in West Medford. The rain came in fat summer drops like a Hollywood musical. The men, just children, with open mouths feeling the salty wet on their tongues their wide brim hats working as waterfalls and the gutters running heavy into the sidewalk. The birds squawking, indignant in their nests inside thirsty old maples. A brown dog licking happily from a dirty puddle while eager faces pressed against windows as if the stars had descended to bring them presents. Earthworms eager participants crawling out of the cracked sidewalk and churning their way across the pavement. A bird. Blue, with light red in its chest waited patiently on a mailbox. There was nothing much else it could do. There was no song, no whistle and when the sun creaked out of the clouds, it flew. Wings desperate for air, leaving nothing and everything, behind.

It had ended and all that was left was mud and hope. That white hive would be full and angry tonight. It was not even noon and West Medford was being bullied by the sun. Willie kept the blinds open despite the heat starting to pour in. He had made promises. Things that could not be undone. He watched them from his desk. Their eyes cast shadows that reached out across the entire stretch of West Medford. They cast it all away and just kept looking to that shining white monument.

Kyla finished the last of the dishes. She had not heard the sputtering end of rain, or the men full with disappointment. The whispers were at her again. The thin black lines crackling voltage at her. Laughing. They knew about the fire. They knew about her story. Her fake-book. They wanted to tear it all apart. They wanted to burn it all again. Her fingernails crawled along her skin. The hiss at the back of her neck and then a fire in her calf. Her shift ended and Kyla had no choice but to find him. He had written her book and now she would be finished.

Willie Huff could not stay in the small wooden box. This town, this memory, this mother, this story was killing him. He closed his eyes from the blinding sun.

His mother was wearing an old dress. She had worn it for him when Willie was just out of first grade. The summer cut through the fabric as she settled with the sun on the porch. Father would be home. The heavy Buick turning about the gravel drive. The bottles were clinking together in the ice bucket. His father could no longer see her. His eyes had been clawed out by another. The car turned hard into the driveway and the door slammed. His shirt collar was open and the tails let loose. At the front porch, he looked at her and spit. He took the beer inside. Willie listened to his footsteps on the worn-out stairs. She was waiting for him sprawled out like a black squid. He really had no choice. His mother was a heap of tears on the porch swing.

Leone drove with a pain in her body that was near crippling. Her hands were shaking violently when she dared to loosen her grip on the steering wheel. The road was burning a white-hot streak between her breasts and the heat was making her sweat. She had no bandages and the blood was holding fast to her clothing. She was fighting to stay awake. She could see her father squinting hard against the sun.

Leone was glaring at a strip of highway through the small window above the kitchen sink. The Winnebago was trying its best to hold itself together. The dishes were rattling. The trunks were humping against each other, and the golf bag full of walking sticks was talking about running. The Winnebago had been huffing fumes for at least twenty miles and she was beginning to worry. Her father seemed further from the road than usual. His eyes clearly seeing more than just asphalt and yellow lines. He had not been the same since the incident with the man in the tall white hat. His heart could not stand the space it was in anymore. They went for days and towns and counties, even states, without talking. The tires sounded worn to Leone. She had not seen a car since they left the edges of Missouri with a wooden box full of coins. His voice came through to her in cannon. "I dreamed of your mother last night. It must have been those coins. She always loved interesting coins. Once in Texas or New Mexico, an Anasazi made her a necklace with an old native coin on it. I was pretty sure it was junk. Total junk but she loved that damn thing. She wore it until the thread broke. I remember it. In New Jersey, the same day we left the hospital with you. It just slipped from her neck. It made such a delicate sound when it broke. She almost dropped you trying to catch it. After that she wouldn't hold you for a month. She felt horrible. She clawed at her own skin. Got all scratched up. She use to smack her thighs with the back of her hairbrush. I grabbed her arm once, almost broke the damn thing, trying to stop her. And you, you never made a goddamn sound. Just laid there looking through the bars of your crib. I thought something was wrong with you. She kept telling me to mind my tongue, like you weren't mine as much as hers." Leone was absolutely still. If she had moved, everything in her body would break like glass. She felt the edges of her bones vibrating. Her father's voice was penetrating well past any part of her she had known before. The only thing keeping her up was the edge of that tiny sink in the Winnebago. She held onto it until her fingernails began to break. She had been waiting 18 years for her father to speak like this. "Then she. . . Well I know you have an idea. You've heard people talk. Your cousins. Those kids are shit. Just shit. Don't you end up like them. Your mother was a good woman. Something just changed in her. It was there before. There all along I saw it. She would stick a pin in her arm. And not a prick like a child. Wrap a piece of cord around her thigh. Once while you were down in the afternoon she cut herself wide open in the kitchen. Twenty-two stitches. It was after that I couldn't leave on my trips anymore. She just couldn't stop. I begged her. Holding you against my chest. I begged her." Leone did not dare move. The pain in her hands was unbearable and her father, for the first time, in that small metal home on wheels, was out of her reach. "The damn coin necklace. It broke her when it hit the ground. Broke us. I pray baby, I pray it didn't break you too."

Leone felt the change in movement. The Winnebago aching as it turned off the straight and onto a rural route. She opened her eyes, ripe with tears. A bold wooden sign read: West Medford, A Return to Values.

Yusef knew his father would be waiting in that big white tent. He did not want to see him. He would not understand all of this. He never had before. His camera was full of empty memories. He could not wait. In his blood he knew things would change tonight. He looked for Kyla from his window. The small apartment was still her disaster. She had saved his life with this mess. That last push might have taken him. It was much harder to catch his breath now. He felt his heart racing while he dressed and his hands were getting hard to control.

The rain had left the air thick and warm. Yusef felt his shirt pressed against his back. The evening was slow to come to West Medford tonight. The sun still full-on orange and lingering above the horizon. He left the building, not looking, not turning, holding tight to his camera. He followed the sun to the place where everything would be.

Kyla had no desire to be in that tent. The lights, the cameras, the video monitors, the lights, the microphones, the speakers, the cables. Thousands of feet of cables. They all would be talking loud enough for her to hear. She sat in the bathtub with the door open. The water cold on her pale skin but she did not care anymore. She knew what had to be done. She no longer bathed when her mother was in the house. She did not want to tell her the story. Her truth. She loved her skin now. She was a beautifully crafted tome. A lesson, an allegory. A rapturous lie. All that was left was the epilogue. She had written it out a thousand times in her head. A hundred times on clean white sheets of unbound paper. A dozen times on delicate paraffin paper. After her bath she would write it carefully one last time on a sheet of thin acetate.

Kyla dried in the mirror and read her story over and over to herself. Watching her own lips move from memory and the swell of her breasts with each pronunciation. She took careful time with the tender passages. The spot about her father's mysterious death in the African jungles and her mother's resulting pill addiction. Her own time with alcohol. Then of course the whispers had their say. Those scratchy metallic voices written on the round of her hip, tucked in at the underside of her arm, hiding behind the tender skin behind her knee. They had exclusive rights to the spot on her calf with that thick raised melanoma they left. There were stories that even kept them away. She sat on the toilet and spread herself. The short bit ran up the inside of her thigh all the way to her clitoris. It was a simple language and crudely scrawled. *I let Yusef lay with me. He said he loved me. I tried to cut him once in his sleep. They had taken him. He woke up early.* The other side was much more clear, a bolder line with much larger letters, *I am sorry mother. I let Willie Huff come inside me. I am full up with lies.* She dressed and went to the kitchen. Her throat was already hot and burning.

The men all wore matching shirts. A light blue polo with piped trim and a single breast pocket bearing a dull grey crucifix. The woman had a similar blouse and a simple pleated skirt in a matching grey. It was a stark contrast to the enormous white belly rising up out of the dusty earth of West Medford. This town was ready to burst wide open. There was music falling out of every corner, tumbling down and ringing against the metal chairs with the clang of cymbals and the round clarity of brass. Willie Huff watched the people billowing out of West Medford. They followed the sound of pre-recorded choirs and the smell of deep fryers. The sun was keeping its vigil at the edge of it all. That thin brutal eye refusing to sleep. The lights were coming up. The generators, sweating metal beasts, barely catching their breath. The heavy thick black cables, snakes in the dry grass.

The men were keeping people in lines. The men were taking money. The men were smiling. West Medford was eager to put their hands out, passing through the erected white promenade, and into a promise for salvation at the cost of twelve dollars. It was the smell that got to them first. The warm sweet hold of sugar on freshly fried dough. Their faces brighten up with child-like smiles. There was music, of course, rolling out from the tent with swimming long hymns and rhythms. Everyone says hello. Everyone has a kind face. The sun is losing this game and the light from beneath that wondrous white tent is like syrup leaking out into the night of West Medford.

Leone stumbled out of her car, legs a weak mess of burning muscles. She never made it to the front door. The sun was toying with her as she lay on the path in a pile. It was just at the edge of her reach. Her father was sobbing wildly next to her ear. The kind of sobbing that makes you sick. Leone turned and retched into the bushes, her stomach a knot in her lungs. Leone pulled herself up by the door handle. The house was hot. She fell into the shower and the water came out ice cold. She tore at her clothes. The cuts on her thighs where still fresh. The marks on her breasts were old company.

You have to keep telling yourself things. You have to keep ahead of everything. Keep telling yourself things. Moving and telling. Telling yourself what these things are that you are working for. Keeping it right on the shelf. Keeping it right on the shelf. Just keep telling yourself. Everything in this world is understandable if you can keep it on the shelf. Quiet and on the shelf. Your mother knew about it. She would have told you. She wished she told you. Told you about all of this. This thing you are doing. You have to put it on the shelf. It can't be this anymore.

When Leone left the shower, the bleeding had finally stopped, and her legs found themselves. The sun was just a single bright orange flare burning at the center of her apartment. She was standing there. This time, right at the window, her face a color of white Leone had never seen. Leone dropped the hairbrush in her hands. She walked to the window, her legs feeling new. It was the first time she had seen her mother cry and in that thin line of light across her face they came out ran down her cheeks like fire. Leone would have wept if she was not so determined now to kill herself. She knew they would write newspaper stories about this.

Yusef was filling roll after roll. His arms were aching but he was convinced to ignore it all. The light was leaving him. Pulling him forward towards that hot white tent. The sides starting to billow with music and hope. He did not fool himself. The lens was honest. His fingers moved so quickly over the shutter, the aperture, he was determined to focus. It was all becoming much clearer. The edges of the negatives cutting a sharp line. They filled the thin tender negative with wide-open faces. White fans strumming the air rapidly. Sagging dress shirts open at the cuff. Sundresses soaked through the back. Handkerchiefs blotted dark with sweat. She was there. The last sliver of sun catching her hair on fire. Her face had not changed much since that first photograph. She was watching him. A small piece of her in every negative. Her smile hiding at the edge of every frame. The blood burning in his arm. The black camera pressed to his face. He swallowed her whole through the lens. The shutter devoured her. The negatives held her against his heart. Yusef knew she could keep him safe. Yusef knew everything was ready to change. He photographed his father, barely a shadow against the setting sun.

Willie worked the crowd helplessly. He drifted with that star burning on his chest through well-uniformed workers and the faces of West Medford. They were scarred by having so much hope. The tent was literally humming. The generators, the lights, the cables, microphones, wires, amplifiers, instruments, and consoles all ready with anticipation. Willie touched his gun. Kyla was holding on to his arm. He no longer cared about them. He looked down to her face. Her eyes were alight. She pressed herself into him and her body felt awkward for the first time. He knew it could not end well. He held onto her as tightly possible. Yusef devoured them blindly, pressing the shutter with ferocity as the sweat poured down his back. Her body was a gorgeous flame next to Willie Huff. A story to be told.

The music came full on with pipe organs and a bellowing choir. There were hands clapping loudly and the crippling heat of West Medford's hottest summer. Their gowns were already soaked through and the song was just hitting its stride. Yusef watched Kyla leave Willie Huff. She just slipped silently away. Her mouth barely whispered goodbye but Yusef heard her so clearly. He would see it all, a perfect document, refracted and forever.

The chorus hit its crescendo and he came upon the stage like a cannonball. Everyone saw him, from the closest seat to the farthest folding chair it was clear who he was. This was the man. The man who had them all at his fingertips. The man who filled this tent with the buzz. The man who had their hope balled up in his sweating fist. His voice was a long drawn bombast. He was exactly what was to be expected. There was no subtlety here. No hidden meaning. No disguises except the obvious. He was a tall man. His arms reached out with every full-throated word and this man, he could touch every hand in that tent. That billowing white church with its temporary glowing steeple and mobile parish. The church so full of steam and sweat. The church full of wilting fans and Sunday shoes. He had no idea the story about to be told.

Leone had no time left for West Medford, for her father, for her secret. She loaded the pistol and walked towards the middle of it all.

Willie would not take his hand from that holster. Yusef had his eye to the camera. Kyla was pressing a match against the strike. The sulfur hit her nostrils as the entire book lit up. It was as easy as she had remembered. The trail of gasoline was fast. She would not have to wait anymore. The flames jumped all over that humming box of wires and coils. The sound was immediate. It gurgled and choked, dying like a beaten animal, blood rushing into its open lungs until they exploded. The sounds were glorious and she opened her eyes until the whites almost disappeared. The flames traveled independently of recourse. Rushing high into the air in search of oxygen and running fast through dry hip-high grass, desperate for fuel.

When the second generator exploded, Kyla felt her body being hurled through the summer. She landed ferociously on a chest of props and costumes, the wooden slats splintering and jabbing into her. The second explosion was distinctly louder than the first. West Medford was at a panic, flooding from the tent like mice. They tripped over cables and extension cords. All those wires wrapped at their ankles with venom just inside their insulation. The concession area took hold next and the grease traps burned with the smell of funnel cakes and donuts. The tie downs were beginning to burn.

Willie Huff ran with his hand on his gun. He shouted but in this panic everyone was deaf. He fought to right himself against the flood. He should have taken her away from this place years ago.

Leone would have pulled the trigger. She told herself so. She was focused and sorted about it. Then the whole town exploded. She could see the flames rocket into the air from her front porch, then another, then the smoke, then the smell, and finally the sound of all those people. She was intimate with the sound of so much pain.

Yusef was having trouble with the aperture. The fire kept dominating the smoke. Then the smoke dominated the fire. The light meter was moving wildly inside the frame. He watched it all through a two inch square. Willie Huff caught mid-stride with his hand still on that gun. Mr. Stevenson holding his five-year-old daughter, arm's length above his head, as his wife wrapped her hand around his belt. Daryl from the hardware store helping Mrs. Adeline Johnson up from the ground only to be pushed aside by a well-used farm hand. The tent was next. The tie-downs on the right side snapping and then whipping about in the breeze. They licked and hissed against the sides of the canvas until finally getting their way. The flames began smoldering in the folds of the billowing white cloth. Then a sudden draft like a secret lover, brought them inside. The smoke began to choke the entire place. Yusef's eyes were burning. She was standing just to the side of it all not looking the least bit upset. Her body laid bare and her skin alive with flame. The acetate had carved its way into her flesh. For the first time West Medford, all of West Medford, could hear her low slender voice. They could all read her magnificent story. Then Willie Huff shot her.

Leone was startled to hear a gunshot other than her own. She dropped the pistol immediately and ran toward the town despite the pain in her legs. She would help them. She would try to save all of them. She would open her doors to them. She would kiss their faces. This is what her mother would have done. Leone could see everything so clearly now through the hot tears burning her eyes. Things were changing. She would begin building something for real now. She could change this monster inside her. She was ready. She had been prepared.

Willie had done it. Standing there like a training video with his legs held apart and both hands on the handle. He had never fired his revolver. The smell of the gunpowder struck him suddenly and he was sick, turning to the side to vomit slightly. Then she was there. Kyla with her hands holding herself together. The blood seeping into her clenched hands. The white tent behind had collapsed. The smoke and flames at his back and people screaming unbearably. He holstered his weapon and turned from her body and ran into the tent. It was the only thing he could think to do.

Yusef was right there. His arms aching uncontrollably the pictures struggling to stay still. He had photographed her so many times before. This one, would change everything. This one, this single frame of her perfect lips as she spoke in a low slender voice was a testament. From here it was all beginning. Her confession. Her only truth. This story was all a lie.

Leone, just on the boundary of disaster, heard a second shot.

There was no song. No whistle. And when the sun creaked out of the clouds it flew. Wings desperate for air leaving nothing, but everything, behind.